MY MASQUERADE WITH THE DUKE

A Steamy Regency Romance With a Sci-fi Twist

THE REEVES OF REEVES HALL
– BOOK 2 –

M.M. Wakeford

THE REEVES OF REEVES HALL

What lies within the walls of Reeves Hall, a grand estate in a lonely corner of Cornwall owned by the mysterious Reeves family?

These steamy romances are set in Regency England—with a subtle science-fiction twist. Follow members of the Reeves clan as each of them take the risk of falling in love while protecting their family's great secret.

Each book can be enjoyed as a standalone, or read in series order for added depth and connection.

Book 1 – **My Captive Duchess**

Book 2 – **My Masquerade With the Duke**

Book 3 – **A Not So Convenient Marriage**

Book 4 – **A Most Reluctant Widow**

PROLOGUE

❧ ❦

A NOT SO INVIGORATING CUP OF COFFEE

July 1821, London

AS HE WOVE his way through the busy thoroughfare of Lower Thames Street, ignoring the clamouring cries of street vendors peddling their wares, Jos could not shake the conviction that he had made a grave error. He walked on, following the path of the river in a westward direction, and reflected on the matter. Yes, it had been a mistake to confront the man as he had done, making loud accusations and threats.

At the time, Jos had thought that a show of determined strength was the way to resolve this intractable problem. Now, he could see that his approach had not only failed, it had also exacerbated the situation. Soon, he would have to come clean with his master and tell him just what a mess he had made of things. He hated the idea of it. For more than three decades, Jos had served the Reeves family diligently, earning their trust and working his way to the position he now held. What would they think of him now? Would he be stripped of his duties and sent back to Reeves Hall in disgrace? All because he had underestimated this enemy and played into his hands.

Some minutes later, he arrived at his home on Barton Street. The elegant townhouse belonged to the Reeves family, but Jos and his wife, Esa, who worked as the housekeeper, had been assigned generous quarters on the top floor. His heart heavy with the burden of his failure, he traipsed up the stairs and let himself into their private parlour, where Esa waited for him as usual, a pot of tea and a slab of cake on the table. Without a word, he removed his shoes and set them neatly by the door, then went to his armchair and sank gratefully into its timeworn depth.

His wife gazed at him in concern. "Long day?" she enquired.

"Yes," he replied. "Long day." That was all that was said. In their long years of marriage, the two had learned the art of unspoken communication. He did not need words to tell her that something was bothering him, and she did not need words to bring him comfort. Instead, she poured him a cup of tea and cut a slice of cake, placing them on the small table beside him. He grunted—his version of a thank you—and drank the hot brew.

Perhaps, he reflected, the situation was not so dire. On the morrow, he would go to plead his case again, maybe use some of his precious store of coins to grease a few palms. Yes, that was what he would do. On that hopeful thought, he retired to bed and sought solace in the familiar embrace of his wife.

But there was to be no chance to plead his case.

Early the next morning, he trudged down to the kitchen, and as was his habit, ate a thick slice of buttered bread with a wedge of cheese. Their maidservant, Nessie, brought him a steaming cup of coffee. He liked it bitter and black, with enough strength to invigorate him for the day. He drank from it, enjoying the sharp, biting taste, and smiled gratefully at the young lass. She was new to the position, having knocked on their door a few weeks previously in desperate need of employment. His master had done a good deed in giving her a job, and she had repaid them in kind.

He got to his feet, his head beginning to spin a little. He steadied himself with a hand to the back of the chair. There was no time to lose. Matters were pressing. He took three steps to the kitchen door, which opened onto a narrow side alley, then another half dozen steps, only to collapse on the cobbled stones of Barton Street.

CHAPTER 1

A FAMILY OUT OF THE ORDINARY

THAT AFTERNOON, FOUR people were gathered in the large parlour of Reeves Hall. One gentleman leaned a hand casually on the mantlepiece as he spoke. Another lounged on a graceful-looking armchair, a leather-bound volume clasped in his hands as he listened intently to what was being said. The third man in the room stood at the window observing the extensive grounds, though it was clear from the stiffness of his stance that his attention was also fixed on the words being spoken.

The final occupant of the room was a lady. Tall and slim, with walnut brown curls and fine, intelligent eyes, she sat ramrod straight at a chair by the fireplace, her gaze alternately set on the gentleman speaking and down on the floor.

A cursory look at this scene would impart nothing out of the ordinary—four well-dressed persons of quality convened in an elegantly appointed parlour in a prosperous-looking country house. But if one looked a little closer, one might notice some strange things about this room and these people.

On the far wall, at waist height, there appeared to be a small square of light continuously flashing green and then red. Higher up on that same wall was a small rectangular grille through which cool air wafted into the room, keeping the temperature low even on this hot July day as the sun speared the windows with its powerful rays. And a closer inspection of the leather-bound volume in the seated gentleman's hands would show it to be not a book but an unusual contraption with a flat glassy surface on which different symbols appeared and then went.

This was no ordinary family, for the Reeves of Reeves Hall had a closely guarded secret. They were not from this world—not from England, nor from Great Britain, nor from the continent of Europe nor from any nation on this great sphere called Earth. The Reeves family hailed from a world called Uvon two million light years away. On that world, their name had been Reevas, but this was changed to the more English sounding name of Reeves shortly after their arrival in England.

As might be expected from a society able to engage in interplanetary travel, the world of Uvon was highly evolved and far more scientifically advanced than England in the year 1821. One might wonder then what such a family was doing living in a country estate in the heart of the Cornish moor. How had they got here and why?

Quite simply, the Reeves family had been banished from Uvon and sent into exile to the only other habitable planet in the universe: Earth. This was a planet that had been colonised by Uvonians hundreds of thousands of years ago, in the early phase of their space exploration, with the hope of forging some mighty, interplanetary empire. With this in mind, thousands of felons from Uvon's overcrowded prisons had been shipped to Earth as a first step towards building a new and enlightened civilization there. The plan had failed; the distance between the two planets far too great for such an ambition—and the stranded felons soon forgotten, left to fend for themselves in a land populated by large reptile creatures.

Over the many centuries that followed, Uvonians had sent the occasional unmanned missions to orbit Earth and gather data, but nothing more. From this data it was known that the felons and their descendants had ended up building civilizations, though whether these were enlightened was debatable. And it was to one of these civilizations, to England, that the Reeves family had been banished.

Why this happened was a story as old as time and all to do with an insatiable lust for power. The matriarch of the Reeves family, a high-ranking member of Uvon's governing body, had been involved in an unsuccessful plot to seize permanent control of the government. Found guilty of treason, she had paid the ultimate price with her life and that of her husband. All four of their children—Broek, Liora, Horis and Simor—had been spared death but forced into exile. With heavy hearts, the bereaved members of the Reeves clan, their ages ranging from fifteen to twenty-three, had left Uvon, accompanied by a retinue of devoted family servants, and embarked on a three-year journey in space to this distant planet that was to become their new home. They had arrived in England in the summer of 1814, discreetly and without fanfare, and set about establishing themselves as members of the landed gentry; their new seat, Reeves Hall.

It had been a derelict estate some six miles east of Newquay which they had purchased and upgraded to their Uvonian standards, installing a security system around the perimeter to prevent outsiders from entering. Its location in the midst of uninhabited moorland, the sleepy village of Penhale a mile away, was perfect for their needs. Of necessity, the family had to keep their true origins to themselves and to guard against anyone finding out about their way of life. Whatever knowledge Earth humans may have once had of their true Uvonian ancestry had long since been lost in the drifts of time. The people of England had no inkling that there existed a planet, impossibly far away, on which lived their brethren humans. And they did not know that secretly amongst them, there lived a family of humans come from that planet on a spaceship, with scientific capabilities beyond their wildest imaginings. They could not be allowed to discover such a fact. This then was the closely guarded secret of the Reeves family.

This secret was a weight on each member of that family, not least on Liora, the lone female among the four siblings and the lady seated ramrod straight in the parlour of Reeves Hall that day. In the years since her arrival in England, Liora had had to contend not only with the loss of her ancestral home on Uvon, but also with a reversal of her status both within the family and in society at large.

For Uvon had been a world where women had an important role to play, not merely be wives and mothers, or chattels of their husbands. Liora had been on the cusp of adulthood when tragedy had struck. All her life up until then, she had been groomed to follow in her powerful mother's footsteps. It had been expected that she too would one day rise to a prominent position on Uvon's governing body. To that end, she had received the best education that money could buy. From early childhood, she had learned to speak fluently all the dialects of her world so that she could address the people she was one day to rule. She had been schooled in every facet of the law, as one day, she would be promulgating new laws of her own. She had studied her people's long history as well as science, for the leaders of Uvon were expected to be steeped in deep knowledge. In short, Liora had been poised for a magnificent future. Faster than the blink of an eye, all this had changed.

Banished from her planet, the bright future mapped out for Liora was suddenly gone, but she had adapted. In the course of their long journey to Earth, she had tried to prepare herself as best she could for her new life. A proficient linguist, she had applied herself to learning English. Knowing that a career in jurisprudence or government would be out of the question for her in England, she had pragmatically set to studying engineering systems, a skill that would prove useful in the setting up of their new home. However, no amount of study could prepare Liora for the reality she had found in England. Here, she could no longer live as she had before. Her freedom was abominably curtailed. She had to adhere to the strict rules that English society set for women from the clothes she wore to the preservation of her virtue and reputation. For someone who had been used to leading a carefree life, answering to few people but herself, this had come as a profound shock.

Again, she had tried as best she could to adjust to her new circumstances. To all appearances, she had succeeded in doing so, living a quiet life at Reeves Hall and letting her brothers take precedence when it came to external matters. But it rankled. Even after several years, the resentment had not been totally erased. This might help to explain why she acted as she did that afternoon on hearing the news of Jos's sudden death.

Standing by the fireplace, Broek, the eldest sibling, was saying, "It is imperative one of us goes to London as soon as possible and takes over the running of the shipping business—at least until we can appoint a permanent replacement for Jos." He looked around the room, casting meaningful glances at his two brothers. It was usually Broek that dealt with business matters, but he did not wish to do so this time. Newly married and still in the early period of domestic bliss, he was reluctant to subject his new bride to a likely stay of several weeks in London. His brothers could take on this responsibility for a change. But before either of them could do so, Liora spoke up. "I will go," she stated firmly.

Her announcement was greeted with surprised stares and a growing scowl on Broek's face. In stern tones, he addressed her. "As capable as you are, Liora, I'm afraid it's a man's world out there."

She was not to be fobbed off with that excuse again. Oh no! Seven years she had spent in subservience at home because she was told England was a man's world. No more.

Raising a stubborn brow, she lobbed back, not thinking the matter through, "Then I'll have to become a man, won't I?"

CHAPTER 2

AN ECCENTRIC DUKE

THERE WAS THE sound of a throat being cleared, then a voice behind him spoke. "Your Grace?"

Marcus Cavendish, eleventh Duke of Coleford, looked up from the bed of nasturtiums he had busily been pruning in time to catch a faint look of disapproval on his butler's face before it was quickly masked with his usual austere countenance. "What is it, Grimshaw?" he asked, thinking not for the first time just how very apt that name was.

"Letters come from London, Your Grace," the butler replied in a clipped tone. "I have taken the liberty of placing them in the front parlour along with a few refreshments."

"Thank you," Marcus said with a smile. "I shall be along shortly."

Grimshaw bowed stiffly and turned on his heels. For several moments, Marcus stared blankly ahead, deep in thought. What news might Mama and Julia have for him in their letters? They were the only persons in London with whom he corresponded, apart from the occasional missive from his solicitor, a Mr Oakley. There were no prizes for guessing what the letters would say. He was needed in London and must join them there post-haste.

The feeling of serenity, which always came over him when he worked in the garden, dissipated quickly. Sighing, he finished his task, then stood, brushing clumps of dirt from the old buckskins that he liked to wear when at work outdoors. He should probably wash and change before making an entrance in the front parlour. He had no wish to scandalise the servants any more than he already had. With a grim satisfaction, Marcus took a final look at his handiwork. Along this wall, he had planted tomatoes, a new plant he was experimenting with. The red fruit was ripening nicely and would soon be ready for eating—much to the disapproval of Wilkins, the head gardener, who contended it was a poisonous fruit, no doubt because of its colour.

He had knocked heads with Wilkins a time or two since inheriting the dukedom and coming to live at Coleford Hall. It was never his intention to raise anyone's hackles, yet the tending of a vegetable garden was something he had always done and done well. It was one of the few areas where he could say with confidence that he had achieved mastery of his subject. Marcus was not much of a scholar, nor much of a sportsman, but here in the garden, he excelled.

At Ashby, his old home, it had been known to all that the vegetable garden was his domain. Papa had often teased him about it, saying he had raised a yeoman farmer for a son rather than a gentleman. The words were never said with any malice. Mr Cavendish senior had been far too kindly a soul to ever want to cause offence. And Marcus had taken none, for they were not far from the truth. He did not engage in the usual gentlemanly pursuits. There again, nobody had much cared what the son of an impoverished country vicar, with a small living and an even smaller estate to his name, might do.

There had at first been thoughts that Marcus would follow in Papa's footsteps and take holy orders. Such ambitions had been quickly dismissed, however, when his poor scholastic abilities came to light. A career in the army was proposed next, but there had been insufficient funds to purchase a commission for him, and in any case, Marcus had had very little wish to become an officer. Better that their modest funds be spent on dowries for his sisters. He would be content with living a rustic life on his small estate in Hampshire. Nobody then had had any notion that he would become a duke a few short years later. Why would they? He was but distantly related to the previous duke, a man cut in his prime after a horseback accident. It was merely happenstance that Geoffrey Cavendish, first in line to inherit the dukedom, had died of an apoplexy that very year, and that his son, Edward, followed him to the grave soon after, the victim of a virulent fever. And then there was Papa, taken from them just over a year previously. That left only him, Marcus Cavendish, to inherit the title, lands and vast fortune of the late duke.

He had had little inkling of this when a letter from a Mr Oakley had arrived at Ashby just four months ago, informing him of his new circumstances. Soon after, he had set off for Coleford Hall in the company of Mama and his three sisters, and taken possession of his new home. And only a few weeks later, he had escorted his family to his newly inherited townhouse in London so that Portia—the eldest of his sisters—could make her debut in society.

With her good looks, and now a tidy dowry too, Mama had been hopeful of his sister making a good marriage. Would that the Good Lord proved her right. All he could say on the matter was that after enduring two weeks of the social whirl, he could take no more. Marcus was generally of a friendly disposition and got along with most people, but he had found the snobbish ways of the *ton* hard to stomach. He had missed the fresh country air and the pleasurable toils in the garden, but over and beyond this, he had found himself the prey of ambitious mamas hunting for a rich duke to marry their daughters. It had been too much. He had had to escape. Once he had seen Mama and his sisters properly established in London and all their needs catered for, he had taken his leave and returned to Coleford Hall—where his singular habits in the garden had raised eyebrows among the servants. Ah well, no matter, he told himself as he hurried back to the house.

Twenty minutes later, clean and dressed in tightly fitting cream pantaloons, a starched shirt and cravat with a double-breasted tailcoat, he made his entrance in the front parlour, spying the letters on the salver. While Grimshaw ostentatiously poured him a cup of tea, Marcus broke the wafer and unfurled the first of the missives. It was from Mama. He took several moments to decipher the words, written in his parent's fussy scrawl. It was as he had thought. Mama requested his return to London to attend the Maybury ball next week, the last major event of the season before he was to escort them all back to Ashby—for though Mama was proud as punch at having a duke for a son, she would rather continue to reside in the shabby comfort of their rambling country house in Hampshire than in the grandness of Coleford Hall. It was only Marcus who would take up residence in this cold and majestic place. All the more reason for taking charge of the vegetable garden, the one place where he could feel at home.

He opened the next missive, finding it much easier to read, for Julia, sweet sister that she was, always took great care to shape the letters clearly and simply for him.

Dearest Marcus,

I am sorry to have to tear you away from your country idyll, but needs must. Mama insists on your escorting us to the Maybury ball, and I do believe she may be right about it. Sir Luke Stafford, it seems, is on the verge of proposing. With a handsome duke of a brother in attendance, Portia will be sure to cut quite a dash at the ball. That should clinch a proposal, no doubt. And you shall need to be there when Sir Luke comes to request permission to pay his addresses.

So you see, we cannot do without you. Do come soon. I promise to help keep the worst of the matchmaking mamas at bay, though you know, it will be your turn next. A duke must marry and carry on the line, after all. No, I joke—or only a tad. But in any case, I wish so very much to see you. I have missed you, dear brother.

Your loving,

Julia

Marcus smiled, despite the sinking feeling in his stomach at the thought of attending this ball. Of course, there was no debate as to what he would do. He had shirked his duty long enough as it was. He went over to the desk in the corner and rummaged for a fresh sheet of paper, pen and ink. With slow deliberation, he then wrote a reply to Mama.

Deer Mama,

I will set out for Londen on the morow and be whyth you by the end of the week.

Your lovyng son,

Marcus

He sealed the missive with wax and carefully copied out the address, then summoned Grimshaw, handing it to him with the instruction, "Please see that this is despatched as soon as possible, then send word to the stables to have my travelling chariot ready first thing tomorrow. I leave for London."

The butler bowed his head in acquiescence and left to do his master's bidding. Sighing gently, Marcus went to find Stubbs, the diligent young man he had recently employed as his valet. Prior to becoming a duke, he had never thought to have nor been able to afford the services of such a person. However, shortly after his arrival at Coleford Hall, the necessity of having a good valet was brought to bear upon him. He had bowed to the inevitable and engaged the services of Stubbs.

At first, Marcus had dreaded the prospect of someone fussing over his appearance, but Stubbs had shown the requisite wit to grasp both the nature of his master's character and his requirements. With minimal fuss, he had ensured the new duke was kitted out in a manner befitting his station.

Marcus found his valet in the anteroom to his chamber, pressing a shirt to neat perfection. "Stubbs," he said without preamble. "Prepare a baggage for me. We leave tomorrow for London, and I am to attend the Maybury ball, so I shall need suitable attire."

The valet's eyes shone at the mention of the ball. "Of course, Your Grace," he replied. "It shall be done."

And so it was. Very early the next day, with a dizzying number of trunks stowed securely onto the carriage, Marcus set off for London.

Chapter 3

❧ 3 ❧

THE MASQUERADE BEGINS

LIORA INSPECTED HERSELF in the looking glass, considering her new appearance. Standing bare of all clothing, covered only in the bodysuit, she could scarcely credit the astounding transformation. Gone were her long brown locks of hair in which she took secret pride. They had been shorn and arranged in the fashionable Brutus style. Gently, she brushed her fingers over her head, then ran them down her forearms and chest which were now covered in a masculine dusting of dark hair, courtesy of the bodysuit.

"What do you think?" Krilea watched her with barely repressed curiosity. She had just helped Liora put on the male bodysuit, a thin layer of artificially constructed material that covered her chest, arms, back and thighs. It was lightweight, designed to fit comfortably like a second skin over one's body. Sealed into place, the suit had inflated to broaden Liora's shoulders and chest.

When yesterday she had blurted out her intention to become a man, there had been numerous expressions of doubt and surprise, not least in her own mind. Could this masquerade work?

Of course, Broek had been set against the idea, but Horis, her middle brother and a trained medical physician, had pointed out that the transformation was technically possible. Back on their home world of Uvon, it was commonplace for some females to wish to live life as a man, and multiple procedures had been developed to cater for such wishes ranging from a permanent transfiguration to the more temporary method of wearing a bodysuit.

Simor, her youngest brother, had been amused but supportive of her wish. With his encouragement, she had been able eventually to overcome Broek's objections to her plan. She would be the one to go to London to manage the shipping arm of their business, and she would do so as a man with the assumed name—Lionel Reeves.

Now her gaze slid further down to the apex of her thighs, where the most startling change was to be seen. This morning, in a medical procedure overseen by Krilea, their assistant medic, a long and thick prosthetic had been attached to her nether regions, in true-to-life mimicry of the male organ. Looking at it now, Liora wondered to herself if it was not a trifle too large. Prior to undergoing the procedure, she had chosen her preferred length and girth, shape and colour from pictures on the gender reassignment programme files in their data bank. The prosthetic of her choice had been created in the replicator and then fitted to her body. It hung now, an unfamiliar weight down her groin. Perhaps she should have gone for something smaller. In her new incarnation as a man, she had wanted to look powerful and potent, and so she had chosen a larger than average male organ. Liora wanted there to be no doubt in people's minds that she was indeed a man.

"Well, what do you think?" repeated Krilea.

Liora did not reply at once. Inspecting herself in the looking glass, she was filled with a mix of sensations. On the one hand, there was discomfort and a sense of alienation from her true body—but there was also a building excitement at the prospect of what she was about to do. She twirled around, studying her reflection, trying to see it from an outside perspective. Did she pass muster? Would anyone looking at her be able to detect the artificial nature of the attachments to her body?

Finally, she spoke. "I think, Krilea, that this will do nicely. Even to my knowing eye, it looks real."

Krilea nodded emphatically. "Yes, it is very life-like, even to the touch." She placed a hand on Liora's enhanced pectoral muscles and gave them a little poke. "It feels warm to the touch and firm, like a human body would," she marvelled, impressed with her handiwork.

"Not that I intend anyone to get this close," Liora replied.

"Perhaps not, but should you do so, be reassured that everything is in working order, even down below. Have you given it a try yet?"

Krilea was referring to the functional nature of the prosthetic male organ. During the medical procedure, it had been cleverly connected to Liora's body, enabling her to use it like any man would their own male organ. For instance, it could become erect when she was aroused. It could also allow her to discharge urine. For all intents and purposes, she was now a man. A man! Her heart pounded in her breast. She tried to ignore it and attend to Krilea's question. "I have put it to the test," she said. "It works, though the effect is not immediate. I shall have to practise it some more."

"That is quite normal," Krilea assured her. "According to the data, it can take anything from a few days to a week for the communication between your nervous system and the prosthetic's computer to work effectively." She gave her a sly look. "But once it is all in working order, will you not use its functionality to the full?"

Liora gazed at her askance. "You mean to fornicate with a woman? I have no desire to do so."

Krilea shrugged. "But you could with a man of a certain persuasion."

"No, I could not," Liora said firmly. "Quite apart from the risk of a malfunction during the act, it would be a dishonesty to become intimate with a person on false pretences."

"Is it not the reason why you are embarking on this adventure in the first place? I thought you wanted the freedom to have sexual frolics."

Krilea was partly right, of course. Liora had missed the freedom she used to have on Uvon, but she was not about to say so. Instead, she stated rather primly, "My intention is to go to London to take care of our business affairs, Krilea, and in order to do so, I must pass as a man. That is all."

"Hmm," Krilea snorted, unconvinced.

This spurred Liora to explain further. "Yes, it is true that I sometimes wish I could have sexual dalliances without fear of social repercussions, ultimately to find myself a suitable mate. However, I cannot do so in the guise of a man. That is not my true identity; it is merely a disguise."

"Then why go to all this trouble?" demanded Krilea.

"Why? Because I shall experience more freedom to do things than I do stuck inside these four walls," insisted Liora. "It will make a welcome change to be out and about in London, to rub shoulders with a vast swathe of humanity, to feel alive!"

Krilea gazed at her in sympathy. "Yes, I do see."

"And this is merely a temporary situation. Once our business affairs are set right, I shall return to Reeves Hall and live as a female again." Liora turned towards the pile of clothing on the bed. "Now help me dress in my newly acquired male attire."

A few minutes later, she stepped once more in front of the looking glass to survey herself. Simor's shirt and tailcoat fit well on her newly masculine frame, if a little loosely. Her cravat was tied, a trifle inexpertly. Her legs were encased in pantaloons and shiny boots. She made a well turned out gentleman.

"Very stylish," approved Krilea.

Liora smiled, "Thank you," and sketched a manly bow.

Then it was time to make her way down to the drawing room, where the family was gathered, waiting for her. She walked in and felt a touch of smugness at the stunned expressions on their faces.

Simor set down his teacup upon sight of her. "You make quite a man, Liora," he chuckled.

Horis smiled his agreement. "That you do."

Most impressed was Jane, Broek's new wife, who gasped, "Oh my!" then came closer, looking Liora up and down. "Quite astounding," she murmured.

Jane Reeves was not from Uvon. In fact, until her marriage to Broek, she had been the Dowager Duchess of Coleford. Widowed tragically earlier this year, all that had been left to her by her late husband was a run-down house, Penhale Manor, which neighboured Reeves Hall. The rest of the entailed estate had passed to the new duke, some distant relation of her late husband. No matter though, for upon moving to Cornwall, she had fallen in love with Broek. Now they were married and happily settled at Penhale Manor, the house having undergone much improvement.

There remained only Broek to respond to the sight of Liora in her male form. Stern-faced, he came to stand before his sister and grunted, "I cannot dissuade you from this madcap idea?"

"No, you cannot."

He sighed and fumbled for something in his pocket. "Then you had better have these." He handed her two small discs made of a clear, soft material. "They are listening devices which I have newly designed," he explained. "Once tucked inside your ear, they are near invisible. Keep them on at all times, so we may be in constant contact with you."

Liora was touched at the thoughtfulness of the gesture. "I will, Broek," she said, unable to hold back the quiver in her voice. "And thank you."

He nodded briskly. "Come along then, let us get you ready for your journey."

CHAPTER 4

A PROMISING START

THE STUBBY SHRUBS on the endless expanse of moor passed by in a blur as Liora gazed absently out of the carriage window. Every so often, she looked down at herself in her masculine garb, catching sight of the bulge at her groin. "I am a man," she reminded herself. "My name is Lionel Reeves, travelling to London to manage the family business." Perhaps if she told this to herself often enough, she would embody the part she was playing more convincingly.

"Liora." Simor's voice spoke into her ears through the new listening device that Broek had given her. She tapped the signet ring on her finger to activate transmission of her voice.

"Yes?"

"How are you bearing up?" asked her younger brother.

"Good," she said. "We have not come across anyone yet on the journey, though we should be approaching Bodmin soon to stop and refresh our horses."

"All will be well," he responded soothingly.

"I know. Of course, it will be."

"It is natural to feel some nerves," reflected Simor. "You are stepping out of the habitual life you have led here and are doing something audacious, even for you."

"I need to do this," she said on a deep exhale.

"Yes, I know, and all will be well. Once you have accustomed yourself to this new persona, you will find it comes easily to you. And any sign of trouble, get in touch with us immediately."

"I will."

"Good luck," her brother said, then ended the transmission.

Liora sat back in her seat and concentrated on taking deep breaths in and out. Already, she could see signs of village life, indicating that they were on the outskirts of the town of Bodmin. Soon, the carriage drew up in front of the White Hart Inn. Ignoring the flutters in her stomach, she swung the carriage door open and jumped out, making sure to walk in a confident manner. An ostler hurried towards her. "Good man," she called out, taking a silver crown out of her pocket. "Have sturdy horses saddled at once to take me to Exeter." she handed him the coin for his trouble then added, "There will be another crown for you when you return my horses to Reeves Hall in Penhale."

"Yes, sir," he replied, already beginning to unharness the horses from her carriage.

Liora turned and headed inside the coaching inn, summoning a young maidservant. "A tankard of ale with bread and cold beef," she instructed imperiously, aping the mannerisms of a gentleman. "And make it quick," she added, dropping a shilling into the maid's waiting palm.

The maid bobbed a curtsy and went to do her bidding, first ushering her into the parlour where she took a seat at a table in the far corner. Liora's hand came down reflexively to arrange her skirt before she remembered that she was not in fact wearing a dress. She covered the error by pretending to brush some dust from her pantaloons, before seating herself at the table. Her heart was pounding frantically in her chest, and she tried to settle it down, looking quickly about the room. Would this be the moment where she was found out for the fraud that she was?

Only two other tables were occupied. She exchanged glances with an elderly gentleman at one of them, who nodded at her in acknowledgement. She returned the nod then stared pensively at a wooden beam, tapping her feet under the table, until the maid brought her the tankard of ale. Liora took a quick gulp, trying not to grimace as she swallowed the drink down. She had not yet developed a taste for such a beverage. At home, purified water or herbal teas were her drinks of choice, with the occasional addition of freshly squeezed juice, but of course, these could not be procured at a coaching inn. At least the bread and meat, when it came, was of a tolerable standard.

She consumed her refreshments then stood, remembering in time not to pat down her non-existent skirt. Giving a brisk nod to the other occupants of the room, she strode out, asking for directions to the privy. After being pointed towards a small wooden structure at the back of the inn, she entered it carefully, her nostrils tightening at the noxious aroma. Already, she dearly missed the modern and fully sanitised washrooms at Reeves Hall—another sacrifice she would have to make for the sake of a little freedom, at least temporarily until she reached the comforts of their London townhouse. With fumbling fingers, she released the fastenings of her pantaloons and pulled out her fake male appendage. Closing her eyes, she focused her mind, transmitting the thought from synapse to synapse until it stimulated a reaction in the nether regions of her body. Finally, a small trickle of urine came out of her prosthetic organ, slowly getting stronger until she was done with this task. Sighing in relief, she tucked herself back into her pantaloons and exited the privy.

Eyes cast down, she found her way back to the front of the inn where her carriage and horses awaited her. She climbed back on board and soon, they were on their way again. As they rolled along the rutted road, Liora breathed in and out slowly to let her agitation subside. She had done it! She had passed this first test with flying colours. She only hoped the rest of the journey would go as smoothly.

IT WAS EARLY evening, after two more equally uneventful stops for a change of horses, when she finally reached Exeter, where she was to stay the night. The carriage pulled up in front of the Black Horse Inn, and she requested a private room and a bath, again with no mishap. Liora was slowly getting accustomed to her new masculine persona and growing in confidence. Upstairs in her bedchamber, two blushing young maids brought in steaming jugs of water, which they poured into a small cast iron tub. She nodded her thanks, tossing them a sixpence each. One of them paused to bat her eyes winsomely at Liora on her way out. "Anything you be needing, sir, just you ask for Annie. That be me," she giggled.

"Thank you, Annie," Liora said firmly, seeing her out. She supposed she did make quite a handsome gentleman, and there was no shortage of pennies in her pocket. She should not be surprised, therefore, if young wenches flirted with her, though it was certainly a strange sensation. A short laugh escaped her. If only these maids knew who they had in reality been flirting with!

Once they were gone, Liora locked the door securely. Only then did she divest herself of her clothes and remove the bodysuit, letting it de-inflate at the touch of a discreet button. It felt strange to be back in her female form—apart from the prosthetic still attached to her groin, which could not be removed until she returned to Reeves Hall and underwent a second medical procedure. Liora touched her small breasts, freed at last from the confines of the suit. It was oddly comforting to feel the soft give of flesh under her fingers, a reassurance that she was still, after all, a female.

Shaking these disturbing thoughts away, she gave the bodysuit a quick wash and hung it to dry, before easing her tired and sore body into the small tub. Briskly, she scrubbed herself clean then stood, reaching for the folded towel the maidservant has left for her. Once dry, she opened her valise and took out a cotton night shirt, slipped it on, then got into the lumpy bed. She laid her head on the pillow and closed her eyes, going over the events of the day. Not once had anyone looked askance at her. The disguise had held well.

"Liora." It was Broek this time, speaking through the listening device.

She tapped her ring to transmit, then spoke in a low voice, lest it carried across the thin walls of the inn. "Yes, Broek."

"Tell me how you are," he barked into her ear.

"All is well. I have put up for the night at the Black Horse Inn."

"Has anyone bothered you or looked at you strangely?" he demanded.

"No. It has gone remarkably well," she responded tartly. "Broek, I believe this guise is going to work."

He sighed loudly. "You will tell me if anything bothersome happens?"

"Yes," she muttered.

He gentled his voice. "Liora, it is not that I do not have faith in you. I do. Only a brother can worry."

"Yes, I know," she murmured. "And I am glad that you care enough to."

"I do," he said, his voice gruff. "Take care and goodnight. Expect a call from me again tomorrow evening."

She chuckled quietly. "Goodnight, Broek."

CHAPTER 5

◈

AN INTERESTING ENCOUNTER

THE FOLLOWING DAY'S journey went by without mishap, and Liora made it in good time to Ilchester, where she spent a marginally more comfortable night at a local coaching inn. Next morning, she set out straight after breakfast, wanting to get a good day's travel before sundown. She was feeling increasingly at ease in her masculine guise and no longer palpitating with tension each time she reached a coaching inn and interacted with other people—for she was Lionel Reeves, a gentleman with business interests in London. She could almost begin to believe it herself.

Her luck only lasted so far.

On her third day of travel, all seemed well at first. She made good time, reaching Wincanton just after noon and stopping for a light luncheon. Then she was once again away with a fresh set of horses, eating up the miles towards Amesbury, where she planned to stop for the night. It was early evening but still light when Liora felt the carriage slowing down to a standstill. She looked out of the window, puzzled at first, until she spied the reason for their halt. On the road was a carriage on its side, one of its back wheels detached. Three men were busy pushing it back upright, intending no doubt to move it off the road, out of harm's way.

She opened the carriage door and jumped out to investigate. As she reached the men, she saw their efforts succeed, the carriage tilting back upright, though it was unsteady, missing

27

one of its wheels. Nevertheless, they managed to push it to a verge on the side, just off the road. "Good evening," she addressed them with a polite smile. Now that she was up close, she could see that one of the men was dressed expensively in tight-fitting pantaloons and a well-cut tailcoat, though looking a little dishevelled from his recent exertions.

The gentleman returned her smile. "Good evening, though as you can see from my predicament, it is not such a good evening for me."

"No, indeed not," she said, coming a little closer to examine the carriage. Immediately, she noted the damage. "Your axle has broken," she remarked, "probably when the carriage fell onto its side."

"Yes," replied the gentleman. "You are quite right." He sighed in vexation. "I am very much afraid this chariot is not going anywhere today, not until we can repair it and refit the wheel." He looked at her hopefully. "Would you be so kind as to give me a ride to the nearest town so I may get some assistance? I believe Amesbury is not too many miles distant."

Liora swallowed her dismay at the idea of having a companion in the close proximity of her carriage, but to refuse would arouse suspicion. "Of course," she mumbled.

His smile grew wider. "Thank you, though I do not yet know to whom I am indebted. Let us make the introductions." He sketched a quick bow. "Marcus Cavendish, at your service."

Liora bowed in return. "Lionel Reeves, of Reeves Hall in Penhale," she replied, then paused. The name, Cavendish, was a familiar one. "You would not, by any chance, be a relation to Jane, the Dowager Duchess of Coleford? Though she is no longer known by that name, for she has recently wed a kinsman of mine." A kinsman, not a brother, for it had been agreed before leaving Reeves Hall that her new persona, Lionel Reeves, would pose as a cousin of the Reeves siblings.

"Ah, yes." The gentleman appeared momentarily abashed. "There is a connection," he said, "for I am the new Duke of

Coleford, though I'm afraid that I have not yet had the honour of making the Dowager Duchess's acquaintance." He went on to disclaim, "I had no knowledge until my arrival at Coleford Hall that the late duke had a wife and a young daughter. It pained me to learn that they had been compelled to move away, in order to cede the house to me. I would not have wished matters so."

So, this was the person that had inherited Jane's home and the dukedom after her late husband had tragically died in an accident. Liora studied him more closely. He was young, somewhere in his mid-twenties, with an unruly mop of sandy-coloured hair and a handsome countenance tanned by the sun—as if he spent much of his time outdoors. Though he was tall and broad of stature, he regarded her with gentle brown eyes, and she was immediately disarmed.

Liora replied with a shrug, "All's well that ends well, as they say, for she is now happily wed to Brook Reeves, my kinsman." With outsiders, Liora always used the name Brook for her eldest brother. Upon their arrival in England, all the family had acquired anglicised names to help their assimilation into society. She had taken on the name Laura, though of course at present, she was Lionel.

The duke nodded. "I am glad to hear it."

While they had been speaking, the other men present had been busy moving several trunks from the defunct carriage and stowing them aboard her own. Just how much baggage did a duke require? It took an extra piece of rope to secure the final trunk above the carriage roof. Liora stared at it in silent perturbation. All that extra weight in the carriage would slow them down. It would take at least an hour now to reach Amesbury, though hopefully it would be before darkness fell.

The duke followed her look and said once more, "I thank you for your assistance, Mr Reeves. I am much in your debt. I hope that you will do me the honour of dining with me this evening. It is the least I can do to repay your kindness."

Liora gave a slight bow of her head in acquiescence, then pointed to her carriage, "Shall we be on our way?"

They walked together to the vehicle. The duke insisted she climb aboard first, so Liora hurriedly got in and moved across to the edge of the seat to make room for him. She heard him instruct his post-boy and valet to ride on to Amesbury behind them. Then he joined her, closing the carriage door behind him. He settled onto the seat beside her, his large frame taking up space, and immediately, she was conscious of his scent. It was not unpleasant, something earthy that spoke of the outdoors with a hint of lemony cologne, but it permeated the narrow interior of the carriage, making his presence feel all the more inescapable.

Liora was silent at first, not knowing quite what to say. How did she converse with this near stranger who was snatching a ride in her carriage? What was it dukes liked to talk about? She was at a loss. The best she could manage was, "So, you are travelling to London?" Her voice, unfortunately, came out as a squeak. She hastily cleared her throat to try to cover up her misstep.

"Sadly, yes," he replied, turning slightly in his seat to face her.

"You do not wish to go?" she queried in confusion, her voice this time a throaty growl.

He let out a short huff. "I am not one for crowded cities. I much prefer to be out in the fields or gardens of my estate."

"Then why do you go? You are a duke, are you not? A man possessed of much wealth and power who can surely do as he pleases."

At her words, the duke burst out laughing, then seeing her frown, hastened to say, "Forgive me, Mr Reeves. I did not mean to mock. It is simply that I find it diverting to think of myself as a man of great power. No indeed, that I am not! It is duty, nothing more, that sends me to the smoky metropolis. Should you ever meet my mama or my sister Julia, you would know that it is nigh on impossible to refuse them."

"I see," she murmured. "So you go at their request."

He sighed. "There is a great ball, the last big event of the season, which they wish me to attend as their escort."

"You do not like a ball? I had thought music and dancing to be something that most people enjoyed."

He brushed away a messy strand of caramel hair that had fallen over his brow, and her eyes strayed to his large, strong hand. It was tanned and calloused, the hand of someone that laboured manually with it from day to day. But how could that be? He was a duke. Nothing about this person tallied with what she had learned about the English aristocracy.

He tucked his hand into his lap, and now her eyes were drawn to the bulge in his pantaloons, which was quite as large as that made by her own fake appendage. She felt a sudden rush of arousal. No! She must not. She reminded herself that she was Lionel Reeves, not Liora. She could not afford to be attracted to this man—to any man—not while she was in this disguise. Quickly, she turned her face away to look out of the window, hoping the duke had not noticed her strange behaviour.

"The music and dancing I do not mind," he said, responding to her question. "It is the other things I dislike."

She was curious enough to cast a quick glance his way. "What other things do you mean?"

"Oh, you know how it is with the *ton*. It is rife with gossiping matrons, and snobbish airs and graces which I cannot abide."

She shook her head. "I'm afraid I do not know, for I do not move in quite the same circles as you do, Your Grace."

"Well then, count yourself fortunate." He smiled then, and her breath caught. Then she reminded herself again that this man was out of bounds. The reaction she was having to his proximity was the result of years of enforced celibacy. That was all. She looked out of the window once more, and for a few moments, silence reigned between them.

He cleared his throat. "And yourself, Mr Reeves?" he enquired.

"Myself?"

"You are travelling to London?"

"Oh," she said, with dawning understanding. "Yes, I am bound for London, but not to attend any social function. It is for business that I go. My family holds many mercantile interests there."

"Do please tell me more," he said with that charming grin. "It sounds mightily more interesting than the Maybury ball."

"As to that, I cannot say. We ship a great many goods from around the world—rubber from Ceylon, sugar, tea and spices from the East Indies, coffee and cocoa too. We also trade in barrels of wine from the Continent and wool, all of which we store in a great warehouse at London Docks."

"Well," he replied. "That is indeed a great many things."

"The only things we do not trade in," she added thoughtfully, "are tobacco and any goods produced on slave plantations."

He examined her curiously. "The slave plantations, I can quite understand. Dreadful practice. But why not tobacco?"

Liora eyed him scornfully. Truly, the level of ignorance among these Earth humans was astounding. "Why not?" she retorted. "Have you not thought that tobacco could be injurious to one's health, not least because it causes a desperate dependency in those that habitually smoke it?"

He scratched his head, pulling her gaze once more towards his big, strong hand. "I had not thought of that," he said, mulling the matter over in his mind, "but come to think of it, what you say makes sense. One of my maternal uncles loves nothing more than to smoke tobacco with his pipe. I do recall an incident one day several years ago when his young son accidentally dropped the pipe on the floor and broke it in two. How angry my uncle was! Not so much at my cousin but at the fact that he would not be able to smoke his precious tobacco until the pipe was replaced."

"What you describe is a classic symptom of tobacco dependency," she concurred.

He studied her as if she were some great curiosity. "How is it that you are so knowledgeable about such things?" he wondered out loud.

"How is it that you are so lacking in knowledge about them?" she parried back, then rebuked herself for her lack of tact.

He flushed and gazed down at his clasped hands on his lap. "I am a very poor scholar," he responded quietly. "I'm afraid I have no great knowledge of things except in the one area that interests me."

"And what is this one area of interest?" she asked, a little more gently.

"Gardening," he said simply. "Anything to do with the growing of plants."

"Ah," she said.

He glanced at her quizzically, so she went on, "Now I understand why you are so tanned and your hands look like they are used for daily toil."

He examined them sheepishly. "Yes, I see." He held them up in front of him. "I suppose these are not the hands of a gentleman."

"Does it matter?"

He sighed softly. "It is frowned upon. I have scandalised my servants and the local village folk with my doings in the garden. I am not what they expect of a duke."

"Again, I ask you. Does it matter?"

He furrowed his brow. "Shouldn't it?"

"May I remind you, Your Grace, that you are a duke, a man with great wealth and power. Beside pleasing your good mother and sister, there is nothing standing in the way of your living life according to your own wishes and desires. If I may say so, you are very fortunate indeed to be in such a position."

His brow cleared. "I had not thought of it in that way. The title and estate are still new to me, so I have not had much time to accustom myself to my changed circumstance."

"Once you have done so," she said with certainty, "you will realise just how fortunate you are. Even though people may gossip about your eccentric habits, your wealth and title will insulate you from overt criticism. This is not a luxury afforded to the rest of us." She could not stop the hint of bitterness in her tone.

Scholar or not, he was quick to pick up on this. "You speak from experience, Mr Reeves? What is it that you are not free to do?"

She could not, of course, respond with the truth. Instead, she stated, "Most of us are constrained, in one way or another, by the rigid rules of society."

Still, he persisted, looking fixedly at her. "How is it that *you* are constrained?"

"I—I am not free… to love as I would wish," she said softly, barely above a whisper.

But he heard her words. A thick silence enveloped them as the import of what she had said sunk in. She cursed her loose tongue, even more so when he murmured, "Ah, I see."

She cursed herself again. Why, oh why had she spoken so? Finally, he broke the oppressive silence with a wry smile. "I am sorry for it, Mr Reeves. It would seem a dreadful shame not to be allowed to love as your nature and soul intends." A moment later, he changed the subject of conversation, switching to that universally safe topic—the weather. "I believe there is a slight chance of rain tonight. What think you, Mr Reeves?"

In this vein, they continued their journey until they reached Amesbury some minutes later, talking trivialities while they both ruminated silently over what had been said; Marcus wondering who it was Mr Reeves was not free to love, and Liora wondering how on earth she had managed to give the duke such a false impression about herself.

CHAPTER 6

A SPLENDID PROPOSITION

AS SOON AS they arrived in Amesbury, Marcus sprang into action, arranging with a local blacksmith for the retrieval and repair of his chariot, though it was as he had feared. The chariot would require at least a few days for the repairs to be effected, which was time he did not have if he wanted to be in London for the Maybury ball. Instead, he resolved to hire a post-chaise for the rest of his journey, but here again he ran into snags, for there was not a single chaise available for hire. It seemed he would have to wait for his chariot to be repaired and hope that it did not take too long. Perhaps he could pay the blacksmith an additional sum to hurry the matter along. Or perhaps there was another alternative.

Evening came, and after a wash and change of clothes, Marcus joined Mr Reeves for dinner in the coaching inn's dining room. On seeing him again, he was struck by the gentleman's appearance, even more so than on their first meeting earlier that day. He examined him surreptitiously as he took a seat across from him. He noticed how Mr Reeves's complexion was pale and smooth, almost ladylike, as if he had the services of an excellent barber at his disposal, though journeying on the road, this could hardly be the case. Marcus concluded that he must be one of those men that did not naturally grow whiskers on their face. He had come across such individuals a time or two in his life, so it was not entirely uncommon.

The gentleman's eyes had a lively intelligence and were of a brown so dark as to be almost black. Marcus found himself drawn to them constantly over the course of the meal, wondering what secrets lay behind them. His attention was also captivated by Mr Reeves's delicate, long-fingered hands which were in odd juxtaposition with the broadness of his stature.

At first, the gentleman was cautious in his speech. Marcus was certain that he rued their conversation in the carriage. A shame, for he did not think any lesser of the man on learning that he was one of those persons that were attracted to their own sex. It did surprise and disconcert him, of course, for he had never before known anyone with such inclinations. Then it occurred to him that no person would choose to love so unnaturally and risk the wrath of society unless they were compelled to do so by their very nature. It must be part of God's mysterious plan, just like he, Marcus, was born with this strange predilection for gardening and with little talent for reading.

It had not been for lack of trying that he could not master his letters. He had put such effort into it, not wanting to disappoint either of his parents, but it had been no use. He had railed at his thick headedness and called himself a clodpate at least a dozen times a day, until one morning, seeing his son's distress, Mr Cavendish senior had taken him aside and said gently, "You are what you are, dear boy, and it is no use fighting it. If God, in his infinite wisdom, decided to make you this way, then who are we to question it? Let us instead put our minds to where your true talents might lie." It was shortly after this conversation that Marcus had been given free rein over the kitchen garden.

Yes, Marcus now thought, it must surely be part of the Great Lord's plan. One needed only to look around at nature to see this pattern replicated everywhere, with subsets within groups not conforming to the main characteristics of that group. Why was it, for instance, that some plants thrived in wet grounds while most others in the same family grew better in dry conditions? To his mind, this variation was what made nature so profoundly interesting. He was unlikely therefore to judge Mr Reeves for not conforming to society's expectations about whom he should love. On the contrary, it made the gentleman more interesting in his eyes, like encountering a rare species of a plant.

Marcus watched observantly as Mr Reeves took another sip of his wine, grimaced and set the glass down. He could not help but ask, "You do not like it?"

The gentleman looked a little flustered. "I am sure it is perfectly adequate," he said by way of reply.

"You must be accustomed to the highest quality vintages, given your family's business interests."

At this, Mr Reeves emitted a reluctant laugh. "No, indeed I am not." He considered for a moment, then came to a decision. "At home, I rarely drink wine," he confessed. "My beverage of choice is water or herbal infusions."

Marcus nodded his head vigorously in agreement. "I too am a great proponent of drinking herbal infusions," he disclosed, adding, "I make them myself from the herbs I grow in my vegetable garden. I pick the leaves and dry them in my glass house." With a triumphant smile, he took out a thin leather pouch hidden in his coat pocket and withdrew from it several small packets wrapped in wax paper. At Mr Reeves's look of enquiry, he explained, "I carry these herbs on my person, for whenever I am in need of a refreshing or revitalising brew. See here, I have peppermint, camomile, fennel, nettle and this last one is a mixture of black tea with spearmint. Which would you like to try?"

Mr Reeves's eyes were wide in wonder. "Do you mean to say you go about everywhere with these herbs on your person?"

"I do!" With an imperious wave of his hand—Marcus was a duke after all and must use this privilege when the need arose—

he summoned the serving maid. When she reached their table, he asked, "Would you be so good as to bring us a pot of boiled water and some tea cups?"

"Boiled water?" she questioned, a puzzled frown on her pleasantly plump face. "Would you like me to bring a pot of tea then?"

"No, not tea. Only the water, as hot as you can make it."

She looked a little doubtful at this but went to do his bidding. Marcus turned his attention back to Mr Reeves. "So, what shall it be?"

There was an amused glint to the gentleman's eyes. "I think I shall try the black tea and spearmint," he said.

"Excellent choice." Marcus took out two packets of the herbal infusion, then stowed the rest back in the pouch and returned it to his pocket.

Mr Reeves studied him, a smile tugging at the corners of his mouth. "Your Grace," he said, "you are a man full of surprises."

"Growing plants in the garden is the one thing at which I excel," Marcus replied modestly.

The gentleman's smile widened. "So it seems," he murmured.

When, a short time later, the maid returned with the hot water, Marcus poured it into the two cups, then added the herbs, swirling them with a spoon. They allowed the infusion to steep for a short while before taking their first drink. Marcus watched Mr Reeves carefully to observe his reaction. The gentleman set the cup down, nodded approvingly, and gave him the highest praise. "That is a very good brew indeed."

Marcus was inordinately pleased. This prompted him to put forward a proposition he had been mulling over in his mind. "Mr Reeves, I have enjoyed your company tremendously this evening and during our short journey here," he said with complete honesty. "I would like, if I may, to travel with you the rest of the way to London. It would do me a great favour as my chariot will sadly be out of commission for several days, and there is no post-chaise available at present to hire. I will, of course, cover the full cost of the horses as well as our room and board, in payment for your trouble."

As he was watching him intently, he did not miss the fleeting look of consternation on Mr Reeves's face before he replied, "I would be honoured, Your Grace."

Marcus felt a burst of pique, for he considered himself a personable man, well-liked by most people of his acquaintance, but quite clearly, Mr Reeves preferred not to have his company on the journey to London. Ordinarily, Marcus was not one to impose himself on others, and he so very nearly gave Mr Reeves an opportunity to withdraw gracefully from this situation. But he did not. Already, he felt a great fascination for this gentleman and had an unexplained urge to continue on this voyage with him. And so he pretended not to notice his reluctance.

"Splendid!" he said in a most jovial manner.

CHAPTER 7

A SURPRISINGLY COOL CARRIAGE

LIORA SETTLED INTO another lumpy bed—clearly, these coaching inns did not know such a thing as a well-sprung mattress—and reflected on the events of the day. In particular, her thoughts returned time and again to her new acquaintance, the Duke of Coleford.

He was nothing like any duke she had ever imagined. Liora had studied the culture of English society, both from afar on her long space journey to Earth and since arriving here. She had seen something of the ways of the aristocratic class. From what she had learned, she expected a duke to be coldly imperious, arrogant and puffed up with self-importance. She expected him to be profoundly aware of his elevated station in society and to act in accordance with that knowledge. She expected a duke to be lily-livered, weak and pampered, with no sign of any manual toil on his smooth and soft hands. Marcus Cavendish, Duke of Coleford, was none of those things.

Her recollection of his big, calloused hands was interrupted by a voice in her ear. "Liora." It was Broek, checking up on her again.

She tapped her ring and answered. "Yes, Broek."

"Is all well?"

She hesitated a fraction too long, and her brother was on the scent immediately, like a bloodhound. "What is it?" he asked sharply.

"Calm yourself, Broek," she said in a low voice. "All is well."

"Something is up. Tell me!"

She let out a long breath. "I have made the acquaintance of someone on the road, someone who is distantly connected to us."

"Who?" his question was razor sharp.

"The new Duke of Coleford," she said softly.

"Yol have mercy," she heard her brother mutter under his breath. "What of this cad? What has he done?"

"Nothing, Broek, he has done nothing. And he is not a cad. Not a bit."

Her brother made a growling noise of impatience into her ear. She rushed to explain, "I came across the duke after his carriage overturned on the road. He was in need of assistance, so I invited him to ride with me to the nearest town. We rode together to Amesbury without any mishap, and he asked me to dine with him." Broek made a huffing noise, but she chose to ignore it and continued, "He was perfectly civil, extending me every courtesy. Not a cad at all."

"And that is all?" asked Broek coolly.

No, that was not all. He was not going to like what she had to say next; that she knew. "Not quite," she hedged.

"Out with it!" he snapped. Marriage to Jane may have softened her brother's edges somewhat, but he was still a grump, as she often liked to call him.

"Oh, very well," she responded with thinly veiled impatience. "It may take several days to effect the repairs on his travelling chariot, and as there is no post-chaise available to hire, he has proposed to travel with me in my carriage the rest of the journey to London."

"And naturally, you refused."

"I... did not."

"What were you thinking, Liora?" he spluttered. "To have a stranger in close quarters with you for hours on end? Think of the possible peril you would be putting yourself in."

"I could hardly refuse without seeming churlish," she remonstrated, "especially when he has been so kind and courteous. And what exactly do you mean by peril? I am fully trained in *raiko*, so could hold my own in a fight, not that there is likely to be one. Do not forget also that Galok is with me."

Galok was one of them from Uvon. He was in charge of the horses at Reeves Hall, and Broek had insisted he travel with Liora to London as a postilion, riding one of the horses at the front of the carriage. She had not argued the decision, for she was glad to have a familiar face on this journey with her. He was a quiet man who mostly kept to himself, even within their closed community at Reeves Hall, but she trusted him implicitly.

They shared a little history too, for in the early days of the family's exile, Liora had sought solace in his warm embrace and hard body. She had been much younger then, only twenty-one years old, and still reeling from the grief of losing both her parents. He was a good-looking man and exuded a soothing calm which worked wonders on both animals and humans alike. He had helped her then, providing comfort and physical pleasure when she needed it most. Their short-lived affair had reached its natural conclusion long before they landed on Earth. It had ended amicably, and by then, Liora had also realised the pitfalls of becoming intimate with a person who worked for her family as a servant. It was best not to cross such a line again. Since then, she had sought physical satisfaction with a sex bot in her favourite holographic programme. It was much safer that way—not a perfect situation, but she had found it to be adequate.

"I do not like it," Broek said testily. "In such close proximity and for so many hours of travel, what if he notices something of your disguise?"

She tried to reassure both Broek and herself when she replied, "I have checked my appearance from top to toe, examining every angle in the looking glass. Even to my critical eye, the disguise is convincing. Nobody suspects I am not a man, and I have not had anyone regard me with suspicion on this journey."

This did not entirely allay her brother's worry. "Be meticulous in checking your appearance every morning, Liora," he urged. "Ensure the bodysuit is correctly sealed each time you wear it, and look out for any possible malfunctions."

"I will."

He took a calming breath. "Very well, then. I shall speak to Galok and ask him to keep a sharp eye on this duke."

"There is no need—"

"There is every need," he cut in quickly.

Now it was Liora's turn to growl, "Great Yol but you are a meddlesome brother."

He responded with a curt, "Goodnight, Liora," and ended the connection. Agh! She loved her brother deeply, but by Yol, he had the infinite power to rile her. With a grunt of annoyance, Liora extinguished her bedside candle and tried to get some sleep as best she could.

NEXT MORNING, THEY set off on the next leg of their journey, departing early, soon after the sun had risen. The duke greeted her with a warm smile and settled beside Liora in the carriage, which was once again laden with his surfeit of trunks. Riding at the front was Galok, and sitting on the rumble seat at the back was the duke's personal valet.

Outwardly, the Reeves carriage was modelled on the design of a common travelling chariot, with one padded bench seat on the interior and shuttered windows to the front and sides. But of course, they had made their own, subtle modifications to it, using Uvonian technology. It was a necessity to do so, for it had been a profound adjustment for the family to go from the electric powered vehicles and drones they had been used to on Uvon to travelling by horse-drawn carriages.

Very early on after their arrival in England, Liora had determined to do something to make this lesser mode of travel more comfortable and reliable. In her workshop at Reeves Hall, she had designed a travelling chariot with much improved suspension and a sophisticated springing mechanism between the axle and carriage body, as well as rubber air bags to cushion the carriage from the many ruts and bumps they might pass upon. The wheels had reinforced metal spokes and thin, partly concealed pneumatic tires over the rim to make for much smoother travel on the road. The carriage body itself was well insulated and contained an auto-recharging, battery powered heating system. For hot days, she had incorporated a cooling mechanism that drew out excessive heat and blew a soft breeze of cool air into the carriage body. And for a final master touch, she had included a concealed refrigeration compartment for keeping drinks and food fresh along the course of a journey. She had wanted to install a screen and console for entertainment, but Broek had vetoed that idea, claiming it was too risky—which was probably wise.

In their short ride the previous day, the duke had not noticed much of this, but today, as they sailed smoothly over the rough road, his curious gaze took in the apparent differences. Finally, he spoke. "Such a comfortably appointed carriage, Mr Reeves. Might I ask who constructed it?"

Liora had found it best to stick as closely to the truth as possible when asked tricky questions about her way of life. So it was she said, "I bought this carriage off a Mr Samuel Hobson, who is known in these parts for the quality of his craftsmanship. Then I made improvements to the design, as I have an interest in engineering. The nature of our business requires frequent travel, and I wanted to make this vehicle as comfortable and reliable as possible."

He looked around him again and said, "Then may I congratulate you, Mr Reeves, on the excellence of the improvements you have made. We are rolling along so smoothly, it almost feels like we are flying above ground." He laughed at that, and Liora refrained from telling him that in reality, flying felt much different to this.

He stretched his long legs out before him and sighed happily. "Well now," he said. "I am almost glad of my accident yesterday, if it means I am to travel the rest of the way in such comfort."

Her comfort, on the other hand, was much diminished. She was wedged as far to the side as possible, so as to avoid any physical contact with his large frame. And now, for the next several hours, she would have to converse with him, making sure to remember to keep her voice at a manly low register, when she would otherwise have been able to listen to a Uvonian novel or music through the receivers in her ears. It did not help at all that she could smell his earthy scent, now discerning within it a hint of aromatic wood spice along with the notes of lemon, nor that within the line of her vision were his powerful thighs on which rested his gargantuan hands.

She had dreamt of them last night, or rather she had dreamt of him using them on her, enfolding her entire breast with one hand while the thick fingers of the other plunged deep into her core. It had been a vivid dream. She had woken from it decidedly hot, her pulse racing and her cunt dripping. What had been even more disconcerting was that her intense arousal had triggered the mechanism on her attached appendage, making it rise and swell. For several minutes, she had lain there in the lumpy bed of the coaching inn, trying to regain her breath and to will her inconvenient erection away. She had reflected then that there were definite limitations to the design of the male anatomy.

These thoughts followed her now, as she sat beside him in the narrow space of the carriage. She could not escape them, much as she wanted to. They made her cheeks burn hot and a layer of sweat form on her brow. And of course, he had to take notice of this. "Dreadfully hot, isn't it?" he stated conversationally. "Would it not help to lower the windows so we can get some air?" He reached out a hand to the window beside him, looking for the laces that would lower it.

She stopped him quickly, crying out, "No, sir!"

He lowered his arm and brought his puzzled gaze back to her. She rushed to explain, "There is a cooling mechanism that I installed in this carriage, but it requires the windows to remain shut."

He frowned. "How so?"

Now this was problematic. How did she describe to this unenlightened human the specifics of the cooling process that compressed and evaporated a refrigerant chemical in order to absorb the heat in the air and expel it out through a condensing fan that was discreetly located on the roof of the carriage? He would not understand, and worse still, he would then have questions in his mind as to how she had come to have such knowledge. Great Yol, this was the very reason why Broek had always insisted they kept their distance from the native population.

Perhaps unwisely, she opted for the following response. "Would you mind very much if I ask Your Grace to take my word for it? The science behind this invention is quite complex and difficult to explain in simple terms, moreover I have not yet obtained a patent for my invention. But you are right, it is hot. I shall adjust the mechanism and shortly, the air will become cooler." She turned away from him, shielding the discreetly concealed control panel from his view as she quickly changed the temperature setting.

Liora turned back to face him again. He had not spoken a word in reply. He simply stared, his brown eyes shining with an emotion she could not at first discern. Cool air flowed through the carriage from the vents tucked unobtrusively up in the ceiling. He must have sensed it, for he put his hand up to feel it brush against his skin. Still, he did not speak. He lowered his hand and sat quietly, looking straight ahead.

She directed a few glances at him, wondering what he was thinking. There was a sinking feeling in her stomach. She had revealed too much, but also something else. She had hurt his feelings. She could tell that was what she had seen in his eyes just now as she watched him tighten his jaw and flatten his lips. Finally, he said in a gritty voice, "That is quite extraordinary, Mr Reeves. You are clearly a man of superior intellect; far beyond my simple level of understanding."

She was simultaneously mortified and annoyed. She did not like to cause anyone injury, but his words were true. Their scientific knowledge was far beyond his understanding. Was it not?

The silence endured between them as the carriage ate up the miles, cruising smoothly over the road, cool air fanning their cheeks. Eventually, she could take no more. "Your Grace," she said softly. "It all comes down to a simple concept, that heat energy can transfer from one place to another. I use a mechanical fan to circulate the air over a metal tube containing a special substance that can absorb the heat and transfer it out of the carriage. This cooling substance I created in my home laboratory after various experiments with chemical reactions. That is the best explanation I can give you."

The duke stared some more. Then, he whispered, "Show me."

She raised a brow in question. "You mean now?"

"Now. At once."

She returned his stare. Should she trust this man she hardly knew with this knowledge? Reason would dictate caution. Broek would insist on it. Yet she decided to follow some innate instinct. Liora knocked peremptorily on the front window, and Galok took this as a signal to slow them down to a halt. She pressed a button on the control panel to stop the fan, then pointed to the vent in the ceiling. "There is a fan there, made of a small rotating part that creates a flow of air. Here, let me show you." She took out a small screwdriver that she always kept in one of her pockets and carefully unscrewed the cover, removing it to show the duke what lay behind. He craned his head to see, then brought a curiously deft hand up to touch the tip of the rotor, making it twirl.

"Yes," he said. "I see."

Next, she carefully removed the rotor to show the duke what was under it—metal tubes set in a narrow wave pattern. "Touch them," she instructed.

He did as she commanded, emitting a cry of surprise at the ice-cold feel of the metal. "Amazing," he said in wonder. "And it is the substance you created flowing inside these tubes that make them feel so cold?"

"Correct," she said.

He stared in concentration at the tubes, then voiced his next question. "Let me see if I have this right. The rotating blade makes the air flow over this cool tube, cooling the air inside the carriage. What happens to the heat?"

She smiled, impressed at the quickness of his thinking. "It is absorbed by the substance in the tube and carried through to the roof of the carriage, where there is another rotating blade to disperse the hot air away. Then, the process begins all over again." There was more to it than that, but she stuck to this simple explanation of the cooling process.

"Fascinating," he murmured. Instinctively, she knew what he was going to say next. "May I see it?"

She laughed as she carefully returned the rotor into place and screwed the vent cover back on. "Of course. Follow me." She hopped out of the carriage, the duke at her heels. Nimbly, she jumped up onto the rumble seat at the back, startling the valet who sat there. "Excuse me," she said, and put her foot on the seat rail to hoist herself up onto the roof of the carriage, much to the valet's amazement.

The duke hesitated behind her. "Will it take my weight?" he wondered.

"It is very sturdy," she assured him. Moments later, he joined her up on the roof of the carriage. She showed him the fan, which was active again since she had turned it back on before leaving the interior of the carriage. She let him feel the hot air blowing out through the vent.

"Extraordinary," he muttered.

Their eyes met, and something happened in that moment. She could not quite describe it. It was like a meeting of two minds in complete harmony with each other, if only for that one instant. She understood his joy and wonder at the marvels of science. It was an emotion she felt herself.

They gazed at each other in happy recognition. Soon, the moment was over, and they rapidly scrambled down from the carriage roof, brushing the dust away from their clothes as they set foot on the ground once more. They got back inside the carriage and were soon on their way again.

The interlude had broken the awkwardness between them. She found herself having an animated discussion with the duke, or Marcus as he bid her to call him, about all manner of things. He was insatiable in his curiosity, but also full of perception about things he had observed in life. Liora began to revise her estimate of him as yet another of those clueless humans. Of course, he did not know what she knew, yet he was not lacking in intelligence nor in insight about the world around him. She was careful though not to reveal too much about who the Reeves really were. That would be taking her trust a step too far. And of course, he remained unaware of one vital thing—that she was a female.

In this way, the time passed quickly. Once they had exhausted their talk, they dozed or simply watched the endless fields go by. They stopped several times for a change of horses and to refresh themselves at the coaching inns, but they made good time. Early evening, they arrived at the Royal Oak in Camberley, where they were to stop for the night. They jumped down from the carriage, eager to stretch their legs. As they stepped inside the building, the innkeeper greeted them with an ingratiating smile, seeing from the cut of their clothes that they were both gentlemen of quality.

"Evening!" boomed Marcus, still in high spirits, taking a few coins out of his pocket and placing them in the innkeeper's grasping palm. "Prepare us each a room for the night and a warm bath. Then we shall be wanting a meal in your fine establishment."

"Of course, sir," replied the innkeeper. "May I ask, who do I have the honour of addressing?"

Marcus pulled himself upright, and for the first time, Liora saw a hint of the haughty aristocrat in him. "You are addressing the Duke of Coleford," he said loftily. Pointing to her, he added, "And this is Mr Lionel Reeves esquire of Reeves Hall in Penhale. Now, how about that room and bath?"

The innkeeper inclined his head. "Your Grace, it is an honour. We do have our best room ready and can send up hot water for a bath shortly. However, as we have several guests staying at the inn presently, I am sorry to say there is no other room available for Mr Reeves."

"Only one room?" she asked in horror.

The innkeeper hung his head in apology. "Only one room," he confirmed.

She heard Marcus chuckle beside her. "Not to worry. Mr Reeves will share the room with me. Come now, let us go and freshen up before dinner."

Share a room? No, that could not be. But already, the innkeeper was leading Marcus up a set of stairs. A throat clearing behind her reminded Liora that his valet was standing, waiting for her to proceed so he might bring up their valises. On wooden legs, she followed up the stairs and entered a cosy room furnished with just one bed — one bed — as well as a small dressing table, an armoire and an armchair in the corner. The innkeeper bowed himself out, promising to send up the hot water immediately.

She stood in the middle of the room, as if turned to stone. Marcus, in the meantime, was already sitting on the edge of the bed and letting his valet pull off his boots. "Ah," he sighed. "That is much better." He looked to her. "Do sit down, Lionel," he commanded. "Let Stubbs pull off your boots for you."

She let herself sink into the armchair and allowed the valet to assist her with the removal of her boots. It was a relief to have them off after wearing them all day in this heat. However, she was still in shock, trying to grapple with this situation. How on earth was she to share not only a room but a bed with Marcus Cavendish, Duke of Coleford?

CHAPTER 8

A LESS THAN PRIVATE BATH

HERE WAS HER situation. She was stuck in the company of Marcus for one night in this coaching inn. He was about to bathe in this room and probably expected her to bathe too. Later tonight, they were to sleep in one bed. She glanced at it assessingly. The bed could fit two people, but it would be snug, especially taking into account the size of the duke. It would be difficult to avoid accidentally touching unless she slept on her side right by the edge of the bed—not a recipe for a comfortable night.

Then, there were other considerations, chief of them her disguise. The bodysuit she wore was built for endurance and could withstand being immersed in water. In theory, she could bathe with her bodysuit on. It would not, of course, clean the skin covered by the suit. It had been a hot day, and she had felt the sweat form on her body. Without removing the bodysuit, she could not wash properly. That would have to wait until she reached London the following evening.

Could she discreetly unseal the suit while submerged in the water and try to get clean underneath? No, that would be too risky. She would have to make do and wash as best she could. The bodysuit was porous, allowing her skin to breathe, so a wash in the bath would achieve some modicum of cleanliness.

Then, there was the question of undressing in the duke's presence. She was not inordinately modest though it had been a very long time since any man had seen her nude body. In this case however, she would not actually be naked, covered as she was by the bodysuit, only appear to be so. Would her disguise hold without any clothes? She had to believe so. The bodysuit was very lifelike. Though it would be best to avoid any lengthy exposure to the duke's eyes.

She took a deep breath, calming her mind. This would work. As long as she was careful and maintained her self-possession, there should be little danger of being exposed for the fraud that she was. She looked up from her stockinged feet which she had been staring at and found that while she had been deliberating things in her mind, Marcus had removed all his clothing and put on a large, patterned robe, belted at the waist. She half wished she had caught a glimpse of his bared body before he covered it up, then decided perhaps it was best that she had not. Liora had no wish for a return of the rosy cheeked arousal she had experienced earlier today in the carriage.

The duke sat now on the edge of the bed, his valet busy trimming and buffing his nails. He met her eyes, humour twinkling in his. "Poor Stubbs," he said jokingly. "He has had quite the task in trying to make me look presentable as a duke, especially with these hands of mine. It is his great mission to refine their appearance, is that not so?"

"It is my duty, Your Grace," responded the valet.

"Notice that after bathing, he will have me immerse my hands in a specially made lotion to soften the skin. Milk of Roses, it is called. Am I wrong, Stubbs?"

"Indeed not, Your Grace. If you will allow me to, of course," murmured his valet.

Just then, there was a knock on the door heralding the arrival of two maids carrying copper pitchers filled with steaming water. They deposited them beside the tub, curtsied and then hurriedly departed.

"Splendid," beamed Marcus. "Shall you bathe first, Lionel? I am sure Stubbs will want to spend further time on my hands, so I will not mind going second."

"Oh no," she demurred. "I would not wish to deprive you of the privilege of going first."

"Not at all, Lionel. I insist."

There was nothing for it. She would have to make it quick. "Thank you, Marcus," she said with a respectful nod of her head, then hurried to take out a fresh set of clothing, a towel, washcloth and soap from her valise. She placed them on a nearby chair, then poured the contents of the first pitcher into the tub.

This was it. There was no turning back. Facing away from the duke and very much hoping that he did not watch her, Liora swiftly disrobed and stepped into the tub, lowering herself into the hot water, which was in no way sufficient to cover her body. Hunched forwards, with her knees bent to fit inside the copper basin, she focused on her task, trying not to think of the two other people present in the room. She heard Marcus chatting amiably with his valet in the background as she took the washcloth and rubbed it with soap, then briskly scrubbed her body.

A shadow loomed over her, and she looked up with a start. It was Stubbs, the valet. He was holding the second pitcher in his hand. "Shall I rinse you, Mr Reeves?" he asked politely.

Her heart pounded wildly in her chest. She knew he expected her to stand in the tub, while he poured clean water over her to rinse away the soap. There was no possibility of hiding her body. He would see all of her, clad in the bodysuit. She sent a quick prayer to Yol that there would be no malfunction to her disguise. If ever there was a test as to its efficacy, this was it. She placed her hands either side of the tub and slowly rose to her full height. Carefully, the valet poured water over her body, leaving enough contents in the pitcher for the duke. She kept her eyes down, looking at her body. Her gaze took in her form in the bodysuit, the enhanced musculature of her chest covered in dark, wet hair that formed a trail down to her pubic area, the natural mound of curling hair there, and below that, her fake appendage glistening pinkly from the bath. She sensed the valet holding out the towel to her and stepped out of the bath hurriedly, murmuring, "Thank you, Stubbs," as he draped it over her.

He stepped away as she began to dry herself. *It had worked.* Her heart could not seem to stop racing. Quickly, she slipped on a linen shirt that dropped down to mid-thigh—only to find herself face to face with Marcus. There was an odd intensity to his eyes as he untied the belt around his waist and slipped off his robe. Then, with a slight smile, he shifted past her and stepped into the tub she had recently vacated. The glimpse she had of him was swift, but already, it had imprinted itself in her brain. Holy Yol! A great broadness of a chest and long, powerful legs, all covered in smooth, tan skin. He was a work of beauteous art, everything in perfect proportion, but large. And running all over that fine golden skin was a dusting of fine golden hair. Oh Great Yol. She was rendered momentarily breathless.

Something else also afflicted her body. Glancing down, she saw a tenting in her shirt where her fake appendage had risen, reacting to the myriad nervous impulses communicating her arousal to the nether regions of her body. Fortunately, nobody was minding her, as the valet hovered solicitously by the tub while the duke scrubbed himself clean. She rushed to finish dressing, pulling on breeches and stockings, then arranging her neck tie. She breathed deeply to try to calm her agitation. "All is well, Liora," she told herself over and over. As soon as she was fully dressed, she excused herself, promising to meet the duke in the dining room, then she made her escape.

"ARE YOU SURE you know what you are doing?"

Startled, she looked around from her contemplation of the field before her, dotted with mounds of wheat sheaves. A few moments ago, she had come outside for some fresh air to help clear her head. Now standing next to her was Galok, a worried frown on his face.

"Sure? Maybe not, but I am doing it all the same," she responded softly, not wishing anyone to overhear their conversation, even though there was nobody in sight.

"Be careful, Liora," he said. "We do not know enough about this duke to put our trust in him."

"Did Broek put you up to this?" she demanded.

There was a flash of anger in his eyes. "This is me talking to an old friend I care deeply about," he said shortly.

She exhaled a breath, already regretting her words. "I know," she whispered. "I am being careful, but I have to see this through."

"Why are you really doing this, Liora? Is your life at Reeves Hall so lacking in excitement that you would endanger yourself like this?"

She turned to face him and hissed, "It is but half a life I live there, Galok, and you know it. Things had to change."

"You'll be careful, won't you?" Galok searched her face with serious eyes.

"I will." Then she added, "But I am glad that you are here with me."

He huffed, "If Broek hadn't ordered me to go, I'd have demanded it myself."

She smiled sadly. Galok was a good friend. She wished it could have turned into more, but the feelings were just not there—at least not on her part. She was not sure how it was with him.

"I had best go inside," she said.

He nodded. "Be safe, Liora."

She turned and headed back towards the inn, making her way to the dining room. There, she found Marcus sitting quietly at a table tucked into the corner of the room, a teacup held in his hand. As she approached, she inhaled a floral scent emanating from the steaming cup. "Camomile?" she queried, taking the seat opposite him.

A smile lit up his face. "Exactly so. Would you care for some?"

She nodded her head in acquiescence, and he poured her a cup from the teapot on the table.

"Thank you," she said.

The first course of their meal arrived, and they ate in companionable silence, broken eventually when Marcus said, "I hope you do not mind too much having to share a room with me tonight."

"It is what it is," she replied. "Travelling always involves some sacrifice of one's creature comforts. We will make do."

"Yes," he agreed. "We shall."

More silence followed, a hint of their prior awkwardness returning. He cleared his throat. "Lionel, may I ask you a personal question?"

"Yes, of course."

He looked over her shoulder, towards the fireplace on the other side of the room. "When was it you knew?"

Mystified, she replied, "I am not sure I understand what you mean."

In a hushed voice, he asked, "When was it you knew that you were attracted to… to other men?"

Ah. That. If only he really knew. But she was stuck in this falsehood and must carry on. She thought back to her childhood and tried to pinpoint the time that she had felt her first quiver of sexual attraction for another. "It was when I was around twelve or thirteen years old," she said. "There was this boy with beautiful brown eyes that captivated me. He was the son of a family friend, come to visit us for a few days, and I was enthralled by him. I followed him everywhere he went, even though he was a few years older." She smiled fondly at the memory then looked directly at Marcus. "Why do you ask?"

He shifted uncomfortably in his seat. "Mere curiosity on my part; do forgive me for prying."

"Am I the first of my sort that you have had occasion to speak of this with?" she asked curiously.

"It is not something one admits to openly," he responded with a frown. "You, Lionel, are the exception."

"I had not meant to be, I assure you. There is something about your manner that invites confidences. You would make an excellent spy, Marcus."

He snorted self-deprecatingly and looked away, uncomfortable with the praise. Soon, however, his gaze was back on her, wanting to know more. "Are there many such people as you?"

She could not help but laugh. These Earth humans amused her sometimes with their ignorance of the basic facts. "It is not as uncommon as you might think it to be," she informed him. "I would hazard a guess that at least a handful of men—or women—of your acquaintance are attracted to their own sex."

His mouth gaped in surprise. "How… how do you know?" he mumbled, looking around the room to ensure nobody was within hearing of what they said.

"I have made it my business to educate myself on such matters, that is all," she scoffed.

He shook his head in wonder. "I have never met the likes of you before, Mr Lionel Reeves. You are a singular individual."

She smiled as she drank the remainder of her camomile tea. "The feeling is mutual, Your Grace. I have never met a duke quite as singular as you either."

He chuckled in response, and in this merry mood, they completed their meal. They lingered over port wine, which she was slowly developing a taste for, regaling each other with tales of childhood pranks and mishaps, but soon enough it was time to retire upstairs to that one room with that one bed.

CHAPTER 9

A ROOM WITH ONE BED

THERE WAS A strange tension in the air as they retired to bed. Could it be something to do with the unexpected desire Marcus had experienced when he had watched Lionel come out of the bath? He had not meant to stare. Indeed he had not. Lionel's body had been thick and powerfully built, covered in part with a coating of coarse black hair. He did not quite know why he had found this sight fascinating, for never before had a man's body held interest for him, except that everything about this particular man held him captivated—his wit and unusual knowledge, the small tilt of his lushly full lips, the mystery in the darkness of his eyes.

As Marcus had moved past him to get into the tub, he had felt this disquieting sensation. He almost shook now thinking of it. How could that be? How was it that he had felt desire… for a man? Never before had he done so. He was not devoid of experience in the bedroom with certain females of his acquaintance—experience that he had lustily enjoyed. But a man? That was why at dinner, he had posed the question to Lionel. When was it that those desires had become apparent to him? His response had not helped Marcus solve his quandary. Lionel's knowledge about his sexual inclinations had come early, in childhood. What then of a twenty-six year old man? It was true that in some aspects, Marcus had been slow to develop and achieve. He had been late to walk, according to Mama, and very late to read and write, never quite managing the fluency that others did. Could this be another thing that he was late at developing—a desire for other men?

These unresolved questions stirred inside of him as they made their way up to their room. Stubbs awaited them there. Efficiently, he assisted him out of his clothes and into his nightshirt, all the while Lionel discreetly disrobed on the other side of the bed. Once they were done, Stubbs worked busily around them, putting away soiled garments and laying out tomorrow's clothing on the armchair. Marcus relieved himself into the chamber pot which Stubbs placed outside the room to be collected by a chambermaid. Then both Lionel and he took turns to cleanse their teeth, though in Lionel's case, it was with an odd looking paste rather than the customary tooth powder most persons used. Stubbs bowed, wishing them a good night, and took his leave. Finally, they were alone.

Marcus lifted the covers and got into the bed, choosing the side nearest the door, thinking perhaps Lionel would appreciate being closest to the window on this balmy evening. He did not join him in the bed at once. Marcus watched as Lionel took out a glass jar from inside his bag, opening it and dipping his finger into the contents, a pale lotion which he rubbed onto his face. Catching his curious gaze and looking a trifle flustered, Lionel explained, "It must seem a strange vanity on my part, but every night, I like to spread this lotion onto my face and hands to keep the skin soft and pliable."

Marcus laughed softly. "Is it any better than the Milk of Roses Stubbs has me use on my hands?"

"Oh as to that, there is no contest. It is miles better."

Now Marcus was even more curious. "May I try it?" he asked with a smile. "My rough hands need all the help they can."

"Of course." Lionel came over to him, proffering the jar.

Marcus shook his head. "Would you rub my hands for me, Lionel?"

Lionel creased his brow at this. "I am not your manservant," he observed wryly.

"No, you are not. You are fast becoming a dear friend, and it is as a friend that I ask."

There was that slight tug at his lips again that indicated amusement. Then, giving a little snort, he came to kneel on the bed beside Marcus, dipping his finger once more in the lotion. Marcus held out a hand, which he took in both of his and began to rub the lotion in. It had a pleasant scent. Marcus's sharp nose detected neroli, the oil obtained from the blossom of the bitter orange tree, and small hints of Frankincense, an oil known for its regenerative properties. He congratulated himself briefly on these detecting skills. He may have been a poor scholar of the classics and literature, but botany was something that he knew well.

Lionel's head was bent, intent on his task. Marcus watched him covertly as he rubbed the lotion over each of his fingers then into the fleshy part of his palms, his touch firm yet wonderfully soothing. He traced circular patterns on his palm and then on the back of his hand. Once he was done with one hand, he took the other and began the task again. Marcus continued to study him, admiring the perfect sculpting of his facial bones, the glow of his skin moistened by the lotion and the generous curve of his red lips. He was seized by the urgent desire to clasp him by his delicate neck and kiss him, not in the gently seductive fashion that he had kissed females, but in a rough, hungry, devouring way.

Of course, he did no such thing. He was horrified and appalled. Dear Lord, what was happening to him? It must stop. It could not be. Abruptly, he pulled his hand away. "Thank you, Lionel," he muttered. "That is quite enough."

Lionel pulled back just as quickly as if stung, making Marcus instantly regret his words. But he simply nodded and stood to put away the jar back into his bag. He returned to the bed presently and slipped under the covers, turning on his side and staying as close to the edge as possible. "Well, goodnight," he said, and blew out the candle nearest to him.

"Goodnight, Lionel," Marcus replied, extinguishing the candle beside him.

THEY WERE ENVELOPED in complete darkness. Marcus closed his eyes and tried to settle to sleep, but he could not ignore the presence of this intriguing man beside him, even though said man in question had tried to put as much distance as possible between them. Lionel lay as still as a statue, though paying great attention, Marcus could faintly hear the rise and fall of his breaths. He knew he was not asleep. He shifted to get more comfortable, and immediately, he sensed Lionel move even further to the side. Any more and he would soon be falling over the edge of the bed. It would serve him right, Marcus thought acidly. Why was he acting like Marcus might pounce upon him? Was he a mind reader? Not that Marcus would do any such thing. He was a civilised human being. Moreover, he was not in the habit of seducing persons of his own sex. No indeed not.

He sighed loudly and tried to get to sleep. Minutes elapsed. He was still wide awake—and so was Lionel, damn him. He turned onto his side, evincing further movement from Lionel away from him. The man was now balancing precariously over the edge of the bed. This was ridiculous. The bed was wide enough for both of them to sleep comfortably, and sleep was what they would do, once he had remedied this situation. Without thinking the matter any further, Marcus reached across and took hold of Lionel's body, pulling it firmly towards him.

"What on earth?"

"Hush now," Marcus whispered sternly. "You were about to fall over the edge. You are acting as if I have the pox!"

"I—no. I did not want to disturb you, that is all."

Marcus did not let go of him, suspecting that if he did, Lionel would scurry back to the edge of the bed. Instead, he brought a leg over his to keep him securely in place. "Lionel," he said as reasonably as he could. "It is fear that you will fall to the floor that is disturbing me. Now let us be sensible about this. Stay here so we can both finally get some sleep."

It was Lionel's turn to sigh. "Very well." A moment later, he added, "You may let go of me."

Yes, Marcus should let him go. It was not at all seemly, the way he was holding him. He buried his nose into the back of Lionel's head, breathing in the fragrance of his hair. It must be the pomade he used. It was a fresh burst of herbal extracts. He scented a hint of rosemary, perhaps also some sage and the fruity notes of lemon. Buried beneath these herbal aromas was the smell of him, sweet and musky. Marcus breathed it deeply into his lungs. He ran his nose through Lionel's hair and down to the silky skin of his neck. There, his natural scent was stronger. He rubbed his nose and lips over his neck, all the while chanting to himself, *Let him go. Let him go.*

"Marcus," Lionel groaned.

"Hmm," Marcus grunted, still unable to stop. "Will you please let me hold you for a little more?" he pleaded. "Then I shall let us both sleep, I promise." He dropped soft kisses to Lionel's neck, his earlier need to be rough replaced by tenderness. He felt him shiver under his touch. Lord help him, if he thought Lionel was shivering in fright, then he would let him go at once. But he knew, he simply knew it was not fear but delicious desire that Lionel was feeling. His groans turned to moans as Marcus took a soft bite of his flesh. Marcus's hand drifted downwards, encountering the jutting firmness of Lionel's sex. Oh yes, he was aroused, and Marcus was equally hard.

Lionel stopped Marcus's hand with his. "We shouldn't," he whispered breathlessly.

"I know, Lionel, but you have awoken a hunger I never knew I had in me," Marcus responded huskily. "Tell me to stop, and I will. Or let us find pleasure together this night. No one shall know but us, and when the day comes, we can put this night behind us, never to mention it again. Only let me hold you now and kiss you." So saying, he dropped more kisses to his neck.

"It would be wrong—" Lionel began to say.

"No," Marcus stopped his words with a hiss. "It cannot be wrong when our good Lord saw fit to make you this way, and me too, it seems. Do not feel shame, please, Lionel."

Marcus felt him breathing shallowly, weighing his words. Abruptly, Lionel turned in his arms, and then their lips met. Oh Lord, yes. Yes! Lost to everything but the pleasure of Lionel's taste on his lips, Marcus plundered his mouth, devouring him hungrily just as he had wanted to earlier. He had never kissed anyone like this before. Always, he had been conscious of the strength of his large body and been careful to exercise restraint, but not this time. Lionel was equally strong and powerful. And Marcus was burning with an unrestrained desire.

His tongue found his, roaming roughly over every corner of his mouth, tasting his essence, savouring, making a veritable feast out of him. Lionel met him stroke for stroke, devouring him in turn. It was like a duel between them, a delicious duel that left them reeling with ecstasy. Marcus held Lionel tightly to him, rubbing his engorged cock against him, feeling Lionel's swollen member rub on him. "Lionel," he breathed between kisses. "Oh, Lionel." Lionel bit his lower lip in response and sucked it hard. Marcus groaned. "Oh, dear man, I am so close."

"Me too," Lionel panted.

They rutted against each other and kissed, each kiss followed by another, seemingly without end. Marcus moaned into his mouth and felt Lionel's responding moan. And then he erupted, his seed gushing from the tip of his cock and soaking into both their shirts. He felt Lionel's quivers as he spent in his arms. Sweet, wondrous Lionel.

They stilled, holding each other close. Eventually, Marcus released Lionel to sit up and remove his soiled nightshirt, using it to wipe the remnants of his spend clean. In the dim moonlight, he saw Lionel do the same. Hopefully, it would be dry by morning, and Stubbs would be none the wiser about their activities this night. Marcus settled back under the covers, bare as the day he was born. "Come, my dear," he said hoarsely to Lionel. "Let us sleep." Lionel joined him in the bed, equally bare. Marcus gathered his body to him, dropping a kiss to the soft skin of his neck, and felt him gradually slacken against him. Holding him close, he breathed in his sweet and now familiar scent. Nothing in his life had ever felt as right as this. His heart slowed as he slipped into a deep, contented sleep.

CHAPTER 10

A WISH AND A PROMISE

THE CALL OF the rooster outside wakened Liora from a deep sleep. Tendrils of light drifted in through the half-open sash window, signalling that it was now morning and high time to put this interlude behind them. Carefully, Liora eased herself out of Marcus's arms. He muttered in his sleep but did not wake. As quietly and quickly as she could, she dressed, then picked up the discarded nightshirts on the floor. She threw hers deep into her valise then gave Marcus's shirt, which was caked in his dried spend, a quick clean with a washcloth and draped it on the end of the bed. Then she tiptoed out of the room.

Downstairs, she found the inn beginning to come to life. After doing her business in the privy, wrinkling her nose at the strong smells, she found water to wash her hands with, discreetly adding some antiseptic solution which she kept in a vial in her pocket. Then she made her way to the dining room, empty of patrons at this early hour, where she requested a coffee from the maid who was busily sweeping the floors. The maid put the broom to one side, curtsied and hurried off to do the gentleman's bidding. Then Liora sat herself at the same corner table as yesterday and took a moment to think.

Last night had been a mistake—a passionate, wonderful mistake—which she needed to ensure never happened again. The best thing to do, she decided, was to act with insouciance, pretending nothing had in fact happened.

In her own mind though, she could not keep to this pretence. How could she ever forget last night? Who would have thought the duke, a mere Earth human limited in his knowledge of the universe, would know how to kiss so well? The recollection turned her skin to goose flesh. He had devoured her with such pent-up hunger, as if he had been starved. She took a deep breath to steady herself. Then came another realisation. Starved he may have been, in a sense. Now that Marcus had become aware of his sexual inclinations, feelings he may have subconsciously repressed over the years must be rushing to the surface. That would explain the hunger with which he had kissed her. It had less to do with herself than with the fact that he had finally opened the floodgates to his true feelings for men.

The thought brought a stab of pain to her chest just as the maid came in with the coffee. Liora forced a smile in thanks and took a first sip of the steaming liquid. What an irony that the best kiss she had ever experienced could be due to a man thinking that she too was male. It would be her just deserts for the deception she was perpetrating. It also served as her reminder that no matter how attractive and charming she found Marcus to be, there could be no possibility of anything romantic—or otherwise—developing between them. He was attracted to men, late though he might be in making this discovery, and Liora, despite the efficacy of her disguise, was not a man. He was an Earth human, and she had travelled millions of light years from her own world, which was far more advanced. They could have little in common.

The maid bustled in again, this time bearing fresh bread, butter and cold cuts of meat. Liora thanked her and began to eat breakfast. An older gentleman and his lady entered the dining room, greeting her politely. She returned the greeting then continued to eat. Slowly, the dining room began to fill with the guests staying at the coaching inn, some on their way to London but most on their way home to their country estates now that the season was nearing its end. It was a mix of people. To her right sat a sour-faced dowager with a younger female companion listening subserviently to her pronouncements about the weather and the quality of the night's accommodation. Across from her was a portly gentleman of middle years with his family—a wife and two marriageable daughters by the looks of it. If they had been to London in hopes of making a suitable match, she did not think their trip had been successful. The gentleman looked bored, his lady peeved, and the two daughters were pouting petulantly. Over to her left sat two plainly dressed gentlemen, solicitors or some such other profession.

The door opened, and another guest entered the room. Marcus. He strolled in cheerfully, an amiable smile on his face as he said a good morning to the innkeeper. She noticed the pouting young ladies were now smiling prettily and batting their eyelashes at him. They had all risen to their feet as their father made himself known to the Duke of Coleford, claiming some sort of connection, and introduced his family to him. Marcus made his bows and responded courteously. She heard the portly gentleman invite him to partake of breakfast with them.

Marcus glanced across at her for an instant then turned his attention back to the gentleman. Was she to be thrust ruthlessly to one side, the inconvenient memories of last night brushed casually away? But no. With a gentle smile, Marcus made his excuses. "I thank you, sir, but I am to dine with Mr Reeves, my travelling companion. It has been an honour to make your acquaintance. Good day." Without further ado, he bowed and turned to head towards her.

She rose to her feet at his approach. "Your Grace," she murmured.

"Good morning, Lionel," he responded, lowering his big body into the chair opposite her.

"Good morning."

He perused her face. "Slept well?" he enquired.

She raised her brow at this. He must know the answer to that question. "Perfectly," she said. "And yourself?"

"Marvellously," he pronounced with a wicked gleam in his eyes.

"It must be the bedding," she mumbled. "I found it to be superior to that in the previous inns."

"The bedding?" he pondered. He grinned then. "Of course, it could not have been anything else."

Seriously? What happened to that promise to put last night behind them and never mention it again? She glowered in his direction, but he ignored her and helped himself to a generous serving of roast beef. He appeared to be in fine spirits this morning.

Once their breakfast was over, there was nothing for it but to board the carriage and start the final leg of their journey to London. For the first half-hour, they sat mostly in silence as she watched the fields, hamlets and villages go by. The closer they got to London, the more populated the landscape became. No longer was it a vast moorland she saw outside her window, but a multitude of small villages separated by neatly cultivated fields, their harvests mostly done.

It was a clement day, the July sun tempered by a cooling breeze. She almost wished she could listen to something on her ear device, anything to while away the time and distract herself from the temptation of the man sitting beside her. She breathed in his fresh and earthy scent, one that was sensuously familiar to her after their intimacies last night. Occasionally, she felt him cast glances in her direction, but he honoured her desire not to speak. Until, quite out of the blue, he asked, "Will you come to the Maybury ball, Lionel?"

"Me? What on earth for?" She turned to face him in surprise.

Marcus gazed at her earnestly. "It would be a great help to me to have your company at the ball."

She studied his ridiculously handsome face in bemusement then shook her head. "Quite apart from the fact I do not have an invitation to the ball, I recall telling you that I do not move in the same social circles as you."

"I can arrange to have an invitation sent to you, but please do say you will come."

"I do not possess the social graces for such entertainments, Marcus," she said, shifting uncomfortably in her seat. "I am not sure I even know the steps to all the dances."

He pounced on this. "I am equally lacking in those social graces, Lionel, so that will make two of us." Then his eyes lit up as an idea came to him. "As for the dancing, you shall have to come and practise at my house. I have three sisters who would be most willing, I am sure, to help us both master the steps."

"You do realise, Marcus," she said irritably, "that I am travelling to London on business, not pleasure. There will be much work for me to do once I am there."

He placed a hand on her arm, the molten brown of his eyes shining brilliantly as he pleaded, "Please, Lionel, I promise not to take too much of your valuable time. You shall have the whole day tomorrow to tend to your business affairs, but then you must come to dinner at my house. You can meet Mama and my sisters, and we can practise the dances afterwards."

She stared down at his hand, enveloping her arm. "Why should it matter so much for me to be there?" she wondered, her voice a little hoarse. "It will hardly give you social cachet to be seen in my company."

His hand slid down her arm to cover hers, pressing gently. "It matters, Lionel," he said softly, "because I dread such occasions, and it would be a great help to have a friend there with me."

"A friend?" she snorted. "We have barely known one another two days."

He buried his face in her hair, dropping tender kisses. "I know the sweet taste of you, Lionel," he said huskily, "and the little moans you make when you spend. I think that puts us on intimate enough terms to be considered friends."

She turned her face to him, and he took the opportunity to press his lips to hers. She accepted the kiss, lingered there a moment or two, then she forced herself to pull back. "You said we would put last night behind us and never mention it again," she told him, her tone accusing.

He released her. "You are right, and I am sorry," he said contritely. "I only brought it up to refute your assertion that we cannot be friends on such short acquaintance."

Liora cast him a cold look, trying to demonstrate the firmness of her intent. "We cannot repeat it, Marcus, not ever again. If you give me your promise on that, then I will come to the ball with you."

He considered this then inclined his head. "You have my word."

They resumed their silence, a little more companionable this time. It was not long though before Marcus broke it again with another surprising question. "If you could have one wish granted for yourself, Lionel, what would it be?"

He lounged beside her, his long legs stretched diagonally to fit in the space, his head resting against the window jamb. His languid pose was belied by the piercing scrutiny of his eyes on her. She could feel them burrowing into her, wanting to discover her secrets.

She began to respond then stopped. She was about to say that her dearest wish was to return to her old home, of course not mentioning that it was a planet millions of light years away called Uvon. Wasn't that what she had craved for so long? A return to her old life on Uvon and the freedom to live on her terms? And yet as she came to speak, the words would not come out.

She took several moments to think, to examine her mind and heart. Marcus did not rush her. He waited patiently for her answer. When finally came her reply, what she said was surprising even to her own ears. "If I could have one wish, it would be to find a mate, someone who loves me unreservedly and with whom I can build a life with, a family."

Marcus nodded his head in understanding. "It is a very human wish to have," he concurred. After a pause, he added, "Do you think you might find such happiness one day with a lady of your acquaintance?"

They had circled back to her big falsehood. He was wondering how she could find lasting love with a woman, given her sexual inclinations. She tried to imagine it from this fictional perspective. "It may be possible," she said finally. "Though the lady may not ignite my carnal passions, still we could share a deep love and devotion."

Marcus examined his fingers, clasped loosely together in his lap. "Yes," he murmured. "I suppose it could be so. But what then, should you meet a man that ignited such passions? Could you stay true to the lady in question?"

"Could you?" she countered in response.

His face creased in troubling thought. Then he sighed. "Therein lies the rub," he said. "To live a life unable to express one's true self is not likely to be conducive to lasting happiness, especially if sinful temptation came knocking at the door." He stared at her, heat flaring in his beautiful brown eyes. "I think," he said slowly, "I would find it nigh on impossible to resist the man that ignited such passions."

She felt a sudden compulsion to kiss him and re-live something of last night's passion. She knew he felt it too; the sexual tension crackled in the air. But he had made a promise never to repeat it. She saw the knowledge in his eyes, and the frustration. With an effort, he tore his gaze away. After a moment, he went on, "It would have to be a very understanding lady, one who would turn a blind eye to such instances of carnal passions with another, in the knowledge that in all other ways, I would stand devoted to her and to my family."

"Yes," she said. "That is a possibility, though it is a rare being that would be so understanding."

"The privilege of being a duchess and mistress of Coleford Hall might encourage a willingness to be so," he said with a hint of bitterness. There was no pretence any longer that he was talking about himself. She could see that their lovemaking had spurred him into some profound soul searching, as such things must. It was no easy thing to discover that you held desires that society would decry. Perhaps it would go towards explaining why all these years, he must have instinctively repressed his attraction to males—until last night. And now that the wool had come off his eyes, he could not pretend any longer to be something he was not. Instead, he grappled with this newfound knowledge and what it could mean for him.

Poor Marcus. She felt an urge to hold his large frame to her and to run her fingers caressingly through his sandy mane of hair. Whoever said that big muscled men could not be fussed over and petted? In truth, his situation was not so different to how she had felt all those years ago when she had learned she was to be exiled to a world that did not allow her to live as she had been groomed to. Here on Earth, she had to be meek and subservient, as all decent females were expected to be. She had to efface all trace of dominance from her character. And though she had lived with her fellow Uvonians in the safety of Reeves Hall, still some of the ways of the outside world had seeped in. Broek's over-protectiveness, for instance, was something that would have been unheard of on Uvon. It was from this sense of being smothered that she had attempted to escape with her disguise, though she found herself now trapped between her desire for Marcus and the lie she was perpetuating.

With an effort, she returned to the matter at hand. "If the lady were to be wooed by your title and wealth," she remarked, "then I very much doubt she could show herself to be truly devoted to you."

He laughed, though without mirth. "It is a good thing then," he replied, "that I am not in search of a wife. It is finding husbands for my sisters that is the most pressing matter."

"And once they are all wed, it shall be your turn."

"Perhaps so, perhaps not," he drawled. "With my sisters wed, I can have no further responsibilities on my shoulders except to myself. I could decide to live out my days a bachelor."

She cocked her head to one side as she regarded him. "Should you remain a bachelor, you would not then have sons and daughters of your own. Would that not bother you?"

He shrugged. "I do not know for certain, though I am sure my sisters will provide me with a good many nieces and nephews in due course whom I can devote myself to." He leaned forward and regarded her equally closely. "Now that we have resolved my future, we come to you, Lionel. How are you to be granted your wish?"

"Hmm," she snorted. "Perhaps there is some fairy godmother out there that shall grant me my wish, for I do not believe I shall find that sort of happiness otherwise."

His large hand covered hers. It warmed her skin, soothing something in the depth of her soul. "Then I shall pray that you will," he said very softly.

She found that she had rested her head on his shoulder. It was an infinitely restful place to be. They stayed like this for some length of time, his hand remaining on hers. As the carriage drove smoothly on, she reflected that it was only two days since she had met this charming and thoughtful duke, yet it felt like much more. In that short time, they had forged a singular intimacy. She felt a desperate urge to be frank with him and to tell him the truth. She was Liora, a female of thirty-one years who hailed from a distant planet. She wanted to rip off the bodysuit and show him who she really was beneath it. Of course, she could not.

The carriage began to slow as they approached their next stop. Marcus removed his hand from hers, and she sat up straight. They descended from the carriage and entered the coaching inn, requesting a luncheon. Throughout the meal and the rest of the journey that day, they kept to less weighty topics for their discourse. Yet at all times there ran between them a warm thread of familiarity. It was a marvel how one could be acquainted with someone for years and never know them truly, and other times, one could know the true measure of a person within days. As they rolled down the narrow streets of London and arrived at Marcus's imposing townhouse on St James's Square, she was conscious of this great feeling of knowing him. The tall, handsome duke was no longer a stranger to her but an intimate friend—though the clock ticked over their friendship, which could last only so long as she stayed in role as Lionel.

CHAPTER 11

AN ABSURD NOTION

ONCE SHE HAD bid Marcus farewell, Liora continued the short drive to her own far less imposing townhouse on Barton Street. There, she was met by Esa, their housekeeper, who was also mated to the lately departed Jos. She greeted Liora solemnly, her red swollen eyes betraying the depth of her grief.

Liora embraced her soberly, expressing deep condolences for her loss. "I knew Jos to be a fine, upstanding man," she said, drawing back. "Our family has depended on him for a great many years, and we shall feel his loss, but that is nothing, I am sure, compared to what you must be feeling."

"We were mated for two decades and more," Esa replied, her voice thick with the tears she had recently shed.

"That is a long time. May the great lord Yol lessen your burden."

She nodded, wiping at her eyes with a handkerchief. "You will be wanting a bath after your travels," she said.

"Yes indeed," Liora replied. Casting a look around her, she asked quietly, "Are there any servants in the house I should know about?"

"No, Mistress Liora. There is a young maid that comes to do the cleaning in the mornings, but then it is just myself in the house, so you can be at your ease."

Liora let out a relieved breath. "Good. I cannot wait to remove this bodysuit and have a proper wash, and then I think

I shall remain as myself for the rest of the evening. I will eat my meal in the parlour upstairs and stay in my robe." In a softer tone she added, "I do not require anything fancy, just bread and slices of cold meat will do, perhaps also a piece of fruit?"

"Of course. I have heated the water in anticipation of your arrival, so you need not wait for a bath."

"Excellent," Liora smiled then made her way up the stairs to her bedchamber, where Galok had already deposited her baggage.

The London townhouse was not filled with their Uvonian technology in the way that Reeves Hall was. Being in the middle of the city, with neighbouring houses close by, there was not the privacy to live here in the comforts they were used to. However, there were some discreet upgrades that Liora had designed, such as the self-composting toilet and the water pump in the bathing room that spouted directly from a pipe leading to a large container of water in the kitchen. She had used all her ingenuity to design an internal purification system which cleansed the water then split it into two separate compartments—one for cold water and the other laid over the kitchen hearth for heating. It was an imperfect system, but at least the basics of hygiene were there.

In the bedchamber, she pulled off her boots then hastily divested herself of every layer of clothing until she was able to be released from the bodysuit. Ah, that felt much better. She glanced down at her body, curiously relieved to see two pert breasts rather than the brawny and hairy chest she had sported the last two days. She was herself again, if one could discount the male appendage attached to her nether regions. Naked, she pattered to the bathing room and began pumping hot water into the tub. Once it was filled, she stepped into it with a happy sigh, easing muscles that had been stiff from sitting in the carriage all day.

She soaked in the water for some time, her thoughts returning time and again to the duke she had encountered on her travels. What would he think if he were to see her as she was now? Would he find this version of her attractive, or was it the powerfully muscled Lionel in the bodysuit that he was drawn to? She glided her hands over the smoothness of her body and cupped the softness of her breasts. If it were his big calloused hands holding these breasts, would he appreciate their curvaceous swell or would he miss the broad muscularity of her male form? It was a pointless question, for he could not be allowed to see her as she truly was. And yet she could not help wondering if his desire for her was due to an instinctive sensing of her femininity—her smell, her taste, the softness of the skin on her face. Faint hope. It was best not to dwell.

She sat up in the bath and scrubbed her body with a washcloth, then carefully washed her hair, massaging a scented cleansing solution into her scalp. She emerged from the tub, her skin pink and gleaming but finally clean. After towelling herself dry, she slipped on a silky robe, tying the sash at her waist. Tapping the communicator on her signet ring, she sent a quick message to her brothers telling them she had arrived safely in London, then she headed over to the upstairs parlour.

It was a mid-sized room with oak floors and wood panelling on the walls, giving it a warm, welcoming feel that insulated occupants from the hustle and bustle of the city outside—though it was quieter now in the late hours of the evening. There were several comfortable armchairs and a chaise longue set next to a walnut side table. She went to this table now and ran her fingers over the dials discreetly positioned on the underside, entering the required code. With a small pop, the lock on the drawer disengaged, allowing her to open it and withdraw the small portable console that was kept in there.

She took it out, placing it on her lap as she settled onto the chaise. It took a few moments to energise it, seeing as it had been several weeks since it had been used by Broek on his last visit to London. First, she replaced the fuel cell with a new one she had brought with her, which ought to provide power to the device for the duration of her stay. With that done, she started it up, and began looking through the various sections relating to their business. There was a live sound and picture feed transmitting from two locations, their warehouse at the docks and their company offices on Threadneedle Street, within easy reach of the Stock Exchange. There were recording devices in each of these buildings, well-hidden so as not to be noticed by the people working there. They had been installed by Broek when he first set up the business upon their arrival in England, and he had access to this feed from his own console at home, allowing him to keep an eye on things even when he was far away from London. Right now, as it was late evening and outside of working hours, there was not much to see on the feed.

She moved to inspect another set of files, detailed ledgers of the stock they kept in the warehouse and of their sales transactions. These were notarised by the clerks employed at their offices, working under Jos's supervision. However, only Jos had been authorised to negotiate and conclude any trades. It was Jos too that had collected the payments and either stored the money in their vault, hidden securely in the basement of this townhouse, or deposited funds with Drummonds Bank. It was a measure of how much they had trusted Jos that they had placed such authority in him. And now with him gone, he would be hard to replace. In truth, she could not see anyone other than herself or one of her brothers stepping into the role. Would she be prepared to live here in London as a man for the long term, not just a few weeks? She was not certain she could.

Casting her eyes over the ledgers, she could see that on the eve of his death, Jos had recorded the arrival of a large shipment of raw sugar. They would need to find buyers for it in the forthcoming weeks. Perhaps in the last few days, there had already been several callers to their offices on Threadneedle

Street wanting to purchase supplies of the commodities they traded, and come away disappointed. First thing tomorrow, she would go to their offices and speak to the head clerk there to get a more up-to-date picture of what may have occurred since Jos had passed away and to arrange appointments with prospective buyers. Then she would pay a visit to the warehouse. A busy day lay ahead of her, after which there would be dinner with the duke and some dancing lessons. How she had let him talk her into that, she did not know.

Just then, there was a knock at the door followed by Esa's entrance bearing a tray of food. "Ah, thank you, Esa," she said as the housekeeper placed it on the side table. Liora could see that she had gone to more effort than had been required, as there was a bowl of stew there together with the cold meats and bread, and what looked to be a lemon tart for pudding. "You spoil me."

Esa quirked her lips in the semblance of a quick smile. "Not at all, Mistress Liora. It is the least I can do, and to be quite honest, I find it helps my grief to keep busy."

"Yes," she nodded understandingly. "But thank you all the same." When they had lost Mother and Father, one thing that had helped them cope with their bereavement had been to busy themselves with work.

Esa made to leave, but at the door, she stopped and turned back to face her. "Mistress Liora."

"Yes, Esa?"

"Jos's death. It makes no sense," the housekeeper said falteringly. "He was so fit and strong."

"These things can happen," Liora said very gently, "even to persons seemingly in the bloom of health."

"Not Jos!"

Liora paused in her task as she set the console back in the drawer. What could she say to that?

"He was only eight and forty years old," Esa went on, "and fit as a fiddle. I made sure he ate well and exercised. He was in excellent health. I simply cannot believe that his heart gave out, just like that."

"What are you suggesting, Esa?"

The housekeeper's expression was set in the rigid lines of grief. Taking a deep breath, she shook her head and said sadly, "I do not know. Only that his passing does not make any sense, and that there was something troubling him. I could tell, as only a mate can, though he did not like to worry me with talk of the work he did."

Liora considered this for a long moment. What Esa was implying was unthinkable. Could Jos have died from something other than natural causes? It was an absurd notion. Even had he been fit and in the full bloom of health, there could have been any number of reasons for his untimely passing. Perhaps he had eaten something that did not agree with him — a stale meat pie from the market or some badly smoked fish. After all, the standards of hygiene in this filthy metropolis left much to be desired.

"Is there anything else you can think of, Esa, anything that would cast further light on this matter?" she asked quietly.

The housekeeper shook her head. "I cannot think of anything, except what I have told you."

Liora pressed her lips together. Finally, she said, "I am sorry, Esa. May Yol grant you relief from the pain of your grief."

The housekeeper inclined her head and turned to go. Once the door shut behind her, Liora let out a sigh then began to eat, reflecting on what she had learned. The manner of Jos's passing was sudden and tragic, but, she concluded, it could not be anything more. She decided not to mention the matter to Broek when he next called, not unless she were to discover some new and compelling evidence. Not long later, her meal complete, she wearily took herself to bed.

CHAPTER 12

A SLIP OF THE TONGUE

IT WAS GOOD, of course, to be reunited with dearest Mama and his three sisters. Yet Marcus could not help making an observation. In the company of Lionel these past few days, he had felt himself to be bold and assertive. It was at his suggestion that they had journeyed to London together, and it was his action that had initiated their passionate lovemaking that unforgettable night.

Now that he was back in the heart of his family, Marcus reverted to his old way of being. He was patient and accommodating, pliant and amenable. He had found, over the course of his years, that it made for a far easier life to accede to the wishes of Mama and his sisters than to resist. He was but one male in the midst of four headstrong and intractable females. This had been the case even when Papa had been alive, for his dearly departed parent had also chosen the course of least resistance when it came to his wife and daughters. He must have inculcated such habits in his son, though to be fair, this ascendancy of the fairer sex in his home was of a benign order. Mama and his sisters were interfering, that was true, but they were led by their kind hearts.

No sooner had he sat in the parlour than they began to fuss over him.

"Marcus, do rest your feet on here," said Diana solicitously, placing a padded footstool before him. She was the middle one of his three sisters.

"Julia," Mama said to her youngest daughter, "be a dear and pour your brother a glass of that fine ratafia. Or would you prefer to have one of your herbal infusions?" She did not give him a chance to reply, for quickly she decided, "No, the ratafia would be best on this warm evening."

Julia duly poured the sweet wine and brought it over to him with an impish grin. He took it from her with a corresponding smile, drinking it down obediently. Ratafia was not his beverage of choice, but he had acquired a taste for it, seeing as he was often plied with it.

Portia, the eldest of his sisters and the beauty of the family, glided over gracefully to offer an extra cushion for his comfort. So doing, she remarked, "I noticed when you arrived that you were not in the Coleford chariot. Did you not wish to travel in it?"

"Ah well, you see I had a mishap on the road and had to abandon it," he replied.

"Oh no!" All eyes fixed on him in concern.

He explained what had occurred and how he came to travel the rest of his journey in Lionel's carriage. This evinced a further round of questioning and much curiosity about his travel companion.

"Reeves, hmm," murmured Mama. "I do not believe I know the family. Is he gentleman-born?"

"Oh yes," he assured her. "I am told the Reeves are an ancient landed family from Cornwall."

"But they engage in trade," Portia said with a shudder.

"They hold a vast landed estate called Reeves Hall, so they are undoubtedly members of the gentry. However, as far as I understand, they also own an interest in a shipping business."

"There is no other name for it but trade," insisted Portia.

"I suppose so," he said with reluctance. "Is that so very bad?"

"Such things are much frowned upon by the *ton*," stated Diana, nodding knowledgeably.

"Well, I think it is nonsense. Why should not a family invest in the shipping of necessary commodities such as the coffee you drink each morning? It is as worthy a way of earning a living as farming the land."

"You may think so, dear Marcus," offered Mama, "but that is not what society decrees."

He curled his lips stubbornly. "Seeing as I am a duke and a scion of high society, I believe I may decide such things for myself."

"Tell me more about this Lionel Reeves," interjected Julia, lounging comfortably on the chintz sofa with a book in her lap—no doubt the latest gothic novel. "Is he handsome?"

"Yes, very handsome." He felt his cheeks redden as he recalled Lionel's dark eyes and soft, kissable lips.

Julia sat up quickly, dropping the book to the floor as she clasped her hands together in glee. "You must make him known to us, Marcus." She went to pick up the book and added, "You know how much we enjoy the company of handsome gentlemen."

"But if his family engages in trade, he cannot be a good marriage prospect," lectured Portia.

"Oh, fustian!" retorted Julia. "As if I care about that. Must everything come down to the subject of marriage? Why cannot I simply enjoy the pleasure of feasting my eyes on a handsome gentleman?"

"I quite understand the enjoyment to be had in the company of a good-looking gentleman," replied Mama diplomatically. "But Julia dear, you must care about the subject of marriage, for soon it shall be your turn to find a suitable husband."

"If I don't," said Julia with a stubborn tilt to her lips, "I shall simply live out my days a spinster and take care of dear Marcus."

"I do not need anyone to take care of me!" he expostulated.

At the same time, Mama declared, "It shall be Marcus's bride that takes care of him."

"Perhaps that Mr Reeves has a pretty younger sister whom Marcus could marry," giggled Diana.

He gazed at them all in irritation. The thought of his sisters wanting to flirt with Lionel was not one that he found comforting, nor the idea of marrying a younger sister of his—if she even existed. *He wanted Lionel for himself.*

"Never mind all that," cried Julia impatiently. "Marcus, do invite Mr Reeves over so we may decide for ourselves just how handsome he is."

"As a matter of fact," he replied, his voice stiff, "I have invited him to dinner tomorrow evening, and I shall also write to Lord Maybury to ask that he extends an invitation to Lionel for the ball."

"Excellent," smiled Julia approvingly.

He was not so sure of that anymore. He had wanted Lionel as a friendly companion at the ball and someone to help him navigate what was sure to be a trying evening. It had hardly been his intention to see his sisters nor any other eligible young lady fawn over him. He had not realised until now that he had such a tendency towards jealousy in his character. Seemingly, Lionel had brought it out of him in addition to making him feel bold.

Well now, the deed was done. And it might not be so bad. He would simply have to make sure no lady, in fact no one but himself, monopolised Lionel's company. At least he would get to see him again soon, for already, he missed his company.

Later that evening, when the candlelight was out and he was tucked comfortably in bed, his mind strayed to Lionel once more, remembering the deliciously depraved things they had done the previous night. He should feel ashamed. Most everyone would say that what they had done was wrong. And yet his body heated in remembrance of that kiss, of the hunger with which they had devoured each other. He recalled the softness of Lionel's skin as he had rained kisses on his face and the delicate line of his neck. He thought of how they had rubbed their erect shafts together and Lionel's whimpers as they had both reached completion. His hand was at his engorged cock, stroking feverishly as he imagined it was Lionel holding him so, Lionel kissing him. With a muffled groan, he exploded into his hand, staining the nightshirt with his spend for a second night in succession.

THE FOLLOWING MORNING, Marcus was kept busy with a never ending stream of callers to the house, all of them wanting to pay their respects to the newly arrived Duke of Coleford. Determined mamas and their simpering daughters vied with young, aspiring gentlemen in their eagerness to make a favourable impression on him. It was a good thing that he did not have a predisposition for arrogance, as such attention might otherwise have gone to his head. Having so recently been a penniless man of little consequence, the sudden interest in his person could not be ascribed to anything but the title and wealth he had come into. It was certainly not for his great wit that these fine people were descending upon his house in St James's Square.

He bore it as well as he could, though he was reminded once more why he spent as little time as he possibly could in London. Were it not for his family duties and Lionel's presence in this city, he would hightail it back to Coleford Hall.

By early afternoon, the stream had turned into a trickle, and Marcus instructed Denby, the butler, to turn away any remaining callers. They gathered for their luncheon, after which Mama retired to her chamber for some rest, as did Portia, who followed a strict beauty regimen requiring that she dab her face with a beautifying mask. Marcus had witnessed this sight many a time—a ghoulish looking Portia, lying as still as stone, her face smeared with a strong smelling, clay-like concoction, and her eyes hidden behind green cucumber orbs. At times like these, he congratulated himself on having been born male and not needing to be subjected to such indignities.

In the parlour, he found Diana busy with her needlework and Julia engrossed in a novel. They both looked up at him as he entered.

"I am minded to go out for a ride in Hyde Park. Would any of you care to join me?" he asked, flinging himself down beside Julia on the sofa.

"Now?" Diana raised a brow. "It is much too early for it. Fashionable London does not ride on Rotten Row until five o'clock."

"That is precisely why now is the time to go," he explained, "for I have no wish to mingle with the doyens of society. I have done enough mingling already this day."

Diana smiled. "Yes, it has been a busy morning. However, you must excuse me from this outing, as I wish to finish embroidering these flowers on the hem of my ballgown, which I shall wear to the Maybury ball."

He turned to his other sister. "And you, Julia?"

She popped her book closed and set it down on the side table. "I believe I shall join you," she stated decisively.

"Good. Then be ready in ten minutes, else I leave without you."

Already, she was on her feet, flying out the door with a wave of her hand. He followed her up the stairs and went quickly to his chamber to change into riding clothes. At the allotted time, they met in the hallway and made their way out to where their saddled horses awaited them. Marcus assisted Julia onto her mount then jumped onto his, patting the fine-looking mare admiringly. The previous duke had kept a first-rate stable of horses in London, though to all accounts he himself had not been much of a horseman. All this was now his, and in this moment, he could not but feel blessed at his good fortune. He may have railed inwardly at the pompousness of the *ton* and at the people who sought favour with him because of his title, but he had no need to be told just how fortunate he was.

They began the short ride to the open spaces of Hyde Park, going at a slow trot on the busy cobbled streets. Once they reached the long bridle path known as Rotten Row, they picked up speed, urging their horses into a gallop. There were few others about as they enjoyed a brisk ride, the wind whipping their faces, the pounding of the hooves on the dry earth vibrating in their ears. For the first time since his arrival in London, he felt carefree.

At last, they slowed to a gentle trot, letting the horses cool off from their exertions. Julia turned to him, a wide smile illuminating her face. "That was tremendous!" she exclaimed. "When I am out with Portia or Diana, they never let me ride so fast. Only with you, dearest Marcus. Now you may understand why I very selfishly wanted you here despite knowing how much you despise London."

"In that case, I am glad to be here."

She cast him another affectionate glance then demanded, "Now tell me more about this Mr Lionel Reeves. I can see he has made quite the impression on you."

Had he given himself away somehow? Julia was ever the perceptive one in the family. He decided to stall for time. "What makes you think so?" he asked, his tone casual.

"When you speak of him," she said sagely, "you have an expression almost of hero worship on your face." She smiled at his reddening countenance, and he cursed himself for this inability to hide what he felt. How was he ever going to conceal this forbidden attraction? It was nigh on impossible. He may as well give up and head home to the country at the earliest opportunity before he made a spectacle of himself.

Julia chuckled. One would never think from her manner with him that he was six years her senior. "There is no need to look so put out, Marcus. All I meant to say is that I am most eager to meet this gentleman and find out what it is about him that has you so in thrall."

He could not help but tell her some of it. "He is astonishingly knowledgeable about so many things, and he is a gifted inventor too."

"Indeed?"

He described to her the cooling contraption in his carriage. She listened raptly then declared, "That, I should like to see."

"I am sure Lionel will not mind taking us for a ride in his carriage one day so that you may experience that wonderfully cooling breeze," he said, a tad boastfully. Could he help it if he was proud of his new friend? Or was it his lover? No, no, he had sworn an oath never to repeat the things they had done that night. Lionel could not be anything more than a friend.

But he so wished he could be his lover.

That is, if they lived in a world where such a thing could be a possibility. He hungered for Lionel in a way that went far beyond mere hero worship. It was carnal. He desired him as no man should another. At this realisation, there came a hollow feeling in the pit of his stomach. He glanced at his sister hesitatingly, then ventured, "Julia, have you ever heard talk of men who desire other men?"

She frowned. "I cannot say that I have. I only know a little from what I have read in the papers," she replied, looking curiously his way.

"What have you read?"

"Well," she said, "most recently there was the case of the bishop who was arrested and stripped of his see after being caught rather compromisingly with a soldier."

He nodded. The story sounded faintly familiar. He knew not where he might have heard of it, for he hardly ever read the newspapers. It must have caused enough of a furore to reach even his ears. He still had more questions, and though Julia was young, he knew her to be knowledgeable beyond her years. So, he asked, "What would be considered as compromising? Were they embracing, kissing or doing something else?"

Julia laughed uncomfortably. "As if I would know!" After a moment's pause, she confided, "Do not rebuke me for this, Marcus, but I did once see a salacious cartoon of it. I am sure it was not meant for my eyes, but it happened to be among a pile of papers on Lord Livemoor's desk."

"Lord Livemoor's desk?" he asked, confused.

"The Livemoors are acquaintances we have made during our stay here," she explained. "Their daughter, Helena, had her debut this season, and we have received several invitations to dine with them. Well, one day, Lord Livemoor claimed he had forgotten his snuff box in his study, and being of an obliging nature, I volunteered to go fetch it for him. And once there, I could not resist catching a look at the papers on his desk, for I could see there were colour prints."

"I see. And what was in the print in question?"

"Well, it showed the bishop being caught in the act with him saying 'Do let me go. I'll give you £500'." She chuckled at the memory.

"Was he embracing the soldier?"

"No, but here's the thing," she said, lowering her voice to barely above a whisper, though there was no one about to hear them. "He had his breeches undone."

Marcus pictured it in his mind. The bishop's breeches were undone so he could... do what exactly? Something similar to what Lionel and him had done, rubbing their cocks together until they spent? Or was it something else? The trouble was that he did not know enough about these so called "unnatural crimes" for which some men had been indicted by the law. He had never had much interest in the matter until now. For of course, now that these feelings had awoken in his chest—and in his cock—he wanted to know all there was to loving another man. All there was to loving Lionel, if he would ever allow him to break that oath.

He felt Julia's eyes on him. "Marcus, why do you ask?"

"I am curious, that is all."

"But why?" Julia wore a puzzled frown.

"I... It is just something that occurred which had me wonder."

"What occurred?" His sister was damnably persistent.

He did not respond. He could not tell her. But unfortunately for him, Julia was quick-witted and could put two clues together. "Is it to do with this Lionel Reeves?"

Still he did not speak.

"It is! I am sure of it," she breathed excitedly. Then her mind jumped to the next clue. She gasped. "Do you think this Mr Reeves is one of them, one of those men who desire fellow men?"

"Of course not," he said hotly. Now he was angry, both with himself and with her. He had no right, no right at all to betray Lionel's secret. He growled furiously, "You are talking absolute balderdash, Julia, which is not worth repeating to anyone. Do you hear me?"

"Well then, why speak of him and in the next breath ask about that thing?" she countered mutinously.

"I don't know! It is just the way my mind works sometimes, jumping from one thought to another. It does not signify."

"I do not believe you," she said quietly. "Marcus, I can tell when you are being less than truthful."

"Believe me or not, see if I care," he spit out, still mad. Then, with an attempt at calm, he went on, "But Julia, it is imperative you understand what harm to a person's reputation could result from a loose tongue. I adjure you to keep quiet about this entire conversation. Forget we even spoke of this."

"You do not need to tell me," she said tartly. "I am quite aware." With a spur of her riding crop, she bid her horse to go faster, setting off at a smart pace. Marcus followed in her wake, galloping back the way they came, except this time, there was no joy at the wind whipping his cheeks. He was filled with remorse, mortification and worry. Had he let the cat out of the bag? And would Julia keep this knowledge to herself? What a numskull he was!

CHAPTER 13

A DINNER AND A CONFESSION

A SOLEMN-LOOKING BUTLER ushered her inside the grand house on St James's Square, announcing her name as he opened the door to the drawing room. It was a large and lavishly decorated room, fitting for a duke. Liora's first impression was of decorative mouldings on the ceiling, an ornate fireplace above which hung a gilt mirror, a richly patterned wallpaper and elegant furniture in tones of powder blue and cream. Her eyes were soon drawn to the tall figure of Marcus rising to his feet to greet her. Around him were several richly dressed ladies whom she presumed to be his mother and sisters. He approached her and said smilingly, "Lionel, how good to see you again."

"Your Grace," she replied with a bow.

"Now, now, Lionel, there is no need for formality between friends." He turned to the older lady beside him. "Mama, let me make you known to Mr Lionel Reeves."

The lady in question curtsied gracefully. "Mr Reeves," she murmured. "How do you do?"

"Mrs Cavendish," Liora bowed. "It is an honour to make your acquaintance."

The lady examined her with strikingly familiar brown eyes. "Mr Reeves," she said. "I believe we are much in your debt for coming to Marcus's rescue on the road."

"Not at all," Liora demurred. "It was the least anyone could have done." At this, the lady inclined her head. Her manner was courteous but not overly warm.

Then Marcus introduced her in turn to each of his sisters: Portia, Diana and Julia. It seemed the late Mr Cavendish had been inspired by the ancient Romans when he came to name his children. She felt their curious gazes on her, and she wondered what Marcus had told them about their journey to London. Nothing about their intimacies, naturally, but how had he described her, as Lionel? Had he talked of her at all? Was it in the briefest of terms, or had he expounded about their time together? And why did it matter to her at all?

She took a seat and listened to the conversations around her, responding when a remark was addressed in her direction. There was easy fondness between them; that was clear to see. And what was also clear was that these females ruled the roost, not Marcus. It was done with kind smiles and words of affection, but Liora could not help notice how his mother and sisters made decisions on his behalf all the while making a show of consulting him. For instance, in the matter of their activities the following day.

"Marcus dearest," began his mother. "What are you minded to do tomorrow afternoon? You know, of course, that we are invited to Lady Rockingham's card party in the evening."

"I did not know. Who is Lady Rockingham?"

"She is the widow of the late Lord Rockingham and a highly regarded figure in London society," spoke up Portia. "It is said her word can elevate or destroy the prospects of ladies making their debuts."

"In that case, she must be of great importance to you, Portia," replied Marcus offhandedly. "Has she given you her seal of approval?"

"Thankfully, yes," responded his mother proudly. "Portia has made a favourable impression on Lady Rockingham, which is why we have been honoured with an invitation to her card party. You will join us, of course. It will be expected."

"I would not miss it," responded Marcus obediently.

"But what are we to do in the afternoon?" wondered Diana.

Marcus hesitated, glancing at Liora. "I had hopes to pay Lionel a visit tomorrow."

"But Mr Reeves is here with us tonight, so there is no need for a visit," giggled Diana, looking amused.

"I was very much looking forward to taking a ride to Hyde Park in the open-top barouche," added Portia.

"Well, of course, you must," replied Marcus.

"Yes, and you must come with us too," said Diana.

"Really?" the youngest, Julia, made a grimace. "I would much rather we had another good gallop on horseback in Rotten Row."

Portia considered the matter. "I suppose if you go early enough, there will be time to do both the horse-riding and the barouche ride," she decided.

"Then it is settled, my dears," pronounced Mrs Cavendish. "Do go for some brisk exercise after luncheon, while I take my rest. Then later, Marcus, you can escort all three of your sisters in the barouche."

"Yes, Mama."

Liora was enraged, though she was not sure why. It could have nothing to do with her how these people chose to occupy themselves of an afternoon. But enraged she was, although she tried not to show it. How dare these ladies dictate what Marcus ought to do with his day? And why was he not fighting back? She looked pointedly at him, but he gazed absently at a painting on the wall opposite. She did not know what possessed her to wade into the matter. "Were you planning to visit me at home, Marcus, or to come to the docks?" she asked him.

His gaze swivelled to hers, and a smile broke out on his face. "The docks," he said. "I am keen to see the warehouse and all the great many goods there. I may even make a purchase of your tea and spices."

"Well, I shall be at the docks all afternoon, in case you decide to visit after all."

"The docks?" exclaimed Portia, aghast. "It would not be seemly for a gentleman to venture there."

"What poppycock," responded Julia heatedly. "Marcus is a duke and can go wherever he pleases." For once, Liora was in agreement with her.

She raised her brow challengingly at him. He stared at her a moment then turned to his sister. "Julia," he said with conviction. "You are quite right. I am a duke, and therefore can go wherever I please."

Good boy, thought Liora.

But then he added, "Though I will not forego our ride together. Perhaps I can postpone my visit to another day."

"Yes, my dear," opined his mother. "Another day would be best." The conversation was laid to rest as they were summoned to dinner.

Liora found herself seated beside Julia, who soon engaged her in an animated conversation, wanting to know her opinion on the latest works of gothic fiction, a subject matter of which she was obviously enamoured.

"You have read Melmoth the Wanderer?" Julia enquired.

"I'm afraid not," was Liora's reply.

"How about The Vampyre by John William Polidori?"

"I am not familiar with that work," she said.

"Well, you must know of Frankenstein by Mary Shelley. What think you of it?"

Again, Liora was forced to disclaim any knowledge of such books written by intellectually inferior Earth humans. She was a voracious reader, but her preference was for the higher quality penmanship of Uvonian authors. Julia appeared taken aback by this admission, but she pressed on. "How about poetry? What is your view on the works of Byron and Keats?"

"Oh, do stop, Julia," snapped Marcus from across the dinner table. "Not all of us must have a view on romantic poets or gothic novels."

All eyes turned to him in shock. It seemed the family was unused to Marcus speaking up in this way. Irked, Julia fired back, "It is little wonder the two of you are friends then, seeing as you are both philistines when it comes to literature."

"Julia, dear," admonished their mother.

Face flushed, Julia looked down at her plate. "I am sorry, Marcus," she muttered. "That was not well done of me."

Marcus fixed her with a stern stare, the first time tonight that Liora had seen him look commanding as befitted his station. He was, after all, the Duke of Coleford and the head of this family. Curtly he said, "Save your sorries for Lionel, for I do not think he deserved such an inquisition."

Promptly, Julia raised her eyes to Liora. "Mr Reeves, I had not meant to discomfit you with my interrogation. Please accept my apologies."

Liora laughed, deciding that she liked Julia most out of Lionel's three sisters. The lady was hot-headed, that was true, but there again, so was she at times. And Liora appreciated how she had immediately righted her wrong with an apology. "Do not worry about my feelings, Miss Julia," she told her, "but I was glad to hear you say sorry to Marcus, for I do not think *he* deserves to be called a philistine."

Now Marcus's warm gaze was on her. For the longest moment, their eyes locked as intimately as if in an embrace. Then the moment passed, and the conversation moved on. However, for the rest of the dinner, she was conscious of Julia's enquiring scrutiny.

At last, the meal was over, and the ladies retired to the drawing room, leaving her alone with Marcus to drink their port. It was a strange convention, one that she had derided often. Why should ladies not partake of port if they so wished? Why was it the sole preserve of males? But on this occasion, she welcomed the opportunity for some privacy. As soon as the footman had poured their wine, Marcus dismissed him with a nod of his head, and then they were alone.

The air thickened between them. At first, they did not speak. Liora stared at the tawny brown liquid in the glass before her. Then Marcus broke the silence. "It seems like an age since we have been alone together. I have missed it."

She laughed. "It was all of one day ago, Marcus, but I know what you mean." She lifted her gaze to his. "You are changed tonight, more diffident. Why do you let them browbeat you so?"

He looked down at his hands sheepishly then took a sip of his port. It reminded her to raise the glass to her own lips. She swirled the sweet wine on her tongue, finding it strangely pleasing. Perhaps she was finally developing a taste for the beverage. "It is habit so deeply ingrained that I do not realise I do it," Marcus said softly. He sighed then. "It is not in my nature to argue, for I hate to be at odds with the people I love. But there is more..." He paused, looking flustered.

"What is it?" she prompted gently. "You can tell me."

He stared at the drink in his hand; she waited expectantly. Finally, he expelled a deep breath. "Ever since I was a child," he murmured, "I have struggled with an affliction. It is something that pains me and makes me feel a lesser person." He did not elaborate.

Liora reached across the table and placed her hand on his. "Tell me," she said again.

Haltingly, he spoke. "I have always found it a struggle to read and to write despite all my efforts. What you might read in an instant takes me far longer to decipher. It is the same with writing." In a low voice, he continued, "That is why I did not go to Oxford like Papa, nor get ordained into the Church. The only thing I am good at, as you know, is nurturing plants in the garden."

She squeezed his hand and hissed, "That is not the only thing you are good at, Marcus. You are wise and see the world around you in ways that others do not see. You have a talent for putting people at ease. Take me, usually so awkward around others, but not with you. And as for the reading and writing, what you describe is not uncommon at all. It has nothing to do with a lack of understanding, nothing at all."

She heard his breath hitch. He regarded her with a brilliant gleam in his brown eyes, then pronounced, "That day my chariot lost a wheel and I met you was a wonderfully fortuitous one."

"It was for me too," she murmured under her breath.

He turned his hand palm up and clasped it around hers, then lifted it to his lips. Her heart stopped then started to beat wildly in her chest. She forced herself to remember. *She could not fall for the duke.*

Almost as if he could hear her thoughts, he released her hand and stood, saying briskly, "Let us rejoin the ladies. We have a lesson in dancing ahead of us."

She groaned, and he laughed, pushing her gently towards the door. "Come along now, Lionel, and let us see your moves."

The rest of the evening was spent in practising some country dances, reels, quadrilles and of course, the waltz, while Portia played lively tunes on the piano for them. Liora's claim that she could not dance was not quite true, for she knew the steps to the dances and performed them well enough, if a little stiffly. There were a few occasions where she mistakenly performed the female steps in the dance or forgot to lead her partner, but she was soon corrected on these errors. By the end of the evening, in any case, Diana judged both Marcus's and her skills to be adequate for the ball which was to take place the night after next. Would they see each other in the interim period? Liora did not know whether to hope so or not for she knew—*she could not fall for the duke.*

CHAPTER 14

ANOTHER CONFESSION

HAVING RETIRED TO his bedchamber for the night, Marcus's mind, as ever these days, was fixed on one person. It was like a madness, the way he could not stop thinking about Lionel. While Stubbs fussed around him, helping him to undress, putting away his soiled clothes and laying out tomorrow's garments, Marcus recalled every instant of the evening, sifting through and dwelling on the most precious moment; when Lionel had pressed his hand and told him he was wise. That was not something Marcus was accustomed to hearing said about himself.

He wondered when he would see Lionel again. Would he have to wait two days until the ball? It seemed unlikely that his family would allow him the luxury of time to himself in the busy social whirl of the days ahead.

He sighed.

"Your Grace does not wish for the blue superfine coat?" asked Stubbs, holding out said coat. "Perhaps the claret would be preferable?"

"I trust your able judgement in this matter, Stubbs," he said, still distracted by his thoughts.

"The blue superfine, I think," replied his valet.

"Then it shall be so."

With a satisfied smile, Stubbs laid out the coat on the chair in readiness for the morrow. Soon, he bid his master a good night and excused himself. Marcus got into the bed, settling himself comfortably under the covers. Just as he was about to extinguish the candle on the table beside him, there came a faint knock at his door. It opened, and Julia's face peeked inside. "Still awake? Oh, good," she said softly, coming inside and shutting the door behind her. Nimbly, she came over and perched on the end of the bed, re-arranging the folds of her robe.

"Julia, what is it?" he asked, not best pleased to have his happy reverie of Lionel interrupted.

"Are you still angry with me?" she demanded, eyeing him with a wrinkled brow.

"Certainly, I was cross with you for being unkind to my friend, calling him a philistine."

"Yes, yes, I know," she said impatiently, "and truly, I am sorry. You cannot still be mad about it."

"I am not."

"Well, good."

A pause. "Was there anything else?" he enquired.

"This Lionel Reeves."

"Yes?"

She cocked her head consideringly. "He is a strange fellow."

He took umbrage at the implied criticism. "How so?"

"I cannot quite say, only that there was something odd about him."

"If you are going to insult my friend," he began indignantly, "then you might as well see yourself out."

She held up a pacifying hand. "I did not mean any offence. It is simply that I am puzzled."

"In what way? Would you care to elucidate?"

She rested back on both her elbows, making herself far too comfortable on his bed. "The way he rose to your defence," she said, "and a few times, he cast a most particular look at you."

"What can you mean?"

She nodded her head, as if coming to a decision. "Yes, I do believe you are right. He is one of those men that desire their own sex—a sodomite."

"Hush!" he hissed at her. "Someone might hear."

"There is nobody about," she hissed back, though she obligingly lowered her voice. "I am right, aren't I?"

"A few glances are hardly evidence of anything," he insisted.

"It is not just that. There is also an air about him, a femininity. His face is almost too pretty for that of a man, and did you not notice his hands at dinner when he took off his gloves? So delicate."

It was a fact that Marcus had noticed Lionel's lovely hands many a time, but he was not about to disclose this to his sister. He merely shrugged. Julia continued her speculation, undeterred. "It is known, is it not, that these sort of men are often effeminate in their being." Her eyes burrowed into him. "You must have noticed this too, else why ask me about it on our ride earlier today?"

She was getting far too close to the truth for his comfort. In a last effort, he said, "What I have noticed, Julia, is the opposite of that. Lionel cuts a mightily fine figure with a body so muscled and shoulders so broad that they must be the envy of every man. There is nothing of the effeminate about him."

"Then why bring up the matter of sodomites during our ride?"

At all costs, he needed to shake off Julia's suspicions about Lionel. He could think of only one way to do it, though this threw him from the frying pot into the fire. He never was much of a quick thinker. "It was not to do with Lionel but with someone else," he muttered quickly.

"Someone else? Who?"

Gazing down at the coverlet with undue fascination, he admitted, "I have been wondering if, perhaps, I might not be one such of those men."

There, the truth was out. It was a shocking admission to make, if one was to go by the resounding silence that greeted his confession. He had made such a muddle of things, but at least her attention was now on him, not Lionel. All of a sudden, he heard a loud burst of laughter. "You?" she cried and laughed again.

"It is no laughing matter," he growled in consternation.

"Oh, but it is," she giggled. "How precious!"

"Julia!"

"Oh, very well," she chortled one last time. More calmly, she asked, "What on earth makes you think such a thing, Marcus? I know for a fact that you spent an entire summer chasing the petticoats of Annie Bartlett, that milliner's daughter. And what about the time we went to Bath for the waters and you became infatuated with Miss Wilmington?"

All this was true. Nevertheless, none of those ladies came close to making him feel what he did for Lionel. "It is different now," he said quietly. "Lately, I have been feeling intense desire for a man."

"For Lionel?"

He did not confirm nor deny. She sighed, reading the truth in his downturned gaze. "I see." Another sigh, then, "Oh Marcus." She was at a loss for several moments as no doubt any young lady would be at hearing such a confession. Eventually, she gathered herself to ask, "Is there nothing you can do to fight this unnatural desire?"

"One cannot fight one's feelings. They rise up in me without my volition."

"But it is wrong."

"It feels too right to be wrong, but I will concede it is something deemed wrong by the world at large."

She hesitated. "And what of Lionel? Does he too have such feelings for you?"

Marcus did not answer. He could not implicate him, yet he also could not lie to Julia. She understood at once. "You wish to protect him," she murmured.

He nodded his head. Then for emphasis, he added, "Nothing of this must reach outside ears."

"I will not tell anyone, Marcus. You can rest easy on that front."

"Your oath, Julia."

"I solemnly swear that I will not disclose a word of this to anyone," she affirmed. Shifting backwards on the bed, she came to him and laid her head on his shoulder. "Poor Marcus," was all she said. After a time, she sat up to go. On her way to the door though, she stopped suddenly, as if struck by a thought, and turned. "How about if tomorrow, on our afternoon ride, we stop by the docks instead of going to Hyde Park?" she asked softly.

"I had thought you would wish me to stay away from Lionel."

She smiled wryly. "The most sensible course of action would undoubtedly be to do so, but I confess I am curious about this Lionel and how he comes to inspire such devotion in you. I would like to get to know him better. We shall go see him tomorrow."

His heart leapt at the thought. Only a short time ago, he had been bemoaning the fact he would not see him until the Maybury ball.

"Yes," he said in response. "Tomorrow, we shall go see Lionel."

"Goodnight, Marcus."

"Goodnight, Julia."

CHAPTER 15

AN UNWANTED VISITOR

LIORA ARRIVED AT London Docks a little after twelve o'clock and made her way to the warehouse, which lay on the western side of the North Quay. The area was well-guarded against light-fingered thieves such as the River Pirates or the Night Plunderers that patrolled the waters and ports in search of spoils. High walls and an army of watchmen made sure the valuable commodities stored in these parts were kept safe.

She passed by one such watchman as she entered the principal entrance gate, giving him a nod of acknowledgement as he doffed his cap and allowed her through. From there, it was a short distance to the Reeves warehouse, a large rectangular building four storeys high. She dismounted from her horse and tethered it to a post that stood outside the building, next to a trough of water and some straw. Using keys extracted from her coat pocket, she unlocked the massive set of iron double doors and stepped inside. They did not use Uvonian technology to lock these doors, as the workmen who frequented this warehouse did not come from Uvon. So, an old-fashioned set of keys was what secured the main door. However, Broek did install recording devices throughout the building, discreetly hidden of course, as well as a trigger alarm that alerted them should there be a forced entry. Thankfully, they had not had any intruders in their time here so far.

Inside the building, illumination streamed in from the many rectangular-shaped windows that were secured with cast-iron spiked frames and grilles. It was almost what she imagined a prison to be like. Carefully, she lit the candles of a lamp, projecting further brightness on her surroundings. Such a pity they could not use Uvonian lighting, which at Reeves Hall could be operated with the sound of their voices. But again, it could not be so, as there was insufficient privacy to hide their Uvonian ways from the simple Earth humans.

Around her was a large, high-ceilinged space that allowed for two tiers of storage. The heavier goods, mainly sugar, were stored here in large sacks—sugar from the East, not the West Indies, as they refused to stock anything grown on slave plantations. A set of stairs led down to the basement where they kept vaults filled with wine barrels and shelves of brandy bottles. Up above on the first floor was where their supplies of wool were stored, and the top level was reserved for coffee, tea and spices.

Over in one corner was a hand winch to hoist goods up and down from each floor through loopholes in the ceiling. On the other side of the building was a transit area, where goods were weighed on large iron beam scales, then carefully labelled before either being stored or dispatched to a buyer. They would be busy shortly, handling the surplus of orders that had come through.

"Mr Reeves, excuse me," said a voice behind her.

She turned to find John Atkins, their chief dockworker, together with a handful of other men. They were here to start loading the goods that had been sold into wagons that would deliver them to their purchasers.

"Mr Atkins, good day," she said. "Let us get started, for we have much to do."

For the next few hours, the warehouse was a hive of busy activity as sacks of sugar, boxes of tea and coffee, barrels of wine and crates of timber were weighed, labelled with their destination and loaded onto various wagons. All the while, she recorded the proceedings in a leather-bound ledger, ensuring that their inventory information was up-to-date and correct. Later, when prying eyes were out of sight, she would input the data onto her console, so that Broek could access it from home. Although he was not here in person, her older brother monitored this data closely, keeping a sharp eye on the fluctuating prices of commodities and where the family's financial interests might best lie. It was mainly due to his endeavours that they had become so wealthy since arriving in England seven years ago.

In those first few years while they were making a home for themselves at Reeves Hall, Broek had spent much of his time in London establishing the business, training Jos and eventually putting him in charge. Now, it was her turn to take on this responsibility, and she was determined to do it well. It was laborious work but a welcome change to the dull life she had been leading at Reeves Hall. And not once did she have to worry about being ladylike and demure. Now into the second week of being Lionel, she had begun to wear her male persona like a second skin and to enjoy the freedom it gave her. If only it also gave her the freedom to ravish the delectable duke as she wished she could. She gave her head a mental shake. No, no. She was not going to think of Marcus on this busy day.

By mid-afternoon, they were almost done. Liora was copying out the final sets of figures into her ledger when a shadow fell over her, causing her to look round. Standing behind her was a man she had never met before. He was dressed in dark clothing which although plain, was of good quality. She judged him to be between thirty and forty, with eyes of a watery grey colour and thin lips cast into a tight semblance of a smile.

"Mr Reeves?" he enquired.

"I am Lionel Reeves, yes," she replied.

The man sketched a bow. "Ralph Boyle, at your service." The name meant little to her, nor did he explain who he was, choosing instead to remark, "I was very sad to hear of Mr Jocelyn's passing. And now I understand you have been sent by the great man himself, Mr Brook Reeves, to take charge of the business here. You are his nephew?"

"A cousin," she corrected.

"Well, Mr Reeves, you are most welcome here. I do look forward to fruitful business dealings between ourselves." His eyes darted round the warehouse, landing on the diminishing stack of sugar sacks to her right. Their stock of this commodity was getting low, but they would be able to replenish it just as soon as their latest shipment was released by the excise officers.

"And your business is?" she enquired politely.

"Let us say that I facilitate certain proceedings," he said smoothly. He nodded his head toward the sugar sacks. "For instance, I may expedite the release of various goods now sequestered by His Majesty's Customs—a hundred tons of sugar, I believe."

Her eyes narrowed. "And what would you demand in exchange for this service?"

He put two hands up, saying placatingly, "Demand is too harsh of a word. No, no, I demand nothing, merely propose."

"What do you propose then?" she asked bluntly, wanting this fellow to get to the point.

He put on a pained expression. "Mr Reeves, the party that I represent is a trifle alarmed at the way the Reeves family is actively promoting its East India sugar to the markets as 'not made by slaves', in collusion with those unfortunate abolitionist groups run by Quakers. I am sure you can see how such words cast aspersions on our own sugar from the West Indies."

"Ha! It is but the truth. Our East India sugar is not grown on slave plantations, unlike other sugar on the market, though for the record, we are not in collusion with anybody; we are simply offering our purchasers factual information about the goods we sell."

He gazed at her solemnly. "Mr Reeves," he said, "the party I represent would like to see a cessation of such promotional slogans that are detrimental to our business. In fact, we propose what I think is a very fair bargain."

Her brows rose in suspicion. She highly doubted this was going to be a fair bargain. She repeated her question with a slight snarl, "Again, I ask you, Mr Boyle, what is it you propose?"

He nodded. "Of course, of course, you are keen to get to the facts. Quite understandable." He nodded again, then said, "Mr Reeves, in return for expediting matters with His Majesty's Customs, we would want to purchase your entire consignment of sugar at the very fair price of three hundred and eighty pounds."

"Three hundred and eighty!" she spluttered in outrage. "That sugar is worth five hundred pounds and more."

"That sugar is worth nothing as long as it remains under lock and key at Custom House," he said sternly.

"What you propose, Mr Boyle, is detrimental to *my* business!"

He shook his head. "Mr Reeves, Mr Reeves. Facts are facts. The customs officers find themselves altogether too busy with the inspection of the many goods that arrive at these docks every day—so much so that I am afraid your shipment of sugar may take a very long time indeed before it is released into your possession. We have it within our means to expedite this matter and do you a favour, but you must understand that we will require something in return."

"That something in return being a bribe of a hundred and twenty pounds."

Mr Boyle tutted. "A bribe? Now your imagination is running wild, Mr Reeves. It is a fair price for a consignment of sugar that would otherwise fester for weeks, even months, in the Custom House which is known to be overrun by rats."

Her hands balled into fists at the injustice of it, the blatant corruption. Could this be the matter that had been troubling Jos before he died? She glared at the man standing before her.

Seeing her reaction, he smiled. "I will leave you to reflect on the matter, Mr Reeves. But do not take too long to reach a decision. Good day."

He bowed and left as quickly as he had come. She watched his departing back, her mind seething. If that unctuous man thought they were going to cave in to such outrageous demands, he could think again. They would simply have to find a way to get the sugar released into their possession. If it came to it, she would even grease a few palms with a guinea or two to get things moving. It surely could not be as intractable a matter as Mr Boyle had implied.

She was so lost in thought that she did not realise that there was someone else present until a large hand landed on her shoulder and a familiar voice murmured, "Lionel."

CHAPTER 16

A STUNNING REALISATION

MARCUS AND JULIA had arrived at the Reeves warehouse and entered it, finding a dimly lit open space filled on one side with piles of timber sitting on wheeled planks. His eyes had scanned the space in search for Lionel, but it had been his voice he heard first, which seemed to be in a heated argument with someone. With Julia a silent figure beside him, they had stepped closer, keeping behind a stack of timber for cover, and listened to the exchange. What he had heard made his blood boil.

How dare that man threaten Lionel and his family? Marcus was filled with a rage the likes of which he had never felt before. He had been tempted to plant a facer on the oily man's countenance, but Julia had laid a restraining hand on him. He had taken a calming breath, for she was right. Satisfying though it might be, such an action would not have done any good. Instead, he had waited for the man to leave before approaching Lionel and calling his name.

Now, Lionel whipped around to face the new intruder, his stance relaxing when he saw it was Marcus. His eyes were a dark cauldron of emotion; his cheeks flushed. "Marcus," he said, trying to regain his composure. "I had not expected to see you today."

Marcus ignored this and got straight to the matter at hand. "Who is this Mr Boyle?" he demanded. "And what shall you do about the sugar?"

Lionel looked over Marcus's shoulder and sketched a bow towards his sister. "Miss Julia."

She responded with a curtsy. "Mr Reeves."

"Answer me, Lionel." Marcus was in no mood for social niceties.

Lionel observed him warily. "How much of that did you overhear?"

"Most of it," responded Julia on his behalf. Then she too asked, "What shall you do about it?"

Lionel pasted on a feeble smile. "It is a trifle. Please do not concern yourselves over it."

Marcus ground his teeth. "Lionel, you are testing my patience," he said forcefully. "Now tell me, what is the plan?"

Lionel stared, no doubt astounded at the pronounced change to Marcus's usually affable manner. Then he shrugged with studied carelessness. "I do not have a plan as yet," he said, trying to put a brave face on the matter. "I suppose I must go to the Custom House and have with me a ready supply of guineas to help persuade the persons in charge to release my goods."

"Will that work, do you think?" pondered Julia.

"It must," smiled Lionel. "I do not see why it should not."

Marcus was not convinced. This Mr Boyle would not have been making such a proposition if the matter were so easy. Quite clearly, the person he represented was powerful and had a hold over the customs officers. But he supposed this would be a sensible first course of action.

"When shall you go?" he grunted out.

Lionel pressed his plush lips together, thinking the matter through. "I suppose there is no time like the present," he said.

"I shall go with you," Marcus stated decisively.

"No!" cried Lionel. "There is no need for such bravado, Marcus. I am quite capable of doing this myself, and besides, you have Miss Julia with you."

Damnation! That was true. And he had also promised to take his sisters out in the barouche later this afternoon. Marcus was not in the habit of breaking his word.

Sensing this, Lionel went on, "Do not worry yourself over this, please. Really, it is no concern of yours."

Of course, it was his concern. Marcus bit back the retort, realising how that would sound. Instead, he contented himself with saying, "Tomorrow morning, I shall call at your house, Lionel, and then I shall expect a full report of what has happened."

"You shall expect?" Lionel's expression turned sardonic, but there was also surprise, for he was not used to Marcus speaking in this vein. Neither was Marcus, to be fair. This was not how he was in the habit of comporting himself, but all had changed in his world since Lionel had entered it.

Marcus took a step forward until he was nose to nose with Lionel. "Oh, yes," he said very softly. "I shall expect." And then, he dropped a quick kiss on the tip of his nose.

For a frozen second, the two stared at each other, then with an effort, Marcus turned away from Lionel's dumbfounded countenance and marched to the door, calling sharply, "Come, Julia."

She did not utter a word as they mounted their horses and rode back to St James's Square. Throughout the ride, his mind feverishly examined the situation, trying to work out a plan. How did he stop these foul, corrupt entities from harming Lionel's business? Should he go in person to the Custom House and use his status as a duke to demand they release that sugar? Would it work, or would he inadvertently make matters worse? It was at times like these that he wished he were of a more quick-witted nature, able to strategise and plan. But he could not give up. The matter was too important. He promised himself that he would find a way.

Back at the house, they both headed to their chambers to wash and change before their outing to the park. At the top of the stairs, Julia paused and turned to face him. Her face ashen, she placed a staying hand on his arm.

"What is it?" he gritted out hoarsely.

She stared at him wide eyed. Then, her voice tremulous, she whispered, "It is not merely desire you feel for him, Marcus. You have fallen in love."

Her words hit him like a hammer. In a daze, he stumbled to his bedchamber. *You have fallen in love*. He closed the door and leaned his head on it. *You have fallen in love*.

Dear Lord, it was true.

CHAPTER 17

A PLAN IS HATCHED

MARCUS DID NOT know how he managed to endure the rest of the day—the barouche ride in the park and Lady Rockingham's card party. It all happened in a sort of haze, for pumping through his veins was the constant refrain, *"You have fallen in love."* With a man!

His play at cards was abysmal, his conversation even more so. Yet it made no difference. The young ladies continued to simper in his presence, the gentlemen to flatter. If ever he needed proof of the shallowness of the *ton*, this must be it. His opinion of polite society, never high, sank even further. What did he care for these people? They were nothing to him. They only mattered in so far as it seemed important for his sisters to be well-regarded so as to make good marriages.

On that front, it seemed they were on their way to a first success, for even in his distracted state, he could not fail to note the marked attention that Sir Luke Stafford was giving to Portia. The gentleman had a substantial estate in Oxfordshire that brought in, so he was told in a hushed whisper by Mama, over eight thousand pounds a year. He was a bore and a prig to boot, but there was no doubt as to his eligibility. Portia did not seem to mind his character faults. If anything, she was positively blooming tonight.

At last, the evening ended, and they returned home in two separate carriages. Thankfully, Marcus was spared a seat with an ecstatic Portia waxing lyrical about every word and look given her by Sir Luke. Instead, he rode home in the chariot with Julia, while Mama, Diana and Portia took the barouche. As soon as the carriage door shut, Julia rested her head back on the seat with a loud sigh. "I am glad that is over," she said.

"Evening not to your liking?" he enquired.

"I had things of greater import on my mind." She looked at him meaningfully. "What are you going to do, Marcus?"

He pretended ignorance. "Do about what?"

"About Lionel and your feelings for him."

He wished she would not ask these questions to which there could be no answer. Feelings could not be quelled in the way one extinguishes a candle with a single blow of one's breath. He returned her stare. "What would you have me do?"

"I suppose it is much too late to sever all connection with him and give yourself a chance to overcome these feelings?"

He laughed unamusedly. "Much too late, Julia. For good or ill, I have fallen in love, and I do not think that this love can be undone."

"It is a love that can have no happy resolution," she pointed out, as if he did not know this already.

"Yet still I love him and will continue to do so."

She gazed at him doubtfully. "How can you be sure? Of course, I can see the depth of your feelings at this moment, but unless the affection is nurtured through regular association, it must surely fade in time. We leave London within a week, and after that there shall be no further opportunity for you to see him."

The thought sent a painful dart to his heart, so much so that he was unable to respond. Julia's gaze turned pitying. "I am sorry, Marcus," she said gently, "for I see a great deal of pain ahead if you continue on this path."

"I will deal with it when the time comes," he replied, a little brusquely, "but right now, I must think of Lionel's situation. How may I help him?"

"Are you so certain he needs your help?"

"Need it or not, he is getting it."

She laughed. "That is one good thing to have emerged from this situation. You are stronger, Marcus, more assertive than before. I have not liked the way you have always let Mama and our sisters browbeat you."

"You too," he reminded her.

She had the grace to look a little shamefaced. "Yes, I suppose I too have been guilty of it, but it was never done maliciously."

"I know, else I would not have tolerated it."

She smiled. After a time, he returned to the pressing matter at hand. "How am I to help him, Julia?" He pondered the question for what seemed the thousandth time.

"I have been thinking," she began. "First, we must uncover the identity of the person who is employing Mr Boyle. Once we know who it is, we must then uncover how this person seems to have such power over the excise officers and how to break that hold they have."

"It is someone in the sugar trade, obviously, so that would limit the number of possible suspects," he said, voicing something he had been mulling over. "We would need to employ someone to investigate. A Bow Street Runner, do you think?"

Julia cast him an approving look. "Yes, a splendid idea! Why did I not think of it?"

"I am not entirely mutton-headed, you know."

"I know." She placed a companionable head on his shoulder.

"Tomorrow morning, I shall visit Lionel," he stated decisively. "You, Mama, Portia and Diana will have to do without me for a change. And after that, I shall go to Bow Street Magistrates' Court and ask for their best runner to put on the case."

"I wish I were going with you," she murmured longingly. "It sounds far more interesting than a round of social calls."

"Ha! I am sure it will be, but I am afraid, Julia, that I must go alone."

"You wish to have private discourse with Lionel," she said shrewdly.

"Yes." It had been too long—one whole day in fact—since he had been able to have a private word with him. Much too long.

Julia sighed into his shoulder. "Oh, very well, but you must tell me all when you return."

NEXT MORNING, MARCUS left immediately after breakfast, ignoring his mama's protests, and made his way on foot to Lionel's house on Barton Street. He quickened his steps, eager to get there and see him. Crossing through St James's Park, he continued in a southernly direction towards Westminster, reaching Barton Street shortly thereafter. He stopped in front of number two, a narrow three-storey brick house with bay windows on the upper floors, then knocked on the door.

A middle-aged housekeeper opened it, looking enquiringly at him. "The Duke of Coleford," he said, "calling on Mr Lionel Reeves."

She inclined her head and beckoned him in, guiding him to a parlour room. "I will fetch Mr Reeves," she said, and Marcus detected in her voice a stronger trace of the accent he had noticed in Lionel's speech. Curious. Perhaps she was a longstanding family servant hailing from the same part of the country as him. Cornwall was it?

He took a seat in the parlour and glanced around him. The room was neither large nor small, furnished with an unostentatious elegance. There were no family portraits on the walls, which were bare in fact except for a mirror above the fireplace and a landscape painting of an unusual-looking beach on the other side of the room. Marcus stood and went over to it, scrutinising the landscape. It showed a long stretch of pale, almost white sand and a sea of turquoise blue. Beyond the sand were grassy cliffs, upon which sat a curious-looking house, painted in a pale shade of peach. Its windows were oddly shaped, tall ovals like repeated number zeroes. He had never before set eyes on a house such as this. It must be somewhere abroad, in Continental Europe or even further afield.

"This is the house where I grew up," said Lionel softly behind him.

Marcus whirled around to face him. He was freshly bathed, the ends of his hair curling wetly along the satin nape of his neck. There was a rosy colour to his smooth cheeks, and his dark eyes shone limpidly in the bright morning light.

"Lionel," he murmured.

Lionel's lips quirked. "Marcus," he responded. "Good morning."

"Good morning," Marcus echoed, lost in the depth of Lionel's eyes. They were truly extraordinary, the lashes almost girlish in their length. With an effort, he composed himself and addressed Lionel's earlier remark. "You did not grow up in England?"

"No, I did not."

Marcus turned to examine the painting once more, the knowledge that this was once Lionel's home making him want to memorise every detail of it. "Where is this?" he asked.

"It is a place named Luxzuc."

Marcus turned to him again. "Luxzuc? Where is that?"

It was only because he was watching Lionel so closely that he caught an instant of hesitation before he said, "In Brazil. My family owns vast tracts of land there where we grow sugar and coffee." Marcus was absolutely certain that he had been told an untruth, but he was more intrigued about it than hurt. Why would Lionel lie about his origins? What secrets did he harbour behind those breathtaking eyes? Marcus had known instinctively since meeting him that there was something that he was keeping from him. He had thought initially that it had to do with Lionel's attraction to his own sex, something which must stay hidden from the world, but he could see now that it was more.

He did not call him out on the lie. Instead, he murmured, "It is beautiful. Would you take me there some day?"

Lionel's eyes grew wistful. "I wish I could," he said in a husky tone. Then he cleared his throat. "Marcus, do please take a seat and let us talk."

He followed Lionel to the burgundy sofa and took a seat beside him. They sat close to one another but did not touch. The herbal aroma of Lionel's pomade drifted towards his nostrils along with the unmistakable scent of him, sweet and slightly musky. Marcus thought he could breathe this air for an eternity. In his sight line was Lionel's elegant, long-fingered hand which rested by him on the sofa. He was seized with the impulse to kiss every last finger of that hand then to run his lips up to Lionel's wrist, savouring the soft feel of his skin. If only he had not given him his oath to never repeat their passionate loving. He would have had him in his arms now. With an effort, he reined in his flighty thoughts and asked instead, "How did it go with the customs officers?"

"Badly," Lionel replied. "I spoke to a person named Henry Blunt, who it seems has been recently appointed as chief collector at Custom House. He was polite, charming even, but he would not budge on the matter. I tried financial inducements to expedite things, all for nought. He cannot be bought."

"Quite clearly he can," Marcus disagreed. "And he has been bought by your anonymous competitor."

"If so," Lionel replied, "I do not know how much more it would take for him to switch to my side and attend to releasing the shipment of sugar before it rots. I offered him ten guineas, but he turned it down without a second thought."

"We need to discover the identity of the person behind all this," Marcus said, tapping his fingers impatiently on his thighs.

"I agree."

Regarding him, Marcus asked urgently, "What will you do?"

"I will make discreet enquiries. It can only be one of a few people, if their interests are in the West Indies sugar trade."

"Yes, that is what I thought," said Marcus, nodding fervently. "We must unmask them and find a way to break the hold they have over the customs authorities." His fingers continued tapping, something he did when he was beset by nerves. The thought of this person, whoever he was, pulling strings to hobble Lionel's business set his teeth on edge.

"Marcus," Lionel said gently, then placed his hand over his, stilling the motion.

"I cannot stand the thought of anyone conspiring against you," Marcus told him honestly.

Lionel said nothing but kept his hand over Marcus's.

"I so wish you would release me from my promise, Lionel."

Lionel did not pretend to misunderstand him. "I wish it too," he said heavily. "But it would be wrong."

Marcus exhaled deeply. Lionel's thumb stroked the top of his hand, soothing his troubled soul. His mind went to something else he had been fretting about. "I am due to leave London next week," he said. "After I do, will I see or hear from you again?"

"It would probably be best if you do not," whispered Lionel.

"Do not say that! Please!"

"Very well, then I shall write."

Marcus's lips twisted bitterly. "I am not much good with letters, remember?"

"I will write in such a way that you will find it easier to read my letters," promised Lionel. "And it does not matter to me how many spelling errors you make, as long as you write back keeping me apprised of how you are."

"Letters, that is all?" Marcus despised the hint of desperation in his voice, but there was no help for it.

Lionel hesitated. "Perhaps someday," he added very softly, "I might stop by at Coleford Hall on my way to Cornwall and pay you a short visit."

"Yes, I would like that."

Lionel gave Marcus's hand a final squeeze then withdrew. He tapped gently on the ruby signet ring he wore. In a brisk manner, he said, "I have asked Esa to bring in some tea for refreshment. May I offer you anything else?"

"What sort of tea?" Marcus asked.

"It is a herbal infusion of mine, lemon balm with a hint of camomile," Lionel replied with a smile.

"Herbs for soothing the nerves," Marcus stated knowledgeably.

"Indeed. Would you like to try it or have something else?"

"I will try your herbal infusion," he said.

"Good." Lionel tapped his ring again. After a while, he added, "Then I shall see you tonight, at the Maybury ball."

"Yes, come find us as soon as you arrive. I shall be looking out for you."

Lionel chuckled. "I hardly know anybody else there, so I will surely look for you."

"Make sure you arrive promptly at nine o'clock."

"I will."

"You have received the invitation?"

"I have."

"Lionel, I have been thinking."

"Yes?" he asked.

"As well as stopping by at Coleford Hall to visit me, I might also not be averse to travelling to Cornwall to pay you a visit at Reeves Hall."

"Ah." Lionel said nothing more.

Annoyed and more than a little chagrined, Marcus looked over at him. "Ah? What does that mean?"

Lionel looked contrite. "You do understand, of course, that Reeves Hall does not belong to me. It is my cousin's home, a man who guards his privacy fiercely, and as such, I am not at liberty to issue invitations."

"I see," Marcus said, feeling deflated. Sometimes, he was certain that the feelings he had for Lionel were reciprocated. Other times, he was left unsure, as now.

Just then, there came a knock at the door, and the housekeeper entered, bearing a tray which she placed on the side table. With a curtsy, she then took her leave.

Marcus watched as Lionel poured them each a cup of the herbal infusion in the pot, admiring his lovely hands, their movement spare and efficient. He took the proffered cup and brought it to his lips, inhaling the soothing herbal aroma. After a few sips, he remarked, "This is a good brew."

"On a par with your herbal infusions?"

Marcus smiled. "On a par. There is just the right balance between the citrus flavour of the lemon balm and the stronger notes of the camomile. And, do I detect also a touch of mint?"

"Yes, I have included a very small amount of mint in the mix. Your senses are finely attuned, Marcus. In another life, you could have been a master perfumer."

Marcus laughed, pleased with the praise. "It is one of the few talents I have."

Lionel levelled him with one of his stern stares. "Have we not talked of this before, Marcus? We have already established that you have many, not few talents. Please do not put on a show of false modesty. It ill becomes you."

"I am not used to being praised for my talents, so forgive me if I occasionally fish for your compliments," Marcus said by way of apology. He could feel his cheeks reddening. What was it about Lionel that at once soothed his soul and discombobulated him? He supposed it was his forthright nature. Lionel did not suffer fools gladly, and Marcus was glad of it. In the short time he had known him, every single one of their interactions have been authentic, not couched in the false flattery of the *ton*.

Marcus let out a breath and carried on, "But you may be right about being a perfumer. From a young age, I have always had an uncanny ability to detect all manner of scents. Take you, for instance."

Lionel raised a brow in enquiry.

Marcus hurried to explain. "I am so cognisant of your scent, Lionel, that I can detect your presence even in an empty room long after you have left it. It is one of the many things I love about you. Your scent, your eyes, your lovely hands, the delicate skin of your neck, your kissable lips, your kindness, your impatience with polite chit chat and of course, the greatness of your mind. Added to which, you taste delicious. It is a combination of so many things that has me burn with desire for you." His heart pounded in his chest as he finished this soliloquy. It was a good thing he was not prideful, for his pride was laid bare on the floor. But he could not tell Lionel anything but the truth.

He heard Lionel's ragged breaths beside him as he stared intently at his lap. He had disconcerted him, he knew. But he was still keeping to the boundaries of his promise, or just about.

"Marcus," Lionel breathed. "We cannot. We must not." He stood abruptly and paced to the window, looking out blindly. They did not speak for long moments while each attempted to calm their raging bodies.

Eventually, once Marcus had regained a modicum of composure, he rose to his feet reluctantly and bid Lionel goodbye. "I shall see you tonight," he sighed.

Lionel nodded in acknowledgement. In silence, Marcus left the room and saw himself out.

CHAPTER 18

A FEW DEVELOPMENTS

IT TOOK LIORA several minutes to compose herself after Marcus left. The things he had said. Oh, Gracious Yol! Her heart could not seem to return to an even rhythm. Heat enveloped her body, from the tips of her toes to the top of her head, which felt it was about to explode. She had always suspected it, but now she knew for certain. Words had power—especially when uttered with such conviction.

It is a combination of so many things that has me burn with desire for you.

Great Yol, she was trying not to involve herself with the man. He was handsome and sweet, with a bewitching combination of vulnerability and dominance. A dozen times a day, she reminded herself of the impossibility of being with Marcus. He was a man who believed she too was male, though she wondered. The things he had said that he loved about her—her scent, her hands, the delicate skin on her neck—all these were what one could generalise as feminine attributes. Could he on some instinctive level discern that she was female? If only... but oh, the danger.

Once she had regained a modicum of composure, Liora took herself upstairs to the private parlour and locked the door behind her. She went to the walnut side table and released the secret compartment containing her console. She took it out then went to sit on a nearby armchair, tapping her ring to call Broek.

When her brother's face appeared on the console screen, he was frowning. "I ran several queries through the data," he said, "but I could not find anything on this Henry Blunt. The man is a mystery, as far as we are concerned."

"At times like these I do wish you had not destroyed your nanoprobes, Broek," she replied wistfully. Her brother was the inventor of tiny, nearly invisible probes that could be launched in their hundreds of thousands all over the world, obtaining valuable data for them, spying on private meetings by relaying both picture and sound recordings to his console. However, in what could only be described as a quixotic gesture, aided and abetted by Jane, his wife, he had destroyed each and every last nanoprobe some weeks ago.

His rationale was understandable. The probes had given him almost God-like power to see into every home, every office, every warehouse, to listen in to the most private of conversations without people's knowledge. There had also been ever present the danger that the nanoprobe technology could fall into the wrong hands one day. It had been noble and worthy of Broek to destroy them, but it had also deprived the family of a major instrument they had used these past seven years to establish themselves in this new world and to protect their interests. Had the nanoprobes still been in operation, Broek could have programmed them in seconds to go and spy on this Henry Blunt. With very little effort, they could have obtained the information they needed to leverage this situation to their advantage. But it was not to be, not anymore.

Broek's jaw tightened. Liora suspected he missed the power and the security that the probes had given him, even though he believed he had done the right thing in destroying them. "You do not need to remind me of this, Liora," he grated. "It is indeed frustrating that we cannot resolve this matter quickly as we could once have done, but that does not mean we are entirely helpless. There are other things which we can do." He paused a moment then stated decisively, "We are all agreed, are we not, that to resolve this matter, we need to get to the source of the problem and find out who is employing Ralph Boyle."

"Someone in the West Indian sugar trade, I should think," observed Liora.

"Precisely. And so I have looked through my data, and I have narrowed down our list of suspects to three individuals. All are powerful merchants heavily involved in the West Indian sugar trade. The first two, William Vaughan and George Hibbert are both investors in the London Docks and owners of large sugar plantations in the West Indies. The third is a man by name of Enoch Miles, whose late father was one of the leading traders of enslaved Africans. This Enoch Miles continues in his father's footsteps. Not only does he own several slave plantations in the West Indies, but he is also a major investor in a large sugar refinery located not far from the docks."

Liora pondered this information. "You think one these three merchants is behind all this, and not anybody else?"

"It is possible that this Mr Boyle is employed by some other person, but unlikely, I think," replied her brother. "At any rate, let us start by making enquiries about these three men."

"I will get started on this straight away," promised Liora.

"Report back to me on this tonight," adjured her brother.

She shook her head. "Tonight, I am attending the Maybury ball."

Broek scowled. "Why on earth? Do not tell me it is that wretched duke's doing?"

She felt the colour rise to her cheeks. "Yes, the duke has extended me an invitation to the ball."

Broek's eyes narrowed. "Is this why you insisted on this masquerade, Liora? Because you've secretly been longing to attend a society ball? If so, you should have said, and I would have arranged it long ago without having recourse to you dressing as a man."

She ground her teeth in irritation. "No," she replied gruffly. "I have no great wish to attend society balls and act all demure and proper. At least when I go as a man, I shall not be bound by the same expectations."

"Why then are you going, Liora?"

She looked away from Broek's face on the screen. "The duke wished me to, and I had no objection," she said as nonchalantly as she could.

"Liora." She faced her brother's worried eyes. "Please tell me you have not become involved with this duke."

"I—well, not exactly."

"Liora!"

"Broek," she snapped wearily. "I am all too aware that getting involved with the duke is a bad, bad idea. I do not need to be told."

He nodded, appeased. "Be careful," he admonished.

"I will be. Now, I had better get to work."

"May Yol be with you." Then her brother ended the connection.

Quickly, she put away the console and locked it securely in the concealed drawer. She considered her next actions. First, she would stop by at Threadneedle Street and speak to the clerks in the office. Perhaps they would have useful clues to impart about this matter. Then, she planned to visit a prominent trading establishment called Garraway's coffee house. She had made arrangements to attend a wool auction there, where she would endeavour to get the very best price for the fine merino wool that was currently stored in the Reeves warehouse. She smiled to herself, amused at the thought that she, Liora of the great Reevas clan of Uvon, should be engaged in selling wool at a market auction. It was a curious symmetry between her home world and Earth that in both places, the high ranking people in society looked down their noses at the activity of trade. She did not mind it. There was something to be said for engaging in honest and useful work, and this would be an opportunity too to do some further investigating. The merchants at the coffee house might offer valuable information about those three suspects. She would have to be discreet in her enquiries, of course, but she hoped that soon, she would get to the bottom of who was threatening her family's business.

Determined to put her plan into action, she strode to the parlour door and unlocked it. "Oh, good day," she said distractedly to the maid who stood nearby, polishing the banister. What was her name? She could not quite recall it in that instant. With an absent nod, she brushed past the young girl and went up to her chamber to get herself ready to go out. She had a busy day ahead. And after that, there was a ball to attend. An image of Marcus sprang to her mind as he had sat beside her this morning and spoken those words.

It is a combination of so many things that has me burn with desire for you.

Great Yol, they were branded in her mind.

MEANWHILE, MARCUS WAS putting his own plan into action. After leaving Barton Street, still reeling from that heated encounter with Lionel, he walked in a northernly direction, unerringly finding his way to Bow Street. Earlier, he had looked for it on the large map of London that hung on the study wall at St James's Square. Though he was not much good with deciphering letters, maps were a different matter. Once he had identified two different locations, he could quickly and easily memorise the route between them. No doubt, Lionel would say this was another of his many talents. As he walked, Marcus reflected on how many of his capabilities he had been hiding under a bushel, cast in the shadow of his one great failing at reading letters. It had taken Lionel's stubborn encouragement to shine a light on these other accomplishments. Perhaps he was not quite the dunce he sometimes felt himself to be. One day soon, he might also become worthy of earning Lionel's trust and have him reveal to him what he was hiding.

With great resolve, he arrived at Bow Street Magistrates' Court and entered. The building was humming with activity, crowds of people waiting for their cases to be heard along with gawking bystanders wanting to witness the latest court proceedings. Weaving in and out of the bustling crowd, he was finally able to locate a side-office where a weary clerk sat at a desk heaving with piles of official-looking papers. With an imperiousness that was fast becoming second nature to him, Marcus demanded the services of the best Bow Street Runner for an investigation.

"That would be Mr Quinn," said the clerk without having to think the matter over.

"Find me this Mr Quinn," commanded Marcus.

The clerk scratched his head. "Well you see, Your Grace, it is more a matter of him finding you. There is a tavern that he frequents, the Fleece in Covent Garden, if you know it."

"No, but I can find it."

"Well then, Your Grace," continued the clerk, "leave a message with the tavern keeper that you are looking for Mr Quinn, and he will come find you."

Marcus frowned at him. "And he is the best officer you have?"

"Assuredly so."

Marcus slipped him a coin in thanks and took his leave. It was another battle through the crowds to get to the front doors, and a great relief once he stood outside again, though there was no respite from the noises and noxious smells of this city. For an instant, Marcus thought longingly of his garden back home, but then he reminded himself of why he was here. He had a mission. Lionel.

Covent Garden was a short stroll from the court, and once there, it took but a few moments to locate the Fleece. He entered it with purpose, determined to find this Mr Quinn and obtain his help for Lionel. Inside the dimly lit front room, he discerned a scattering of rustic wooden tables and chairs, some empty and some occupied. There was a loud hum of voices and a strong smell of ale. Eyes followed him with interest, a well-dressed gentleman in their midst, as he made his way to the counter behind which a portly man with a shiny face and ruddy cheeks stood serving the drinks.

"What'll you have?" barked the tavern keeper, not in the least subservient in the presence of a gentleman. An interesting establishment.

Marcus decided now was not the time to be a high stickler for etiquette. "A pint of your finest ale," he replied, then after a pause, added, "and also something else."

The tavern keeper narrowed his eyes and observed Marcus in pointed silence. Willing his courage, for this was well outside what he was accustomed to, Marcus stated his business. "Tell Mr Quinn that I would like a word with him." He counted out six pennies and passed them to the tavern keeper. Quick as a flash, they disappeared under the counter.

"Who shall I say wants a word?"

"Marcus Cavendish," he replied, deciding not to mention his title at this point.

"Take a seat, Mr Cavendish. I'll send your ale shortly."

Turning around, Marcus perused the far from salubrious surroundings for a place to sit. He spied an empty table in a recessed corner of the room and made his way there, hoping it would allow him to be less conspicuous. All around, the patrons of this establishment continued with their business, some laughing boisterously and clapping each other on the shoulder. They cast him a curious glance or two, but beyond this did not pay him much mind after their initial spark of interest. Somewhat relieved, he sat himself down and waited, trying not to tap his fingers and betray his nerves. It was a wonder why a Bow Street Runner would choose a place like this to frequent. On second thought, maybe not. Lurking in the underbelly of the city, no doubt there were many informants that for a price, could bring to light valuable information. He hoped that would be the case for Lionel.

A short while later, a young serving maid brought him his pint of ale. Marcus took it gratefully and gulped a quarter of it down in one go, quenching his thirst and easing his jitters.

It was some time later that a dark haired man of middling age approached his table. "Your Grace," said the man. "I hear you wish to speak with me."

Marcus stood and sketched a bow. "Mr Quinn?"

"At your service, Your Grace." Mr Quinn bowed in return and took the remaining seat at the table, glancing enquiringly at Marcus.

Something puzzled him. "How do you know I am a duke?" Marcus asked him. "I only told the tavern keeper my name, not my title."

Mr Quinn snorted. "Your Grace, it is my job to keep my ears to the ground and know who's who. I am well aware that a Marcus Cavendish has recently come into the dukedom of Coleford and that he is come to London for the season."

Marcus was impressed. Perhaps this Quinn would be of use to him after all. He decided to get straight to business. "There is a matter I would like your assistance with," he began, then went on to explain.

Mr Quinn listened intently, stroking his chin, astute blue eyes studying him keenly. At length, the man said, "You propose going against some very powerful vested interests."

"They must be stopped," Marcus stated firmly.

"As to that, you will get no argument from me." Mr Quinn thought some more. "I will bring you the name of the person behind the threats to Mr Reeves," he assured him. "With regards to the second matter, however, I can make no promises." The second matter being to find a way to compel the customs authorities to stop blocking the release of Lionel's consignment of sugar.

"Find out whatever you can," Marcus told him, "and I shall pay you well. Two guineas upfront, and two more upon successful conclusion of the matter."

Mr Quinn nodded. "Very well, Your Grace."

Marcus took the coins out of his inside coat pocket and slid them carefully towards Mr Quinn. The man slipped them into his own pocket and stood. "Good day, Your Grace. I shall find you as soon as I have information."

In an instant, he had disappeared out of a backroom door. With his pulse racing in hope and excitement, Marcus chugged the rest of his ale, then he too took his leave, nodding to the tavern keeper on the way out. His burden felt a little lighter now that he had someone on the case. With a sense of relief, he emerged into the bright sunlight and began his walk back to the house on St James's Square, taking New Street then crossing St Martin's Lane. He wondered what Lionel was up to at that moment and what turn his own investigations were taking, for Marcus felt sure that Lionel was busily trying to resolve the situation from his end. With the two of them working on this together, they were bound to succeed. That was what he told himself.

And tonight, he would see Lionel again at the ball.

CHAPTER 19

AN EVENTFUL BALL

LIORA'S DAY HAD been a mixed success. On the one hand, she had achieved an excellent price at the wool auction for all their stock of merino wool. She would need to speak to Broek about increasing their supply of this much-in-demand commodity.

However, on the matter of discovering the identity of the person threatening their business, she had made far less headway. Discreetly, she had sounded out the merchants at the auction, trying to find out what she could about the three men under suspicion. All she had managed to obtain was a tenuous snippet of information about one of their suspects, William Vaughan. She learned that on visiting the coffee house last month, someone had playfully handed him a pamphlet which advertised that Mrs. B. Henderson's warehouse in Peckham was selling a variety of ceramic basins that had the slogan 'East India Sugar, Not Made by Slaves' inscribed in gold lettering.

The pamphlet had gone on to claim: "A family that uses 5lb of sugar per week, will, by using East India, instead of West India, for 21 months, prevent the slavery, or murder of one fellow-creature!" On seeing the pamphlet, William Vaughan had erupted angrily, cursing "these pestilent Quakers" for trying to ruin his business. Could this anger have been extended to the Reeves family, prominent traders of East India sugar? It was not very conclusive but seemed to point to William Vaughan being their chief suspect. She resolved on the morrow to focus her enquiries on this individual. Perhaps she could employ someone to have him watched, though she was not sure how she would go about finding such a person to do this. Up until now, the family had relied on Broek's trusted nanoprobes to spy on their business competitors when the need for doing so had arisen. Once more, she rued their loss. Would Galok be willing to abandon his care of the horses long enough to do this surveillance on their behalf? She would have to speak to him about it.

She sat down for an early dinner, then busied herself with work, inputting the day's sales into the data files on the console. Once she was done, she stretched her stiff muscles and decided some exercise would be beneficial. It had been several days since she had engaged in her regular *raiko* practice. Quickly, she changed into a pair of soft and stretchy trousers then returned to the parlour, locking the door behind her once more and moving the furniture out of the way. She made sure the curtains were securely in place before initiating the *raiko* holo-programme on her console. In seconds, her holographic sparring partner appeared before her. They bowed to each other, as was customary, then the fight began. Liora had set the programme to a medium difficulty level, but even so, it took every ounce of her strength and dexterity to keep pace with her opponent. In the end, a victory eluded her, and the fight concluded with a draw. Turning off the holo-programme, she collapsed on the floor in a sweat, trying to regain her breath. She promised herself that from here on, she would keep up with a daily regimen of *raiko* practice, even while in London.

Evening had fallen by now, and it was time to get ready for the ball. She retired to her chamber to wash and dress, taking great care with her appearance. Sitting at her dressing table, she styled her hair and surreptitiously applied some light cosmetics to her face—nothing too obvious, just a dab of tinted cream followed by a brush of powder to brighten her complexion. Next, she fixed her cravat with a diamond encrusted pin, then pulled on a navy linen tailcoat. Taking her hat and gloves, she went downstairs, bidding Esa goodnight as she left the house. Galok waited outside with the carriage and horses. He came forward, opening the door for her.

"Looking mighty fine," he muttered under his breath.

"Do I make a handsome gentleman?" she asked with a smile.

"Far too handsome for my peace of mind," he grumbled. Then, looking at her in concern, he added, "You will be careful, Liora, won't you?"

What was it with everyone asking her to be careful? But she answered reassuringly, "Do not worry. I am being careful. Now, take me to this ball."

"MR LIONEL REEVES." Her fictitious name was announced as she entered the large ballroom at the Maybury mansion. The room was lit by a giant chandelier of glowing candles and several wall sconces which shone a warm golden light. Grecian columns graced the sides of this vast, rectangular space, which was filled with the hubbub of many voices, while in one corner, a string orchestra played a brisk tune. Richly dressed guests gathered in small groups all around the room, bowing and curtsying, smiling and conversing.

She had not come here expecting to be impressed, not when she had memories of the lavish *frolls* that her family had held back in her home world of Uvon. A *froll* was their version of a ball, but it was on an entirely different level. It was not simply one ballroom filled with dancing couples, but several themed rooms in which guests could cavort, play, dance, feast or converse quietly in private nooks. Their music there had played to a different beat, accompanied by talented singers whose voices meshed beautifully with one another to create an inimitable sound. When one had experienced a *froll*, nothing else could quite compare. Liora had not lied to Broek when she had said she had no great wish to attend an English society ball.

It was not something that had been high on her wish list of things to do.

And yet as she got her first glimpse of this ball, she realised there was something to be said for the pent-up feeling of excitement that permeated the room. People here tonight were dressed in their best and determined to extract maximum enjoyment from the final ball of the season. She stood for a moment taking in this scene of revelry and running her gaze over the room in search for Marcus. With his tall and broad frame, he was not difficult to find. Her breath hitched at the sight of him in evening dress, the tightly fitted breeches hugging the contours of his powerful thighs and the perfectly tailored black tailcoat accentuating the perfection of his shoulders. He left every other man here in the shade.

Without thinking, her feet moved her in his direction. His mother and sisters were beside him, dressed in all their finery. Together, they made a striking tableau as a family. Milling around them were a handful of other gentlemen and ladies, none of whom she knew, but it mattered not, for all her attention was on him and his melting brown eyes which regarded her fixedly as she crossed the room towards him. *Do not get involved, Liora.* She gave herself this mental reminder in the faint hope that it would stop the feelings gathering in her chest and threatening to overwhelm her. Faint hope indeed.

Once she reached the vicinity of his group, he stepped to one side, extricating himself from whoever he was speaking to with some polite excuse so that he could come up to her.

"Lionel!" he exclaimed warmly.

She executed a creditable bow. "Your Grace." Then she turned and made her bows to his mother and sisters. She was introduced to various other people, but she did not recollect their names.

Then Julia handed her a dance card, saying with a bright smile, "Mr Reeves, you had better sign me up as your partner for a dance before my card fills up."

"Of course," she said with as much gallantry as she could. She took Julia's card, which was hardly full, and quickly inscribed her name in pencil, reserving for herself a country dance. It would be an odd feeling to play the role of the gentleman tonight, asking blushing young females for a dance—though in this instance the female was hardly blushing, for Julia treated her with the easy familiarity of a longstanding family friend. Did she suspect anything about Liora's relationship with her brother? No, that could not be. If she did, then she would not act in such a friendly fashion. Indeed who could suspect, looking at the tall and broad and powerfully muscled duke, that he had spent a night of passion with another man? A man who was not really a man. The truth was ever so complicated.

She shook these troubling thoughts away and tried to focus on the here and now. Yet more persons approached their gathered group, and more introductions were made. She bowed and said pleasantries, and watched as the ladies fluttered their lashes at Marcus—and some too at her—waiting to be asked for a dance. To her mind, it was a vivid example of the inequalities between the sexes in English society. Men did the asking while women waved their fans prettily and hoped to be chosen. Those that did not got consigned to sitting out the dances, labelled cruelly as wallflowers. Her sympathy went out to them. To be made to feel unwanted, and in such a public way, must hurt the soul. If it were up to her, she would be choosing these wallflowers for a dance rather than the belles of the ball.

It was almost like Marcus heard her thoughts. For as the chords were struck for the cotillion, he deftly guided Liora to one side of the ballroom where several young ladies had gone to sit in the knowledge that they did not have a partner for the dance. He approached one such lady, a scrawny looking thing in a shabby gown of dusky pink, saying to her with a smile, "Miss Vernon, we meet again. I do hope by now you have forgiven me for my pitiful play at Lady Rockingham's card party."

For an instant, the lady looked taken aback at the unexpected attention but swiftly gathered her composure to reply in a high-pitched voice, "Your Grace, no forgiveness is required, I assure you."

"Then perhaps you may allow me to escort you for this cotillion which is now about to start?"

"Oh... Yes, of course." Her sallow face flushed bright with colour.

She stood, and as she did so, Marcus looked pointedly in the direction of another young lady sitting beside her, this one short and plump, and wearing an unflattering floral patterned yellow gown. "Miss Vernon," he continued. "Will you make known to us your fair neighbour, for I feel sure my good friend Mr Reeves here would dearly love to engage her in this dance too."

"Oh." Miss Vernon turned to the other lady in question, who was also now blushing furiously. "This is Miss Wetherington, Your Grace."

"Miss Wetherington," Marcus said, bowing in her direction. "A pleasure."

Miss Wetherington stumbled to her feet and executed a wobbly curtsy, her voice having briefly deserted her. Taking her cue from Marcus, Liora bowed in her direction. "Miss Wetherington," she said, putting on her deepest male voice. "Would you do me the honour of this dance?"

Still deprived of the power of speech, Miss Wetherington inclined her head of bright red curls in acceptance. Liora held out her arm chivalrously and led her to the dance floor, where they took their positions in a square formation with Marcus and his partner. For the first part of the dance, the lady said nothing, and Liora was glad of it, for the cotillion required elaborate footwork. It took all her power of concentration to get it right, but after a few minutes of this, she began to feel more confident in the dance and decided to engage her partner in some conversation. It was a relief to find that Miss Wetherington had also used the time to regain her power of speech, and for the remaining duration of the dance, they exchanged surprisingly witty banter. What a shame that high society did not value a person such as she, thought Liora. She was doubly glad now that she had asked this particular wallflower to dance.

In this fashion, Marcus and Liora spent the next hour dancing with one wallflower after the next. It was as if they were partners in an unspoken mission, and it espoused a warm feeling of camaraderie between them. Her dance partners were not all as witty as Miss Wetherington, yet she enjoyed herself. There was pleasure to be had in doing a good deed while at the same time snubbing the snobbish and entitled people at the top of the society tree. As the evening progressed, she could see they were creating quite a stir. Whispers flew around the room about the Duke of Coleford purposely choosing wallflowers for his dance partners. Some were amused; some were aghast. Mrs Cavendish, Marcus's mama, was most definitely unamused.

During a lull between dances, she marched up to them and chided her son, "Marcus, what can you be about? Everyone here is talking of you, and not in a good way."

Marcus hung his head sheepishly, the habit of pleasing his mother deeply ingrained. "I am sorry, Mama," he said. "I had thought I was doing a kindness to those ladies."

"And so you were, my dear," she retorted, sounding a little less peeved, "but in so doing, you have put the backs up of other, equally deserving ladies." Before he could respond, she went on to say, "And now I wish you to accompany me to speak with Mr and Miss Worsley, and you will kindly ask the lady to be your partner for the waltz."

Marcus was not given a chance to disagree. With the determination of a military general leading his troops into battle, Mrs Cavendish shepherded her son towards a lady and gentleman standing a little way apart, whom Liora recalled being introduced to earlier in the evening. They were brother and sister, the lady a little older in years than the other blushing females that had surrounded them this night. Liora followed in their footsteps, not having anywhere else to be, and observed as they exchanged pleasantries. Soon, Marcus dutifully asked Miss Worsley for the honour of dancing the waltz, to which she gracefully agreed. A moment later, he offered her his hand and ushered her to the dancefloor, casting Liora a quick glance of apology on the way. There was nothing to apologise for, and yet curiously, she was put out.

She watched them from afar, his gloved hand sliding to Miss Worsley's waist while she placed delicate fingers to his shoulder. There was a decorous distance between their bodies as they began to twirl to the music. There could be no suggestion of any impropriety. And yet as she watched them, Liora seethed inwardly. The two were well matched, for Miss Worsley was taller than average, though not as tall as herself. Despite his great size, Marcus was surprisingly light on his feet. Liora observed the lady say something to him that had him laugh. With their elegant figures and sunny smiles, they made a striking couple as they flew around the room to the strains of the waltz. Others were watching them and noting this too. Liora overheard someone behind her speculate about the duke and the particular honour he had bestowed on Miss Worsley by standing with her for the waltz. Could there be a match in the making? More voices discussed this possibility and made conjectures.

"It is Miss Worsley's fourth London season. She can hardly wish to return for a fifth one next year still unwed."

Another voice said, "Yet she has turned down many suitors, some of them perfectly eligible."

Someone else replied, "True, but circumstances have changed. Not only is she older now, and not quite as in demand as she was in her previous seasons, but I have it on good authority that Mr Worsley, her brother, is set to marry this Michaelmas. She will not want to remain in the house where she is now mistress and find her status there relegated. I can well see why she might feel a more pressing need now to find herself a husband."

"And she has set her cap at the duke?"

"So it seems. And what a brilliant feather in her cap that would be."

A poisonous jealousy filled Liora's veins. What if Marcus was attracted to females just as much as to males? That was not uncommon a thing. It would help explain why he had been slow to realise he had a propensity for men too. And if he found this Miss Worsley attractive, then wouldn't she be a much better prospect for his affections than embarking on a dangerous affair with her?

Do not get involved, Liora. Once again, she repeated this chant to herself. There was no happy resolution for the maelstrom of feelings in her breast. The best, most sensible thing to do would be to turn away and keep her distance. Excusing herself, she went in search of some beverage to cool her heated body. She accepted a glass of lemonade from an attendant then wove through the throng of people, in search of a quiet spot to drink, reflect and restore her spirits. In a vestibule not far from the refreshment table, she spied an alcove with a large potted plant which seemed to be deserted at this moment. She went to stand there, taking sips from the lemonade, and tried to let her jealousy simmer down. No matter how sweet, how delectably handsome, how winsome was Marcus, Duke of Coleford, she should truly accept that there could be nothing between them beyond a friendly acquaintance. It was past time she did so.

"Mr Reeves," a cool voice spoke beside her. "Have you come to a decision regarding our little matter?"

Liora whirled to find that slimy toad, Ralph Boyle, standing beside her. How the devil had this man gotten an invitation to a society ball? Or had he barged in uninvited? That would not surprise her at all.

Coldly, she replied, "The Reeves of Reeves Hall do not look kindly upon coercive business practices, Mr Boyle."

"The Reeves of Reeves Hall are willing to see an expensive consignment of sugar rot and spoil, I take it?"

"Ha!" she scoffed. "We shall find a way to get our goods back. That I promise."

Mr Boyle took a step closer, skewering her with a razor sharp gaze. At the same time, she got an unpleasant whiff of stale sweat imperfectly masked by a cloying cologne. Very softly he hissed, "I would not try it if I were you, Mr Reeves, unless you wish for the same fate as your predecessor."

She froze as the import of these words sunk in. So, Esa had been right. Jos's death had been no accident, but caused by this man standing before her and his master. On the heels of her shock came a great fury which engulfed her from head to toe. It took all her self-discipline not to take down that slippery eel of a man with one lethal *raiko* move. Instead, she lanced him with a deadly gaze of her own and spit, "Nobody messes with the Reeves of Reeves Hall. Not only will we get back what is ours, but now, we are also going to take you and your vile master down. That is a promise, not a threat. Now get out of my sight!"

The man stepped hurriedly back, his face set into a sneer. "A grave mistake, Mr Reeves," he snarled, then whipped around and disappeared into the crowd.

Liora stood for several moments, trying to tamp down her agitation. Now that the confrontation was over, a reaction set in. Her hands trembled as convulsive shivers ran through her body. She breathed in and out deeply, and sent a silent supplication. *Great Yol, help me.*

Help came from an unexpected direction. A gentle hand touched her arm, and looking round, she saw Julia, her face creased in concern. Marcus's sister could hardly fail to notice her tremors and the sweat breaking out on her brow. "It's alright," Julia said softly. "It's alright." She took a handkerchief out of her reticule and handed it to her. Liora took it with a muttered thanks and held it to her brow, breathing in a calming scent of lavender—from Marcus's garden no doubt.

"How much of that did you hear?" she eventually asked.

"All of it, I'm afraid. You see, that little nook behind the potted plant is where I went to have a brief respite from it all."

Liora nodded in understanding. She had come here for much the same purpose. "That monstrous excuse for a person had Jos killed," she said, grief and anger ripping through her once more.

"Jos? Your predecessor?"

"Yes," replied Liora. "He was in charge of our business affairs at the docks and had worked faithfully for my family many years."

"I see," murmured Julia. "And now this Mr Boyle is threatening your person. What shall you do?"

"I do not quite know yet, but I will think of something." Liora did not tell her the germ of an idea forming in her head. That would have to wait until she could speak privately with Broek on the matter. Instead, she said, "Now, perhaps it is best we get back to the ballroom. I believe you have promised me the next dance."

"Yes, I have," Julia agreed with a smile.

Together, they made their way back to the ballroom where they found Marcus, his mother and other sisters gathered in a small group. "Where did you go?" demanded Marcus as soon as he set eyes on her. "I was looking out for you during the waltz but could not see you."

More likely he was looking at his fair partner, Liora thought sourly. Then she castigated herself. If there was one of Marcus's traits she knew well, it was his honesty. In a flash, she realised that her earlier jealousy had been for naught. Rightly or wrongly, it was her—or Lionel—that had captured his interest. The thought sent a fluttery feeling in her chest while the voice of reason in her head decried the sentiment, reminding her for the umpteenth time: *do not get involved, Liora.*

Pulling herself together, she replied calmly, "I merely went to obtain refreshments for myself and Miss Julia."

"It was very chivalrous of Mr Reeves," affirmed Julia.

"Oh," responded Marcus, looking slightly mollified. "That was well done of you, Lionel."

"Indeed it was," said Julia smoothly. "And now, if you will excuse us, we must take our positions for the country dance."

CHAPTER 20

❧ ❦

A PAINFUL DECISION

IT WAS LATE, close on one o'clock in the morning, when Liora finally returned home to Barton Street. Stifling a yawn, she went up to her bedchamber and toed off her black leather pumps, wriggling her tired feet in relief. She did not undress immediately though. Broek was probably fast asleep in his bed with Jane, but she had to speak with him. Tapping the communicator on her ring, Liora called him. She heard a groan as he jolted awake, then becoming more alert, he demanded gruffly, "Liora. What is it?"

"I am sorry to wake you, Broek," she said, " but I have news that cannot wait."

"Speak."

As briefly as she could, she told him about her altercation with Ralph Boyle at the ball, then about Esa's suspicions regarding Jos's death. She heard him utter a colourful Uvonian swearword which fortunately for him, Jane did not comprehend. "Why on earth did you not tell me this before?" he exploded.

She sighed. "I thought it was her grief speaking at the suddenness of his passing, and I did not wish to worry you."

"Damn it, Liora!"

"I am sorry, but what is done is done. Let us focus our minds on the more pressing matter of what to do now."

There was a lengthy silence. Then Broek said, his tone turning gentle, "Liora, I do not want you to take this the wrong way, but I am sending Simor and Horis down to London, and the sooner they get to you the better."

"You do not think I can manage this myself?" She felt a puncture to her pride at the idea of having her younger brothers come to the rescue after less than a week of being in charge.

"It is no judgement on you, Liora," retorted Broek with a hint of urgency. "You have nothing to prove to me or anyone else. But you will pardon me for caring that the life of someone I love is being threatened."

"What difference will it make having them here?"

"What difference?" Broek muttered impatiently. "For starters, three heads are better than one. And when there is a threat of bodily danger, it is best not to go anywhere alone. There is safety in numbers."

He was not wrong. Perhaps now was not the time for pride. And yet she could not help but feel a sense of failure. "I suppose so," she said wearily.

"Liora," her brother grunted in irritation. "You must know I have nothing but admiration for the work you have done since taking over from Jos. And you know too that I do not varnish the truth. I say what I mean. You are incredibly capable, sister mine. I have seen the data. The sales you negotiated these last few days have brought us higher returns than ever before."

She knew his words were true. She was highly capable, and had managed things well so far. Most days, she was confident in herself, but there were the odd moments when doubt crept in. It was a very human foible, she supposed. Everyone had vulnerabilities behind the mask they presented to the world. For some reason, this made her think of Marcus. Behind his easy affability and good-humoured smile was a man who carried a world of uncertainty on his shoulders—all because he was born with a condition well known on her home world of Uvon, one in which he encountered a difficulty in deciphering letters. Some of the most intelligent minds on her world had had this condition, for instance Kreis Belas, the man who, centuries ago, had jumpstarted their space exploration with his discovery of the 'distortion drive'. But of course, here in backward England, there had been no concerted research on the subject, and instead, those persons who had the condition were labelled as slow and dim-witted.

Quite clearly, at least to her, Marcus was anything but dim-witted. She recalled how swiftly he had grasped the concept of cooling technology when she had explained it to him on their carriage journey to London. Over the course of that journey too, she had noticed his unfailing capability for taking the true measure of people. At one coaching inn, he had been quick to notice, quicker even than Galok, when the ostler had tried to palm them with tired horses that were not very fresh. And of course, there was the extraordinary way he had taught himself about the natural world, for even though he could not read with ease, he carried in his mind an encyclopaedia of knowledge about plants. Yes indeed, Marcus was far more capable than he appeared, and strangely, it was thinking of him that gave her the strength, right at this moment, to overcome her own lapse in confidence. Let Simor and Horis come to London. Broek was right that three heads were better than one. It implied no judgement on her capabilities. Moreover, she had something else to bring to the table. An idea had been brewing in her mind.

"Yes, I know I am capable," she replied to Broek's earlier comments. "And there is something I have thought of that might help us with our problem. I realise we no longer have the nanoprobes, but do you have any more of the recording devices you installed at our office and at the warehouse? I am thinking we could glean valuable information by placing one such device in Henry Blunt's office at the Custom House, perhaps even another in his home."

"Good thinking!" exclaimed Broek, giving Liora's damaged ego a boost. "As a matter of fact, I do have a few of those devices to spare. I'll send them with your brothers." He thought a bit then added, "They will travel by drone to London. It is the quickest way, and if they leave while it is still dark and operate the cloaking mechanism, the risk of them being seen flying in the drone is minimal. I'll send the co-ordinates to Galok, so he can ride to the landing point on the outskirts of the city and pick them up first thing in the morning."

And there it was, the end to her exciting adventure. Tomorrow morning when she woke, her brothers would be here. She loved them dearly, but she had been enjoying being on her own for a while and being mistress of her own home. It had been too long since she had felt independent.

Resigned to her fate, she bid Broek a good night, though she suspected he would not be getting much in the way of sleep. Then she sat on her bed a long time in contemplation. She pondered their problem with Ralph Boyle and his master, but her thoughts soon turned to one matter only, to one person. *Marcus*. What was she to do about him? About the feelings she had tried to repress, with little success. And about the feelings he had undoubtedly developed for her. Was there any way out of this dilemma?

She had gone over it in her head time and again. And time and again, she had returned to the same conclusion. There could be no relationship between her and Marcus unless she revealed her true self and therefore also her origins on Uvon. That she could not do. Ergo, it was hopeless, and the kindest thing, both to him and to herself, was to cut all ties once and for all. Liora felt a constriction in her chest as she reached a decision. On the morrow, she would pay him a visit and tell him. She would say that watching him dance with Miss Worsley had finally made her realise that she needed to let him go, much as it pained her. She would wish him well, then say goodbye. With the arrival of her brothers, there would be important business to take care of. There could be no time for romantic entanglements.

She stared at the wall, unseeing, and felt a searing sadness sweep through her. Sweet, wonderful Marcus. So beautiful inside and out. She wished he knew just how very special he was and how much he had come to mean to her. She knew that her words next day would cause him pain, and it was going to hurt for her to say them. But it had to be done.

CHAPTER 21

A HEROIC GESTURE

MARCUS STRETCHED HIS arms overhead and gave a great yawn. It had been a long night at the ball, and the latter part of it, he had not enjoyed at all. Something was up with Lionel. He wished he knew what it was. First thing tomorrow, he promised himself he would pay a visit to Barton Street and find out. On that last thought, he slipped under the covers and extinguished the candle before he let his weary body sink into the bed.

Not a moment later, there came a knock at the door. Great heavens, who could want to see him at this late hour? "Come in!" he called out gruffly.

The latch turned, and a small shaft of light streamed into the room as the door eased open. His sleepy eyes took in the sight of Julia, face pale and pinched, holding a small lamp in her hand. "May I speak with you, Marcus?" she whispered softly.

He stifled another yawn and groaned, "Can it not wait until morning, Julia? I am worn out."

She shut the door gently behind her and advanced towards him, holding the lamp aloft. "I do not think it can wait," she said.

"Very well," he grunted, sitting up in bed. "What is it?"

"That horrid Mr Boyle..."

"What about him?" he asked impatiently.

"He was there tonight at the ball."

Marcus stiffened, a sense of dread trickling through him. "Go on," he urged her.

"He spoke to Lionel. I heard it all, for I was hidden behind a potted plant, out of sight. Do not ask me why." As quickly as she could, Julia relayed the gist of the conversation she had overheard.

"Well," she ended, "Mr Boyle did not like it one bit. And he said, 'I would not try it if I were you, Mr Reeves, unless you wish for the same fate as your predecessor.'"

"The hell he did!" Marcus's fists curled around the sheet on his lap as the import of those words sank in. That predecessor had died very suddenly—and quite clearly not from natural causes. Now it was Lionel whose life was under threat. This matter had gone beyond merely fraudulent business practices and entered into the realm of the very sinister indeed.

"Lionel was so very brave," Julia went on. "He promised he'd get his goods back and that he would take Mr Boyle and his master down. I think that Boyle fellow was a bit shook by how fierce Lionel was. In any event, he backed away and left, telling Lionel he'd made a grave mistake."

The grave mistake was ever threatening Lionel's person in the first place. Marcus vowed he would hunt these evil persons down and make them pay for what they had done. But first, he needed to ensure Lionel's safety, and there was not a minute to be lost. He threw off the covers and jumped out of bed, startling Julia, who stared at him in bewilderment.

"What are you doing?" she cried.

Going over to the dresser, he snatched it open and took out a fresh shirt, then rummaged some more for stockings and pantaloons. Throwing them on the bed, he went quickly to the armoire to take out a tailcoat and polished boots, saying in a rough voice, "You had best go now, Julia, for I must dress."

"But it is the middle of night," she demurred.

"Lionel is in danger, and I must go to him now." Remembering the flintlock pistol which he kept in his travel bag, he went to retrieve it, placing it carefully on the dressing table.

Julia's eyes widened at the sight of it. "Marcus," she remonstrated. "Do you know what you are doing?"

He turned to her, fierce in his determination. "I am going to the man I love who is in danger. Do not question me further, Julia, or try to stop me. Now go!"

She threw him one last hesitant glance then rushed out of the room. Hardly had the door closed on her than he was pulling the nightshirt over his head and dressing as quickly as he could. Tying a cravat haphazardly around his neck, he then dug his arms into the coat and pulled on his boots. Finally, he took the pistol, slipping it into his coat pocket. Within moments, he was at the front door, shutting it behind him and hurrying into the dark night. With swift footsteps, he made his way towards Barton Street, a faint glow of the moon lighting his path. There were few people about at this time, and wisely, nobody accosted him. In no time at all, he reached Lionel's home, and without thinking things through, his heart pounding madly in his chest, he banged his fists on the door and demanded to be let in.

In a few moments, the door opened, and there was Lionel. He stepped aside, letting Marcus through and shut the door behind him. Marcus bounded inside, unable to mask his agitation. In an instant, he had taken Lionel by the shoulders. "Lionel," he cried. "Until that murderous villain is caught and put to justice, I am not leaving your side. Do you hear?"

LIORA STARED AT Marcus in shock. Before she could reply, two more persons appeared in the hallway: Esa who had hurried down the stairs, and Galok who had rushed in from the room at the back of the kitchen where he had his quarters, tucking his shirt into his trousers. It was Galok who spoke first.

"What is going on here?" he boomed.

Marcus dropped his hands from her shoulders as they both turned to face Galok, who glowered ferociously. She finally recovered her wits enough to say, "It's alright. I just have a late visitor, that is all."

Galok was not so easily deflected. He stood, a powerful figure, with his legs apart and arms crossed. Addressing her, he asked mutinously, "Why is he here?"

On a breath, she replied, "Galok, trust me. It is fine. Both you and Esa can go back to bed."

Still, Galok did not move. Glancing at Marcus with a frown, he asked again, "Why is he here? It is the middle of the night."

"I am here to see Lionel on a private matter which is of no concern to you," growled Marcus. Subconsciously or not, he too now stood legs wide and arms crossed, facing him down.

Liora's voice took on a harder edge as she grit out, "All is well, Galok. Please go." She met his eyes, willing him to let the matter drop.

He took his time about it, scowling at Marcus. Finally, he grunted, "If you need me, I am close by." The words were both for her and for Marcus, their intent clear.

Soon, the two of them were left alone in the hallway. Liora went to pick up the pistol she had placed on a side table once she realised who was at the door. Wryly, she said, "You gave us quite the fright tonight. I took this out, thinking there might be a need for it."

Marcus watched her closely, a frown on his face. "It is good you have it near you at all times," he replied. Patting his own pocket, he said, "I brought my pistol along too, for that matter."

"So," Liora said, leading the way into the front parlour, "Julia told you."

"That blackguard needs to be brought to justice," he murmured darkly, following Lionel into the room.

She quickly lit the candles in another lamp, then turned to him, looking down at her stockinged feet and state of dishabille. "I am not in a fit state to receive visitors, as you can see," she said lightly. As Marcus did not respond to that frivolous remark, she continued in a more serious vein, "Did you really have to come here in the middle of the night? This could have waited till morning."

Still, Marcus said nothing. He breathed deeply, as if trying to regain his lost composure. Then he stalked towards her, his brown eyes glittering with a mix of emotions—anger, passion, desire and worry. Something about him felt different tonight, as if a dormant beast within him had awoken. He came to stand a hair's breadth from Liora. Softly, he hissed, "When it comes to your safety, Lionel, the matter cannot wait."

Liora scoffed, though her pulse was starting to race. "I am perfectly safe in my house, as you can see."

"And even safer now that I am here with you. A bullet or a sword would have to go through me first to get to you," countered Marcus gruffly.

Liora tried to laugh the matter off, though in reality, her heart was squeezing hard in her chest. "You are being quite melodramatic, Marcus," she said. "And in any case, all that would achieve is getting you killed, which would hardly save me if we were truly under attack."

Marcus ran a finger down her cheek, the gentleness of his touch belying the fierceness of his tone as he rasped, "I would protect you to my dying breath, Lionel. Melodramatic or not, if your life is in danger, then do not ask me to keep away."

"But I must." Flustered, Liora forced herself to step back and turn towards the nearest armchair, inviting him with a hand gesture to take a seat. Once they had both sat a respectable distance from one another, she continued her speech. "Marcus, I am touched that you have come to pledge yourself as my protector, but you need not do so. I am taking the required precautions to keep myself safe, added to which tomorrow, my cousins arrive, so I shall not be alone. Do not forget too that you have a responsibility to your family."

"I have not forgotten," he growled, tapping two fingers to his thigh, a habit she had noticed he had when he was agitated.

"They can do without me this night, and until I am sure in my mind that you are indeed safe."

"I have no plans to send you back out in the middle of the night," she sighed, "but tomorrow morning, you must return to your home."

To this Marcus did not respond. Changing the subject abruptly, he asked, "This servant with the strange name, Galok, what is he to you?"

"He is a long-standing servant of my family," Liora said smoothly.

Marcus stared her down. "The truth, Lionel," he grated. "The man's manner was more than simply that of a servant."

Liora hesitated, but then decided that on this matter at least, she could be truthful with him. "Years ago, he was my lover," she said quietly, "but all that is over now."

"How long ago?" Marcus barked out.

"It has been at least eight years since I have lain with him. It is in the past, Marcus."

The nervous tapping on his thigh continued. He gritted out, "The way he looked at you and spoke tonight, it does not seem to be in the past."

There was jealousy in his voice, but also pain. It was this that propelled Liora to her feet. She went to him then, sinking to her knees and placing a firm hand over his to silence the tapping of his fingers. "It is in the past," she reiterated. "We split amicably long ago, but there remains affection and loyalty, that is all. In any case, Marcus, it should not matter, for it has been clear to me that whatever it is that has sprung up between us must end, for both our sakes. Look at the way you came here tonight. If this goes on any further, people will talk. It is time to put an end to this."

"I have fallen in love with you," Marcus said raggedly, looking her straight in the eyes.

Liora went quiet, though her hand squeezed his tightly. She did not tell him that her feelings were equally strong. There was no point in stoking that fire. Finally, she said, "All the more reason why it is best we go our separate ways. You shall soon be returning to the country, in any case."

"I will not leave or let things go until I know you are safe," Marcus replied stubbornly.

"Simon and Harry, my cousins, will be here soon, and you have seen how protective Galok can be. I will not go anywhere alone from here on, and I will have my pistol with me. Please do not worry."

"But I do." His smile was twisted.

Liora bent her head down and placed a gentle kiss to Marcus's hand. "I worry about you too, Marcus," she said softly. "I worry what people will say about you. I worry about your future and your happiness. Believe me when I say, it is for the best that we part."

Marcus leaned forward to touch his forehead to hers. In a low, urgent voice, he said, "My feelings for you are real, Lionel, even though we have known each other but a short time." His breath caressed her face. "I know it in my heart."

"I do not doubt it," Liora murmured huskily, keeping their foreheads together. The tip of their noses touched just a fraction. "It was the same with my mother and father. They knew from their first meeting that they had met the love of their life."

"Where are they now?" Marcus queried, sensing her grief.

"Long gone."

Marcus sighed, then dropped a gentle kiss to her mouth. "I am sorry." He lifted his free hand to cup her jaw. "It is not just me, is it? You feel it too." He searched Liora's eyes, demanding the truth.

At first, she stayed silent, then she gave a quick nod. Marcus's breath caught. "Lionel—" he began throatily.

But Liora pressed a finger to his lips. "No, Marcus. Do not say it. Our feelings for each other do not change the impossibility of our situation. We do not live in a world where we could give free rein to what we feel, and besides, there are things about me that you do not know."

Marcus stilled, his eyes fixed on her. "I know that you have secrets, Lionel," he said very softly. "You did not grow up in Brazil, did you?"

"No," Liora admitted.

"Where then? And why does it matter?"

She let out a long breath. "It is not within my gift to tell you." At Marcus's insistent stare, she finally relented. "You will have noticed that I am different from most other people you know."

Marcus nodded quickly. "It is one of the many things that makes you special to me."

"There is a reason for it to do with my past," she explained, "but I am bound to secrecy. On the surface, I am Lionel Reeves of Reeves Hall, but beneath the surface, I am someone else. I cannot tell you more."

Marcus digested this information. Very softly, he asked, "Would it be such a tragedy if I knew the truth? You know that you can trust me."

Liora closed her eyes, praying for strength. Then, with a deep breath, she opened them once more and said, a finality in her voice, "I cannot tell you."

The silence between them lengthened. At last, Marcus spoke defeatedly, "I will leave only once I have spoken with your cousins and got an assurance from them that you will not be left alone at any time. You will carry that pistol with you and keep it loaded, understood?"

Liora smiled. "Understood."

"I have engaged the services of a Bow Street Runner who comes well recommended," he continued crisply. "If need be, I can engage two or more such men, until we get a satisfactory resolution to this matter."

Liora's smile widened. "Ah! I had been wondering whose services to engage on this matter. Thank you for this, Marcus." Then she added, "Although I do also have a plan of my own…"

"I am sure you do," Marcus responded quickly. "You ever were a resourceful person, Lionel. With your plan and my man on the case, we will succeed. Have no doubt about it."

His words filled her with renewed confidence. Yes, they would succeed, and they would get justice for Jos. She stroked his hand, which still lay under hers, and blurted the thought in her mind, "Dare I say it, Marcus, but you are showing an assertiveness that was not there when we first met."

"If so, it is you that has brought it out of me." Marcus peppered the praise with another light kiss to her lips.

"Please keep it that way, even once we are parted," Liora pleaded.

The reminder that they must part cast a pall over them. "I will," Marcus promised in a low voice.

Determined to keep firm to her resolution, Liora went on, pouring salt over the wound, "Tomorrow, we say goodbye. For good. No going back."

"Very well," he agreed reluctantly, "but I shall stay in London and liaise with Mr Quinn, the Bow Street Runner, until the matter is resolved. I will not leave until I know you are safe."

"You will apprise me of any information Mr Quinn shares with you?"

"Of course." Marcus gave a light snort. "You shall become acquainted with my terrible writing."

"It does not matter. I will never judge." Liora kissed his hand one final time then rose to her feet. A yawn escaped her. "It is late," she groaned. "We had best get some sleep."

She saw the thought flash in his eyes before he said it. "Will you share a bed with me, Lionel, one final time?"

There was nothing she wanted more, but they could not make love. That was a line she would not cross again, as long as she was not in her true form as a female. She held out her hands and pulled Marcus's hulking form to his feet. "You will share my bed tonight," she said, "but that is all. There will be no repeat of what we did last time." Seeing the conflict in

Marcus's eyes, she added, "Promise now, before we go upstairs."

"Fine," Marcus muttered. "You have my word. All we shall do is hold each other and sleep."

"Come along then." Liora took the lamp and led him out of the parlour. On quiet feet, they went up the stairs to her bedchamber. Once there, they each began to undress, watching each other closely. Liora pulled out one of her nightshirts from the dresser and threw it in Marcus's direction.

He caught it, but could not help quipping with a mischievous grin. "You wish us to be dressed in our bed tonight?"

"It is best we avoid temptation," Liora replied stoically.

Marcus chuckled and pulled his shirt over his head, exposing the glory that was his naked chest. He preened a little at her obvious admiration and drawled, "As you wish, Lionel, but you may as well get a show of what you will be missing." With these words, he dropped his pantaloons to the floor, baring his body fully. His cock was rigid and swollen, standing proudly in a nest of golden brown hair. She salivated at the view, and vexatious man that he was, he did not cover himself with the nightshirt right away, but stood, letting her drink in the sight of him.

"Your turn," Marcus said softly.

With fumbling fingers, she removed her shirt then dropped her pantaloons quickly. She was not in actuality naked, covered as she was with her bodysuit, but he was not to know. He stared at her intently, his face creased in a frown of concentration. "I have never before appreciated the naked form of a man," he whispered. "Not until you."

Guiltily, she slipped the nightshirt over her head, not lingering to give him a show as he had done for her. "Let us get to bed," she said briskly, lifting the covers at one end. Marcus joined her on the other side, waiting patiently while Liora extinguished the lamp. In the darkness, he reached for her, spooning her body to his. She was engulfed by his spicy male scent and by the warmth of his skin. He felt so wonderfully right. She sighed in satisfaction. One more night, she thought to herself. One more chance to feel his body close to hers.

He echoed her thoughts, murmuring in her ear, "You feel as though you were made just for me." He nuzzled her close, dropping tender kisses to the top of her head. "I love you, Lionel," he said.

In the dark intimacy of the night, she said the words back. "I love you too, Marcus."

Marcus's arms tightened around her. "Is there really no chance for us?" he asked, his face buried in her hair, breathing her in.

Her body responded to his embrace, arousal present in every pore, but she kept firm to her decision. "Believe me when I say I have gone over this time and again. There is no possibility of a future for us unless I reveal my secret, and revealing it is an impossibility."

"Can you not trust me?" he pleaded.

Liora sighed heavily. "It is not simply a matter of trusting you, Marcus. The secrets I hold are not mine to reveal."

"I cannot imagine being apart from you," Marcus said gruffly. "In a short time, you have become my entire world." His kiss on the back of her neck sent a quiver down her whole body as he urged, "There must be a way for us to be together. There must."

Liora turned in his embrace and kissed him gently on the lips. "There is not. We must accept it." He must have heard the finality in her voice, for he did not argue any further as Liora turned once more and resumed their previous position with her back to Marcus's chest.

They stayed liked this, Marcus holding her close, their senses alive to the scent and feel of each other. "I wish things could be different," she murmured sleepily. "But it is not to be. In time,

Marcus, your memories of us will fade, and I hope you may find happiness with a worthy lady to make your duchess."

"I cannot think of being with anyone but you," he grunted stubbornly.

"Give it time, sweetheart. Give it time."

She settled back against him, and soon, despite her best efforts to the contrary, she felt herself drift off to sleep.

CHAPTER 22

A STRANGE DISCOVERY AND A GOODBYE

LIONEL'S EVEN BREATHING told Marcus that he had fallen fast asleep. He, on the other hand, lingered in wakefulness, his mind too full of thoughts to slumber. As Lionel slept, Marcus gathered him close, burrowing his face in his silky curls and breathing him in while his hand stroked along his arm and chest. He felt Lionel's powerful, rippling muscles under his fingers and the scratchiness of the hair on his chest as he ran his palm under the nightshirt he was wearing. He wondered at it. For some strange reason, it felt out of kilter with the way he thought of Lionel. Nevertheless, it was a part of him that he tried to map in his mind, memorising all he could before they parted ways on the morrow.

For now, he had to accede to Lionel's wish for them to separate. He seemed adamant that this secret he held represented an impediment to their being together. There were other obstacles in the way as well, Marcus was well aware. Two men could not openly form a romantic attachment, yet he thought with ingenuity and discretion, it could be done. So, the matter really came down to this secret. What could it be? He recalled Lionel's words. *On the surface, I am Lionel Reeves of Reeves Hall, but beneath the surface, I am someone else.* Could this mean he was not really of the Reeves family, but some kind of impostor impersonating the real Lionel Reeves? He hinted it had to do with how different he was to everyone else—the knowledge he had, the subtle accent in his speech, his forthright manner and lack of social finesse. If indeed he was an impostor, could he be up to some nefarious activity? Some criminality? Marcus's mind rebelled against the idea. No, whatever it was, it was not that. But then, what was Lionel hiding? Try as he might, Marcus could not make sense of it.

In the deepest part of his heart, he still held a hope that their separation was not to be a permanent one. Perhaps, over the weeks and months to come, he might find a way to unravel the tangled web of secrets that were keeping them apart. Surely all was not lost? But what if it was? What if this was after all the end to their brief but blistering romance? His arms tightened around Lionel reflexively at the thought. After a time, he sank into a fitful sleep, his mind no closer to any resolution.

A sound jolted him awake some hours later. He opened bleary eyes to tendrils of light streaming in through the shutters. For a few instants, he lay still, trying to gain his bearings. There was that sound again, like the buzzing of an insect. Where was it coming from? Marcus shifted in the bed, noticing Lionel's slumbering form on the far edge of the mattress. They must have moved apart during the night, most likely to cool their heated bodies. Lionel lay on his right side, breathing deeply. Marcus searched with his eyes for the fly that was the most likely cause of the buzzing noise. Nothing. Then the glint of something caught his eye. An odd-looking object lay on the edge of Lionel's pillow. He picked it up gingerly, feeling it vibrate. Undoubtedly, this was the source of the noise. It was a small, transparent disc made of some unknown material—not glass. He brought it closer to inspect, and as he did, the noise it was emitting became louder, almost like it was a voice. Following his instinct, Marcus brought the object to his ear. It was a voice! Tucking the thing deeper into the cavity of his ear, the voice became clearer. It was a man speaking.

"Lior, are you there? Just to let you know Simor and Horis have met up with Galok and are on their way to the London house as we speak. They should be with you within the hour.

Did you hear that?" The irate voice became louder. "Oh, do wake up!"

Lionel grunted, emerging from his sleep. The voice must have woken him too. Quickly, not thinking the matter through, Marcus took the disc out of his ear and returned it to its original place on Lionel's pillow. In the same breath, he lay back on the bed and pretended to be asleep. He heard Lionel swear under his breath, then speak in a low voice—presumably to the man he had heard just now, but how that was possible, he could not fathom.

"I'm here... Yes, alright, understood... Very well, speak soon."

Marcus heard him shift in the bed, mumbling, "Where is that damned thing?" He realised Lionel must be looking for the clear disc that had been in his hands moments before. Lionel sighed in relief as he located it. Meanwhile, it was all Marcus could do to maintain the fiction that he was asleep. He took deep, even breaths, even going as far as to emit a light snore. Had he overdone it? He sensed Lionel's gaze on him, studying his reclining form. Then he was all action, hurriedly getting out of bed and moving about the room. Marcus heard the opening and shutting of drawers, the rustling of clothes. A door opened and shut—one he had not noticed last night. The sound of water. Lionel must be doing his ablutions in the dressing room next door.

Marcus stayed in position, eyes closed, and waited for his return. Sure enough, soon Lionel was back, sitting on the edge of the bed. He heard a light grunt. Another muttered oath. Marcus could tell he was pulling on his boots and having a fine time of it. If only Stubbs were here to assist him, he thought to himself in fleeting amusement. Then, Lionel was on his feet again and coming to his side of the room. He stood there a while, watching him. Marcus felt him lean close and lightly brush his lips to his forehead. A moment later, the door shut behind him, and Marcus was alone in the room.

Slowly, Marcus eased his eyes open. His mind was spinning in reaction to what he had just seen and heard. None of it made sense, yet it all seemed to be leading to that great secret Lionel held close to his chest. He thought back over it. Did he imagine that voice? But he had heard it speak clearly in his ear, coming through that transparent disc. He could not have imagined that, surely? He had heard a man speak of Galok and mention of two other strange names, saying they were on their way to the London house. Lionel's cousins? The man had addressed Lionel as 'Lior'. Could that be his true name?

His heart pounded wildly in a mix of excitement, wonder and fear. How could a disembodied voice speak so into his ear? Some ghostly apparition? Could it be magic? He took deep steadying breaths and tried to think rationally. Lionel was an inventor, an immensely clever one. If he could make cold air stream into a hot carriage, then surely too he had the wherewithal to invent some sort of communicating device in which persons could speak to one another from afar. How it was done, Marcus had no clue. But that must be it. A person he knew, a cousin of his perhaps, was speaking to him somehow through that small transparent disc.

Marcus's mind raced with a myriad thoughts and ideas. Of course, anyone seeing a speaking disc would think it to be some form of occult, some dark form of magic. It was not something that could easily be disclosed to others. It must be kept secret. But he was not anybody. Why would Lionel not trust him with this knowledge? He felt a tinge of hurt at the thought.

Could there be more? There must be. Knowing that Lionel was an inventor of marvellous things could not be what was keeping them apart.

His mind whirred with one idea after another. It occurred to him that if there was a disc that conveyed someone's voice, then too there must be some other contraption through which a person's speech was dispatched. He thought to the times he had seen Lionel tap his signet ring. It too had a clear, disc-like surface. His excitement mounted. Yes, that must be it. When was the last time he had seen Lionel do it? He thought and thought. It was on his visit yesterday. Lionel had tapped the ring and spoken of Esa bringing in some tea for refreshment. They had discussed what sort of tea. A herbal infusion with lemon balm and camomile, Lionel had said. Lo and behold, a few minutes later, the housekeeper had come in with just such a beverage on a tray. Somehow, through that signet ring, Lionel had instructed her to bring it.

So, this would mean the housekeeper, and also the pesky groom Galok, were part of this secret circle of which he was excluded. The thought burned. Then Marcus had another, painful reflection. If Lionel's ring had the capability of transmitting the sound of someone speaking to a receiving device far away, then might he not use this to spy on that corrupt official at the Custom House? Marcus's attempt to resolve the situation by hiring a Bow Street Runner seemed flimsy by comparison. Of course, Lionel and his cousins must have the means at their disposal to glean the information they needed. They could not be in want of his assistance. How foolish of him to think his help was needed!

Once again, Marcus was overwhelmed with his uncertainties. No longer did he feel like the Marcus who was strong and talented, but more like the Marcus who was incapable and dim-witted—the one who was managed by his mother and sisters, and who hid from the world by working in his garden. The feeling was so intense that he hunched over for several minutes, clutching his face in his hands.

After a while, he straightened up, his thoughts bleak. Yes, he was probably the most foolish man in town, but there was no point in wallowing. Determinedly, he got out of bed and strode to the dressing room to wash. He was surprised once more, for what he found behind the door was not a dressing room but a privy and washroom all in one. There was a handle above a bowl, and when he pressed it, water gushed out. He smiled despite himself. Clever Lionel. Quickly, Marcus did his ablutions then got himself dressed as best he could. No doubt Stubbs would be scandalised at the crease in his coat and the simple way he had tied his cravat, but it would have to do.

He exited the bedchamber and made his way down the stairs, where he was met by Esa, the housekeeper. She greeted him politely, her expression inscrutable, and directed him to the dining room. There, he found Lionel at the table, buttering a slice of toast. The fragrant aroma of coffee wafted towards him from the steaming cup laid before him. Lionel put the toast down and rose to his feet with a smile.

"Good morning, Marcus."

"Good morning," he replied.

"Do make yourself at home," Lionel said. "Would you like coffee?"

Marcus nodded politely. "Yes, thank you."

Lionel poured him a cup as he took his seat opposite him. Without asking, he added a dash of cream, just the way Marcus liked. With a murmured word of thanks, Marcus took the cup from him. Lionel was solicitous, plying him with cold cuts of meat, eggs, crisped bacon and slices of toast. Marcus ate his breakfast and drank his coffee, responding to all civilities in monosyllabic words.

He could see Lionel's frown as he puzzled over this change of mood. He wished he could explain it. Marcus was not angry with him. How could he ever be? The closest way of describing it was that he was conscious of a great weight on him—the weight of his inadequacies, the weight of knowing they were about to part, the weight of his worries for Lionel's safety. It was like a cloud he could not dispel, and poor Lionel was the recipient of this dark mood. Well, did he think he was always sunny and bright in disposition? A grave error. Marcus was as humanly fallible as anyone. Perhaps it was best Lionel learned this fact about him from the start.

Finally, he laid down his knife and fork, and determined to break the uncomfortable silence. "Now you see that I can be quite the grump in the mornings when I have not had a full night's sleep," he said ruefully.

Lionel huffed. "I do see, but not to worry, I am well used to it in my family."

"It is not just that I have had little sleep," Marcus continued.

"I know." Lionel watched him intently. "The time is nearly upon us."

"I am not leaving until I have spoken with your cousins," Marcus insisted stubbornly.

"They will be here soon," Lionel replied as he rose to his feet. "In the meantime, let us make the most of these last moments together and not bicker. Come."

Lionel led him up the stairs to a private parlour room. He locked the door then leaned on it, his dark eyes regarding him heatedly. "Kiss me," he murmured.

No sooner were the words out than Marcus had pounced on him, folding him in his strong embrace and bringing their lips together. They kissed. Or more accurately, their tongues and teeth battled with each other. This was no gentle brush of the lips but a show of ravenous desperation. The need for Lionel thrummed in his veins. He was plagued with one thought. How was he ever going to let this man go? Impossible.

With each kiss, their hunger mounted. Marcus bit Lionel's bottom lip and sucked it into his mouth—a retaliation of sorts for his doing it to him that night they had kissed in the coaching inn. His hands held Lionel's head firmly, fingers threaded in his hair while he plundered his fill. He was about to throw caution to the wind and to strip off their clothes so he could have his wicked way with Lionel. His hand fisted Lionel's shirt in readiness. Then a loud knock sounded at the front door. It was as if a bucket of cold water had been thrown over them. They froze, then swiftly pulled apart, repairing their clothes. Looking respectable again if a little out breath, Lionel unlocked the parlour door, and with a backward glance at him, departed the room, making his way down the stairs. Marcus followed him to see two gentlemen had arrived, one of them bearing a striking resemblance to Lionel.

As soon as they caught sight of Lionel, they called a greeting and smiled, holding out their arms for a warm embrace. The one who closely resembled Lionel looked over his shoulder and noticed Marcus. Abruptly, he pulled away, the smile leaving his face. "And who have we here?" he asked pointedly.

Face flushed, Lionel turned to him. "Simon, Harry, let me make known to you the Duke of Coleford," he said.

"The Duke of Coleford?" Simon—or was it Simor—stared fixedly at Marcus then sketched a polite bow. "How do you do, Your Grace."

The introductions were swiftly made, then Lionel ushered them all into the front parlour, where they sat themselves down. They exchanged civilities, but it felt stilted and awkward. It was clear they wished Marcus gone so they could speak freely with each other. Marcus decided it was time to stop beating about the bush. "Mr Simon and Mr Harry Reeves," he said, clearing his throat. "I am fully apprised of the events that have led to your coming here and to the threat that has been made against Lionel's person."

"Oh?" They made a show of surprise at this.

Marcus continued his speech. "I can see you have much to discuss between yourselves, and I shall leave you to it. However, I would like to make a few things clear before I go."

"Yes?" Simon Reeves's lips curled into a cynical smile.

"Firstly, all precautions must be taken to ensure Lionel's safety. I would like your word that neither of you will let Lionel go anywhere alone and without protection until this situation is resolved."

Harry Reeves merely raised a brow at this, but Simon snorted, "Your Grace, Lionel is family, and there is no earthly way that we would allow any harm to come to him, regardless of anything you have to say on the matter."

Marcus fixed him with his stare. "Nevertheless, I would like your word."

Now it was that Harry spoke. "You have our word, Your Grace. Lionel's safety is our highest priority. That is why we are here."

Marcus nodded. "Good. Please also know that I have hired the services of a Bow Street Runner to investigate this man, Ralph Boyle, and his cronies. Should I learn information of any import, I will naturally share it with you."

Harry inclined his head. "We are grateful for any help, Your Grace."

Marcus turned to the man he loved. Despite every effort not to betray his anguish, he could not help the grittiness in his voice as he said, "Lionel, you will let me know of any developments. Do not keep me in the dark on any of this. And let me know if there is anything else at all I can do. You must know my wealth and influence are at your disposal."

Lionel's gaze softened. "I do know. And I thank you, Marcus."

Marcus swallowed, his throat tight. The time had come. Perhaps it was for the best that they were not alone. They had said their real goodbyes earlier in the desperate kisses they had shared in the parlour. He stood stiffly and bowed to each man. One final agonised glance. Then on legs that felt made of wool, he walked out of the room and out of Lionel's life.

CHAPTER 23

◈

ANOTHER PLAN IS HATCHED

"WELL, WELL, WELL," drawled Simor. "Barely a week in London and already, you have made a conquest. Of a duke no less."

Liora bristled. "Do not tease, Simor. I am in no mood for it."

"I do not mean to tease, but I am curious. Does the man have no inkling as to your real sex?"

That was the salient question. She had often wondered if, at a subconscious level, Marcus responded to and recognised her femininity. Who was it really that he loved? Was it her, Liora, or was it a fictitious person named Lionel? She feared the truth would not be what she wished to hear.

"I do not believe so," she replied.

Horis appraised her figure. "The bodysuit looks impressively real," he said, "even to my discerning eyes."

"Yes, as a disguise, it has worked well."

"So, the poor duke is smitten with you, but he thinks you're a man." As usual, Simor was quick to sum up the situation. "Hate to break this to you, Liora, but that's not going to end well." He came over to pat her on the shoulder, then gave the top of her arms a squeeze, testing the muscle tone of her bodysuit. "Impressive," he said under his breath.

Horis had other concerns. Being a medical person, his thoughts went straight to the ethical dimension of her situation. Frowning, he voiced what had kept her twisted in knots these past several days. "Liora, I am not one to pry into your private

175

affairs, so forgive me if I ask this. But have you had sexual relations with this duke?" When she did not reply at once, he went on, the contours of his face unusually stern, "You do realise, don't you, that this presents an ethical dilemma. Engaging in sexual intimacy under false pretences by fooling your partner into thinking you are male—well I cannot say it is anything but wrong."

He was right, of course. "We have not fully had sexual relations," she said in her defence, then admitted, "but we have been intimate."

Still, her brother looked on at her with disapproval. It was not at all a pleasant sensation to be so judged, and yet she knew the truth in her heart. She should not have let things go so far with Marcus. She was at fault. She had let her emotions get the better of her, and now, both Marcus and she were paying the price. Throat tight, she managed to say, "Believe me, I know it was wrong, and I have put a stop to it. Just now, we said our final goodbyes." The reminder that she would not see Marcus again had her take a shuddering breath and blink her eyes rapidly. She would not cry in front of her brothers.

In an instant, Horis's expression turned from censure to sympathy. "Oh, Liora," he murmured.

His pity was the last thing she needed. It was the straw that broke the camel's back. A sob escaped her as she said brokenly, "I tried not to fall for him. I should have tried harder."

Simor's arms enfolded her in a comforting embrace. "Shh," he admonished. "What is done is done. Hush now."

Burying her face in the material of his coat, she took several shaky breaths and tried to regain her composure while both her brothers murmured words of consolation. At last, she raised her head and attempted a smile. "Do not concern yourselves with me, please, " she told them. "It is done now and over with." She gave a decisive nod, to convince them as well as herself. "I am well and strong. Let us talk instead of the real reason why you are here."

They eyed her doubtfully but took her at her word. "Broek has given us the recording devices," said Horis. "We shall need to plant one in Henry Blunt's office as soon as possible. Simor and I will go to see him today, and while one of us distracts him, the other will place the device in a secure place."

"When shall you go to the Custom House?" Liora asked.

"In an hour or so, once we have rested and refreshed ourselves," replied Simor. "While we are out, Liora, you will stay safely home with Galok and Esa. I want you to listen in on our conversation with this Henry Blunt and check the feed on the console once I plant the recording device in his office. Let us know if the device is transmitting correctly before we leave the meeting, and most importantly, after we do, listen and watch for his reaction. He may write a missive to an accomplice or discuss the matter with some underling, who knows? Any information you can glean will be beneficial."

"Very well." She did not particularly relish the idea of waiting at home while her brothers swung into action, but there could be no denying that she would be needed here to monitor whatever Henry Blunt might do. There was another matter too, which they should address.

"I believe we should also consider placing a device at the house of William Vaughan," she said. "He is the most likely of our three suspects." She went on to tell them of what she had learned on her visit to the coffee house the previous day.

"Hmm, it is not exactly proof," remarked Simor, "but I agree he should be first on our list of suspects to investigate." He settled his head back on the armchair on which he sat and stretched his long limbs out before him, stifling a yawn. It was no surprise that, having travelled to London overnight, he was exhausted.

"How shall we manage to place the device though?" wondered Liora.

Simor shrugged. "I suppose we could just pay him a visit, like we are doing today with Henry Blunt."

Liora shook her head at this. "Firstly," she said, "if anyone is to pay William Vaughan a visit, it shall be me, accompanied by one of you. I should like to look this dreadful man in the eye as I accuse him of blackmail, extortion and abetting a murder. However, it may not be as simple a matter as paying him a visit. Should we do so, he would most likely receive us in his parlour or drawing room, not in his study, yet it is there we need to place the recording device if we are to obtain any incriminating information."

"What about slipping the device into his pocket at some point during the visit? It is small enough not to be noticed and would give us a sound transmission, if not a visual."

It was Horis this time who shook his head. "No, that will not do. A wealthy man such as him will wear different coats, so our device might be stuck inside a wardrobe for many a day without providing us with any data. Then of course, there is the danger of an overzealous valet shaking it out and having the device fall to the floor, only to be crushed under someone's shoe."

No, planting the device in William Vaughan's coat pocket would not do the trick, but the suggestion put another idea in her head. "How about," she said, "if we were to plant the device on something he might always carry on his person—his pocket watch, for instance."

Simor stretched his arms overhead. "Hmm, that might work," he got out in between yawns, then took an envelope out of his pocket. From it, he removed a small transparent disc, not too dissimilar in appearance to the listening device Broek had given her, though this one was thinner and had a larger circumference. Simor held it up for them to see. "This," he stated, "could easily be stuck on the glass surface of the watch without anyone being the wiser. We would have to concoct some reason for handling his watch, long enough for one of us to stick this on."

She felt a rising sense of excitement. "It can be done. Leave that to me."

Simor studied her a moment or two, then grinned. "Very well, sister mine. This afternoon, the two us will pay William Vaughan a visit. I trust you can come up with a strategy for what we shall say and do."

"I will think on it."

He inclined his head in acquiescence, then excused himself to go rest in his bedchamber. Horis stood too, but he stopped by her side, a look of concern in his eyes. "Will you be alright?" he asked quietly.

"Of course."

She did not quite manage to convince him. He smiled and dropped a gentle kiss to her cheek. "Speak to me about it whenever you wish, and I promise to listen with a sympathetic ear." Then he too left the room.

Alone, her thoughts returned to Marcus and to their last farewell. Her mind felt heavy; her heart numb. Ending their nascent relationship had been the right thing to do. That was what she told herself. No matter that it hurt. She comforted herself with the knowledge that it would not always feel so. She had endured grief before and recovered. It had forever marked her, true, but she had been able to keep going, and that was what she would have to do once more. The path that Yol had mapped out for her life had ever been riddled with obstacles. She closed her eyes, picturing the anguish in Marcus's face as he bid her goodbye. Recalling the passionate, almost feral way they had kissed, she touched a finger to the soreness of her bottom lip. Into the ether, she sent out a plea. *Oh, Marcus. Forgive me. Forget me. And oh Great Yol, please let it stop hurting so.*

CHAPTER 24

⊰§⊱

A TENSE CONVERSATION AND A PROPOSAL

AFTER SAYING GOODBYE to Lionel, Marcus walked back to his townhouse in a state of numbness. One thought only resounded in his head. He would see Lionel no more. It was over. A tumultuous week in which he had met and fallen in love with a beautiful, mysterious man, had come to an end. Now, he returned to his old, unsatisfactory life—but he was a changed man.

Upon arrival back at St James's Square, Marcus was greeted by Denby, who betrayed no reaction at the return of his master from an overnight excursion looking less than his usual sartorial self. The butler's face was resolutely scrubbed of any expression as he said, "Your Grace, Mrs Cavendish has requested a meeting with you as soon as you are returned."

Marcus huffed a tired breath through his nostrils. Of course, there would be a reckoning for his mad dash to see Lionel last night. "Where is she?" he asked.

"In her private parlour, Your Grace."

Inclining his head in acknowledgement, Marcus hastened up the stairs and across the landing to his mama's door, knocking briskly before entering the parlour. The familiar scent of her perfume, infused with jasmine and honeysuckle, permeated the room. It was a tidy square-shaped space furnished with a plush chaise longue and an armchair, both a deep blue in colour, together with an escritoire set to one corner. Mama reclined on the chaise longue, fanning herself listlessly.

"Good morning, Mama," he murmured, going to kneel before her and taking the hand she held out to him, dropping a light kiss to it. "You wished to see me?"

Mama pursed her lips, eyeing him in evident displeasure. Her gaze took in his rumpled coat and shirt. "Marcus," she interrogated crossly. "What is this I hear of you leaving the house in the dead of night, on foot no less, to go see that strange friend of yours? Have you taken leave of your senses? What on earth could have possessed you to do such a thing, and have you no thought to what people might say?"

Marcus sank into the vacant armchair, bracing himself against this diatribe, and summoned his patience to respond, "I am sorry to have caused you worry, Mama. However, it was unavoidable. I received intelligence which required that I speak to Lionel with the utmost urgency."

"What intelligence?" she demanded acidly. "What could you possibly have to discuss that would require such urgency? I fear, Marcus, that ever since you met that unfortunate fellow, you have not been your usual self."

It was true that he had changed since meeting Lionel. However, there was one thing to which he took umbrage. "Mama, please I beg you, do not speak of Lionel that way. He is a dear friend whom I hold in high esteem. I would not have you disparage him."

"Yet disparage him I must for the deleterious effect he has had on you!" exclaimed Mama, most out of sorts.

"No," he argued, "quite the contrary. I am a better man for knowing him."

"Hmm," sniffed Mama. "In any case, I would adjure you to have a care, not only for your reputation but also for the safety of your person, and not go out to visit anyone in the dead of night, no matter the perceived urgency. Why, you could have been set upon by pickpockets or much worse!"

"As you can see, Mama, I was not," he replied with as much forbearance as he could. "Now, if there is nothing else, will you excuse me? I must go refresh my appearance."

Her disapproving gaze took in his rumpled state once more. "Yes, you must do so," she stated coldly. "But first, there is another matter of which I must speak with you." At his look of enquiry, she went on, "I believe Miss Worsley would make an excellent duchess."

A surprised laugh escaped him. "I am sure the lady is very worthy, but I am not at present in the market for a duchess."

She narrowed her gaze. "Then perhaps you ought to reconsider that position."

"Mama—" he began to say, but she held up a hand to stay his words.

"No, Marcus, I wish you to listen. Ever since you inherited Coleford Hall, I have been vexed with worries about how you will get along there on your own. It is such a grand and formal house, which needs the warmth and loving touch of a lady. If I were younger and less set in my ways, then I might have considered moving in with you, but I cannot. Already, I am longing to return to the calm familiarity of Ashby, our dear home."

"Mama," he protested, rubbing his hand over the stubble that had formed on his jaw, "there is no need to worry. I will manage as best I can."

She sighed volubly. "Therein lies the problem. With the best will in the world, Marcus, you will find it difficult to manage on your own the many responsibilities that come with being duke and master of Coleford Hall. This is where Miss Worsley comes in. I have been immensely impressed with her down-to-earth and practical nature. She is not one of those empty-headed debutantes, only concerned with the latest fashion and gossip. No indeed. And I must inform you that for several years now since the passing of the late Sir William Worsley, her esteemed parent, she has been mistress of her ancestral home, running it on behalf of her brother with remarkable efficiency. There is no better qualified lady to be mistress of Coleford Hall."

"But Mama—"

"No, my dear, do but listen. You must know that I have your best interests at heart. I would never recommend a lady who would not suit you. But I have observed Miss Worsley closely. Her temperament would match yours admirably. She will not interfere with your gardening pursuits nor impose intolerable social burdens upon you. Moreover, with her skills, you may rest easy as to the management of your household and the maintenance of all necessary correspondence. And, most importantly, I believe she is likely to accept your suit given that her brother is now betrothed. I do think this situation is providential, and I urge you to take advantage of the opportunity."

All the while she spoke, he stared morosely down at his feet. Of course, he was deemed incapable of managing his affairs—how could a dunce who could barely read or write be capable of such a thing? Despair overwhelmed him, not so much at his ineptitude but at the way he had allowed his family to develop such a poor opinion of him. He might not be the sharpest person put on this earth, but surely he was able to muddle through well enough on his own! Neither Miss Worsley's great qualities nor the fact that he loved a man he could not have should be a reason to enter into a marriage designed to perpetuate a state of affairs where things were managed for him. Enough of this! He felt his body vibrate with a deep well of rage at the injustice of it all and with frustration at himself for having let it happen. No more.

With a great effort at maintaining his civility, he spoke. "Mama, I am grateful for all you have done for me and appreciate your advice with regards to Miss Worsley." Marcus raised his eyes to gaze at her directly. "However, I need not remind you that I am a grown man of six and twenty years, able to make decisions for myself. If and when I eventually marry, it shall be at my impulse, not anybody else's." He stood. "And now, if you will excuse me." He took his leave, sensing Mama's open-mouthed astonishment. If he were not so heartbroken, he would take a moment to savour this small victory, but instead, he dragged his feet to his chamber, where Stubbs helped him with his toilette, thankfully keeping conversation to a minimum.

Once he was presentable again, he made his way down to the front parlour. Regardless of his heartache, social exigencies would continue to require his attention, and he knew that his presence would be expected should any visitor call at the house. In the parlour, he found his sisters in animated discussion about the previous night's ball. It was a relief to him that their excitement over the ball distracted them from enquiring too keenly about his absence last night, though alone among his sisters, Julia cast him frequent searching glances.

Soon, a visitor did call. With a knock, Denby entered the parlour and announced, "Sir Luke Stafford is here to call on Your Grace."

The announcement was received with gasps from his sisters. It could only mean one thing. Sir Luke was come to ask permission to pay his addresses to Portia. Marcus instructed Denby to show their visitor to the drawing room, and with a sigh, he rose to his feet, ready to do his duty.

He received Sir Luke with civility and in due course, gave his permission to the match. There could be no objection to it, although Marcus did place one condition. Before the betrothal could be announced, they would pay a short visit to Sir Luke's country seat and see for themselves what sort of a home Portia would have in the event of her marriage. To Marcus's way of thinking, one could tell a lot more about a person when one saw them in their own environment rather than in the drawing rooms of London. This way, he would do his duty by Portia and ensure that Sir Luke was indeed as suitable a match as he appeared to be. To this condition, Sir Luke readily agreed, and they shook hands on the matter.

Portia was duly summoned for a private audience with Sir Luke, and his proposal accepted. Over the course of the next hour, the house vibrated with the excitement of the ladies. Portia was to be married! What would she get for her trousseau? When would be a good date for the wedding? What had Sir Luke said when he had got down on his knee? Had it been romantic?

Marcus had had enough. He rose and excused himself, wanting to find a quiet space to lick his wounds. The garden, he thought. It was not a large one, but it was a garden nonetheless. And there was no better place than a garden for calm and reflection. He started up the stairs, intent on going to his bedchamber to get changed, but a call of his name had him pause. Julia. He turned and masked his annoyance as she tripped up the stairs behind him.

"Marcus, do tell me what happened last night," she whispered when she reached his side, but he shook his head. At this moment, the last thing he wanted was to talk, and he had no intention of disclosing the secret he had discovered, not even to Julia.

"Not now," he replied, a trifle irritably.

"But "

"No, Julia!" He tried to temper the rebuke with a light kiss to her cheek. "We will talk soon, but not now," he added more gently. With that, he continued to his bedchamber and bid Stubbs to bring out his old buckskins, which he had presciently made his valet pack for his journey to London. Without a raise of his brows nor any show of censure, Stubbs, excellent servant that he was, assisted him into the old clothes he liked to wear when gardening. And then, he was hurrying down the stairs and through the back door to the garden, walking along the borders and examining the beds, bending down to pick out some weeds and using his scissors to deadhead the stems.

For the next hour, Marcus immersed himself in the work, tending to the plants and letting the familiarity of the task restore within him a sense of equilibrium. One could not say he was happy nor even content, for his heart was much too sore, but he was at peace. At length, he began to reflect once more on the mystery surrounding Lionel and then on to the other matter of Ralph Boyle's vicious threat at the ball last night. Instinctively on learning of it, Marcus had rushed to Barton Street, pistol in his pocket, only to find Lionel perfectly safe and sound in his home. It had been a foolish gesture, had it not? With his two strapping cousins about him, Lionel was in no need of an additional protector. And yet, something niggled at him, a sense that they were all missing some vital clue.

Methodically as he tended to a weedy patch, Marcus sorted the information in his mind, trying to identify the source of his apprehension. Ralph Boyle had threatened Lionel with the same fate as his predecessor, and given that this predecessor had died suddenly, then it was quite clear that Boyle had threatened Lionel's life. But there was something about the choice of the words, "the same fate as your predecessor", that heightened Marcus's sense of unease. Just how had this man, Jos, met his death? Marcus had not thought to ask before, and yet now, the knowledge seemed critical. Had Jos met with an accident on the road? Had a heavy crate of goods at the warehouse fallen onto his head? How was it that up until Boyle's words last night, this man's death had not been regarded as suspicious? The more he thought of it, the more Marcus was filled with a sense of dread.

A throat cleared behind him. It was Denby. "Your Grace has another visitor," he said. "A person by the name of Mr Quinn who is most insistent that he see you. Should I show him to the drawing room?"

Mr Quinn. Just the person he wished to see, apart from Lionel, of course. Mr Quinn might be able to shed light on this mystery, and moreover, Marcus hoped he had new and useful information to impart.

"Bring him out here, Denby," he instructed.

CHAPTER 25

A PARALLEL REALISATION

SIMOR AND HORIS had been gone three quarters of an hour, and Liora had been in the upstairs parlour, with the door securely locked, listening in to their encounter with Henry Blunt. The recording device had been successfully planted in the man's office, and she now had a visual on her console of the customs officer sitting behind his desk.

The meeting ended with Henry Blunt as before refusing to budge on the matter of their sugar shipment, only stating that the goods would be inspected and a duty levied in due course. Her brothers took their leave, and she watched intently, wanting to see what this Henry Blunt would do. He did not disappoint. As soon as her brothers departed, he took out a sheet of paper and jotted a quick message, then sealed it. Although she could not make out the words he had written in the note, the recording device allowed her to decipher the two initials—R.B.—written on the front. R.B. for Ralph Boyle no doubt. Blunt rang a bell to summon an underling, who soon arrived, knocking briskly on the door before entering.

"Jessop," Blunt said, "please have this note delivered to the Sun Tavern in Shadwell. The tavern keeper will know what to do with it."

"Yes, sir," replied Jessop, not batting an eyelid, as he took the note and turned to leave.

Liora's senses tingled. This could be their opportunity. Quickly, she tapped her ring to speak to her brothers, who as agreed, were waiting close by in case something like this should occur. "Horis, Simor," she said urgently, "this might be the clue we need. Blunt has just sent a man called Jessop to deliver a note to the tavern keeper at the Sun Tavern in Shadwell. It's addressed to R.B."

"Ralph Boyle," said Simor at once.

"Exactly. Could you intercept this Jessop and offer him inducements to hand over the note long enough for you to read what it says before he delivers it? He might also be a useful person for us in future within the Custom House."

"We are at the ready," replied Simor.

Then Horis spoke. "I can see a uniformed officer coming out of the Custom House. Medium build, dark hair and eyes, longish nose."

"That's him," she said swiftly.

"Right, let us follow the man and find a way to corner him," said Simor, ending the connection.

She sat back in the armchair and took a deep breath, feeling a sense of anxious anticipation. What might they learn from this note? And once it was delivered to Ralph Boyle at the tavern, what might he do next? Arrange a meeting with his paymaster, a certain William Vaughan perhaps? Or might he not send a response to Blunt and provide them with incriminating evidence?

It was irksome and frustrating to be sitting in this parlour at home and not be out there doing something active for their cause. Surely there was more that she could be doing. With a huff of irritation, she sat back in her armchair, challenging her mind to find something productive to do.

"Agh!"

She could feel the tension rising in her body with each minute she spent cooped up in this room. Perhaps a restorative herbal infusion would help soothe her nerves. Tapping her ring, she spoke to Esa, "Could you send up a pot of my lemon balm and camomile infusion please, Esa."

"Of course," the housekeeper replied. "I'll have Nessie bring it up to you straight away."

Liora stood then and began to pace the room. Was there some vital clue that she was missing? True, the information they had gathered was slim at best, but even so, was there more to infer? Then she hit on an idea. She did not know why she had not thought to do this before. Quickly, she went to her console and summoned the artificial brain, asking for its help and providing it with all the information she had so far. A knock at the door had her quickly hiding the console under a cushion before she went to let Nessie in. The young maid came into the room and deposited a tray on the table.

"Was there anything else, miss?" she asked shyly.

"No, thank you, Nessie. That will be all."

Nessie bobbed a curtsy and left the room. Liora locked the door once more before returning to her console, which by now had the results of her query to the artificial brain. She poured from the teapot and filled the cup, then returned to her console.

"Since it has been established that Jos did not die from natural causes," she read as she brought the cup to her lips, *"it would be useful to determine the method by which that death was brought about."*

Liora set the cup down, a chill running up her spine, and continued reading the artificial brain's analysis.

"Jos collapsed unconscious on the street a few yards from his home and was found dead some time later by a concerned passer-by. The manner of his death suggests that its cause was the ingestion of a poisonous substance. When and how this poison was administered is unclear. Some poisons, depending on the dosage, can act slowly over time; others may have an immediate effect."

Poison. Yes, that would make sense. Why had it not occurred to her until now? Perhaps it was because her mind had been far too preoccupied with other matters. Now though, she focused on the question of who could have done it. Without knowing Jos's regular habits, it was difficult to conjecture. Did he stop by a street hawker and buy a pie or some other food that was laced with poison. Or had it been administered closer to home? Not Esa, surely. That left only that young maid, Nessie. Again, Liora dismissed the idea as far too improbable.

She sighed and lifted the cup once more to her lips. An instant later, she set it down. Best to err on the side of caution. Frowning, she cast her eyes on the console and continued to read the report, but in this endeavour, she was soon interrupted by Simor's voice in her ear. "Ralph Boyle has just entered the tavern and will shortly be given Blunt's missive. We managed to have a quick read of it before Jessop took it inside. Nothing too incriminating there, merely a message informing Boyle that two further members of the Reeves family had paid him a visit and were asking questions about the sugar shipment. Now let us see how Boyle reacts. Once he is on the move again, we shall follow."

"Understood," murmured Liora.

Unable to stay sitting a moment longer, she rose to her feet. This was it, she thought. Their mystery was about to unravel. She could feel it in her bones. She paced the room, her mind churning. What would Boyle decide to do? Would he not want to confer with his master? Now that they were dealing with three members of the Reeves clan, not just one, they would surely need to make an adjustment to their plans. And for that, they would have to meet.

Liora felt a rising excitement. If Ralph Boyle was about to initiate a meeting with his master—most probably William Vaughan—then it was imperative that they have a recording device planted on the man's person. The matter could not wait until this afternoon. There was no time to be lost. She must go to William Vaughan now and somehow plant the recording device before Ralph Boyle got to him.

She reasoned there could be little danger in it; she could hardly be poisoned if she ingested nothing that was given her. Moreover, Galok would go with her, so she would not be quite alone. She pocketed the envelope with the remaining recording device and before putting the console away, looked up William Vaughan's address, which turned out to be on Fenchurch Street, not far from the docks. It was enough of a distance that she would need to ride there. Tapping her ring, she called on Galok to saddle up two horses.

"But—"

"No buts, Galok. This is important. Now do it!"

She returned the console into its hidden compartment then unlocked the parlour door and went to change into riding clothes. A few minutes later, she was heading back down the stairs. On her way, she passed Nessie once more busily dusting the banister. Liora paused a moment, studying the young girl with a frown. Then she shook her head and hurried by. A moment later, she let herself out the door and approached Galok, who had obeyed her instructions and got both horses ready.

"Are you sure about this?" he asked worriedly.

"Yes," she said emphatically. "We are going to William Vaughan's house on Fenchurch Street." In a hushed voice she added, "It is urgent that I plant a recording device there before he meets with an accomplice. It will be fine, Galok. No harm can come to me in the man's house in full view of the servants, and you will be with me the rest of the time. Now come, let us go."

CHAPTER 26

❧ ❧

A SECOND MAD DASH TO BARTON STREET

"GOOD DAY, MR QUINN," said Marcus. "Have you any news for me?"

"Your Grace," he bowed stiffly. "Indeed I have."

"Have you found the identity of the person behind these threats to Mr Reeves?" Marcus asked, barely masked impatience laced into his tone.

Mr Quinn cocked his head to one side as if deep in consideration of the question. He replied, "I have learned of an interesting connection between the customs officer, Henry Blunt, and the shipping merchant, William Vaughan, a man with considerable interests in the sugar trade."

"What sort of connection?"

"My informants tell me that Blunt is William Vaughan's nephew on the maternal side," said Mr Quinn.

Marcus felt a spark of excitement. "So," he deduced, "this would mean that Vaughan is the person behind all this."

"It would seem so," agreed Mr Quinn, "but we cannot be certain. A family connection is not in itself proof of criminality."

Marcus stood, dusting the dirt off his knees and decided, "I shall go pay a visit to this William Vaughan, and it will soon become clear whether or not the man is implicated."

Mr Quinn regarded him with a frown. "Your Grace," he said, "far be it from me to tell you what you should or should not do, however, is it a wise course of action to confront this William

Vaughan? Do remember that he is a man of considerable power and resources."

Marcus crossed his arms to his broad chest. "As am I, Mr Quinn," he reminded him, and for the first time, he felt it too—the power of his privileged station, the power too of being a man of large stature.

"Your Grace, I fear that a confrontation might spark a need for retaliation on Mr Vaughan's part. I do urge some caution in the matter."

Marcus paused, suddenly struck by a thought. "You say that Mr Vaughan might react with some form of retaliation if threatened. I wonder..."

Mr Quinn raised an enquiring brow. Quickly, Marcus filled him in on the conversation between Lionel and Ralph Boyle at the ball, in which the damned blackguard had threatened Lionel with the same fate as his predecessor. He finished his account with a question. "Do you suppose that this man, Jos, could have gone to confront Mr Vaughan and was murdered as a consequence of that action?"

Mr Quinn's expression was grim. "Quite possibly, Your Grace. All the more reason to exercise caution."

"All the more reason to go see this William Vaughan," Marcus countered determinedly. "Let the man feel cornered. That will flush him out quicker than anything else."

"But the risk to your person—"

"A risk I am willing to take," Marcus replied. "The only person whose life I will not put at risk is Mr Reeves, and he is well protected." Or was he? His earlier reflections about the mode of Jos's murder niggled him once more. Lionel was in the constant company of his cousins, all of whom were armed with pistols. His home was well secured. Surely he could come to no harm? Why was it then that he felt a cold sweat of anxiety?

Mr Quinn was quick to pick up on his perturbation. "This Jos—or Mr Jocelyn as I believe he was known," he enquired. "How was it that he met his death?"

Marcus shook his head in frustration. "I do not know precisely, but until Ralph Boyle's words at the ball, it had been assumed that he died of natural causes."

"Poisoning."

Marcus narrowed his eyes at Mr Quinn, his pulse beginning to race. "Poisoning?" he asked, though his mind was quickly working out the missing pieces of the puzzle.

"If the man was murdered but it looked like natural causes, it can only have been poisoning. Arsenic, most likely. It is tasteless and odourless, so can be added to a victim's food or drink without a trace. Whoever it was that administered that fatal dose to Mr Jocelyn could do so again."

Yes, that was it. The thing that had niggled at his mind. Lionel's predecessor had not been violently murdered. He had been poisoned. But by whom and how? A servant? Could it be the housekeeper at Lionel's house or one of the maidservants? He recalled a young lass with blushing cheeks bringing in a fresh pot of coffee while they ate breakfast this morning. His skin prickled. Lionel could be in danger even at home. Marcus began to stride back towards the house, calling out to his visitor as he did, "Mr Quinn, I wish you to have men keep a close eye on the activities of both Henry Blunt and William Vaughan, especially after I go to visit him today. We must get evidence of their guilt and put a stop to their evil activities once and for all."

"Yes, Your Grace," replied Mr Quinn, following him into the house. "I should also like to be close by when Your Grace goes to visit Vaughan, so I can be on the lookout for any wrongdoing."

"First, I must go warn Lionel about the poison and tell him of Blunt's connection to Vaughan. Then I'll go pay that visit to Vaughan."

"In that case, I shall follow along," responded Mr Quinn.

Nodding his assent, Marcus left the Bow Street Runner in the hallway and hurriedly went up to his bedchamber to dress. Within a few minutes, he was back downstairs and striding to the door, not caring to lose a single moment. Every instinct he possessed told him it was urgent he find Lionel. He did not speak to or acknowledge Mr Quinn as he left the house, yet he was aware of his presence, matching him stride for stride as they made their way to Lionel's house.

Only a few hours previously, he had left Barton Street, saying his final goodbyes to Lionel. And now he was going back. What a preposterous decision it had been, to bid each other farewell while this matter lay unresolved—to bid each other farewell full stop. Both of them should have known better. He could not stay away from Lionel, especially if his life hung in the balance.

Soon, he arrived at Barton Street and without hesitation, knocked at the door, which was opened by Lionel's housekeeper.

"I am here to see Mr Lionel Reeves," he said peremptorily.

She did not step back to allow him inside. Instead, with a crease of her brow and in that heavily accented voice, she told him, "Mr Reeves is out at present."

"Out? Where has he gone and with whom?" he demanded, caring little for niceties. His heart hammered in his chest, partly from the exertion of his brisk walk to get here and partly with nerves.

"I—I do not know. He left on his horse a short while ago with Galok."

"And where are his cousins?" he thundered. "Why are they not with Lionel?"

Her expression shuttered at his tone, but she replied courteously enough, "Mr Harry and Mr Simon Reeves went out earlier today, I know not where."

Marcus felt his temper begin to boil. Lionel's cousins had given him their word that they would not let Lionel go anywhere alone. And now it seemed he had done so. He discounted Galok. A groom could not accompany Lionel to all the places he might go, so he was as good as alone. *Damnation!*

Marcus tried to arrange his jumbled thoughts into a semblance of coherence. Where could Lionel have gone if he was not home? The warehouse? His offices near the stock exchange? Or somewhere else?

The clearing of a throat had him whip round to see Mr Quinn standing behind him, the slight glistening of his brow the only indication that he had been walking at speed to keep up with him. "If I might suggest, Your Grace?" he said.

"Yes? What is it?"

"Might it not be possible that Mr Reeves has acquired information about Henry Blunt's connection with William Vaughan just as we have done?" Mr Quinn suggested.

"You think he may have gone to see him?"

Mr Quinn shrugged. "It is a distinct possibility."

Marcus mulled the matter over in his mind and reached the same conclusion. It was not a certainty, but it was their best bet. They would go find this William Vaughan, in the hope that this was where Lionel had gone too. With this resolve, he started off down the street, only to stop abruptly. He had no inkling where William Vaughan's house was located.

As if reading his mind once more, Mr Quinn said beside him, "I believe, Your Grace, we should be heading in the opposite direction if we are to go to Fenchurch Street. It may be quickest to walk to the hackney stand at the next corner and find a carriage there to convey us."

Marcus nodded, a wry smile escaping his lips. "I am grateful to have you here, Mr Quinn," he told him in full honesty as he changed course and headed towards the hackney stand. When they reached it, they were fortunate enough to find a carriage waiting there, and soon they were aboard and on their way to Fenchurch Street. Some minutes later, the hackney deposited them in front of number seventy, a large stucco-fronted house with tall rectangular windows separated by grandiose Grecian columns. It was the house of a man with great wealth, eager to communicate his affluence to the world—perhaps also a man who would protect this wealth at all cost. Marcus was determined to find out.

As he emerged from the carriage and made his way to the front door, he spied a man standing to his right, holding the reins of the two horses with him. Marcus recognised him at once. It was Lionel's groom, Galok, the one who had had a love affair with him many years ago. Jealousy spiked his veins almost at the same time as relief filled his heart. Lionel was here. He had found him. For a brief instant, Marcus locked eyes with this Galok. The man stared back, barely concealed hostility glittering in his eyes. His narrowed gaze followed him as Marcus pulled the knocker on the door. Moments later, it was opened by a stiff-lipped butler.

"The Duke of Coleford," Marcus stated imperiously, "here to see Mr Vaughan." Mr Quinn meanwhile had tactfully effaced himself and slipped away out of sight, though Marcus knew he would stay close and keep watch.

The butler bowed and allowed him to enter, taking his hat then ushering him to a side parlour. "Please wait here, Your Grace, while I inform Mr Vaughan of your arrival," he said in a colourless voice. Soon though, he returned and escorted Marcus to an opulent drawing room in which stood two persons.

CHAPTER 27

AN UNSATISFACTORY ENCOUNTER AND A NEW LEAD

BOTH MEN ROSE to their feet as Marcus entered the room. He walked purposely towards them, observing Lionel's face going from pale to flushed in a matter of seconds. His fine dark eyes swam with emotion as they regarded Marcus, first in surprise then in what he thought was both relief and joy. He was sure these emotions—minus the surprise—were reflected in his own eyes.

Dearest Lionel. He had been gone from his side less than a day and already, he ached for him. It was like missing a limb. No more. He was officially putting pay to the insane notion of their separation. It could not be done. He would not allow it. Whatever impediment it was that stood between them must and had to be overcome.

Marcus was so entranced by the presence of his love that at first, he did not take much stock of the other person in the room. Eventually, he forced his attention towards William Vaughan, a man of indeterminate age with thin lips and a coldly calculating expression in his eyes.

"Your Grace," Vaughan now said, "this is an honour, though an unexpected one. I do not believe we have met before."

Marcus bowed and responded, "No, we have not. Let me remedy the situation at once. Marcus Cavendish, Duke of Coleford, at your service." Not for the first time, Marcus wondered at this ludicrous aspect of social discourse. He was not in any way at this man's service nor did he ever expect to be, yet those were the words that slipped from his lips; the ones that were expected. On the contrary, if indeed this was the person who had put Lionel's life under jeopardy, then he was more likely to want to throttle the man than bow to him, let alone be in service to him in any shape or form.

Vaughan responded with an inclination of the head then turned towards Lionel, about to make the introductions. "This is—"

"I am already well acquainted with Mr Reeves," Marcus interjected, bowing to the man he loved. *The man he loved!* Not so long ago, such a sentiment would have been unimaginable. He'd had no notion even that a man could wholeheartedly love another man body and soul. Of course, he had been aware that there existed these strange, unnatural desires among some people in society, but they had been at the periphery of his sheltered world, and he had paid them little mind. Yet here he was today, his heart singing with unfettered joy at the sight of Lionel, his loins tightening instinctively as he caught the sweet scent of him. What could be more natural than for him to love this man?

He greeted Lionel with a tender smile. "Good day, Mr Reeves. It is a pleasure to see you again." No truer words had ever been spoken.

Lionel bowed in return. "The pleasure is mine, Your Grace."

William Vaughan gestured for them all to sit, and once they had settled themselves down, an awkward silence descended on them. Marcus could imagine the man was wondering why on earth he had received a visit from the Duke of Coleford. He decided to get straight to the point, any lingering diffidence he may have felt eclipsed by the need to stand firm with Lionel. "Mr Vaughan," he began, "there is a reason for our visit today, for Mr Reeves and I are both keen to get to the bottom of a particular mystery."

Vaughan raised his brows and regarded him coolly, his gaze inviting him to explain. Marcus resumed his speech. "As you may know, Mr Reeves has been put in charge of his family's mercantile operations at the London Docks. A few days ago, he received a visit at the warehouse from a certain individual named Ralph Boyle." He paused to see if the name induced any reaction. Vaughan continued to regard him stonily, not a hint of emotion crossing his face. "This Mr Boyle," Marcus continued, "intimated that a recently arrived shipment of sugar in one of the Reeves vessels was being held indefinitely with the customs authorities at the behest of certain interested parties that were unhappy with the way the Reeves were marketing their East Indian sugar as 'not made by slaves'. Mr Boyle then said that he would facilitate the release of this sugar shipment if Mr Reeves would promise not only to discontinue using that slogan but to sell that entire shipment of sugar at a heavily discounted price to Mr Boyle's anonymous master."

Still, William Vaughan betrayed no reaction except for a tightening of his lips. Lionel stepped in with the rest of the tale. "You may imagine, Mr Vaughan, what choice words I may have had for this Mr Boyle. That very day, I took myself to the Custom House and spoke with a Mr Henry Blunt, the chief collector, who was curiously unwilling to expedite the inspection of my shipment, and quite clearly in the pay of Mr Boyle and his master."

Now Marcus interjected, for he had further information to impart. "And then today," he stated, "we learned of Mr Blunt's family connection to yourself, a merchant with vast holdings in the West Indies and a vested interested in the sugar trade. We can only surmise, therefore, that Mr Boyle's employer and the person trying to coerce Mr Reeves over the matter of this sugar, can be none other than yourself."

The accusation was met with a prolonged silence, though Lionel's eyes widened in surprise. Aha, so he had not known of Blunt's family connection to Vaughan. Marcus felt a moment of fleeting pride at having been a step ahead in this investigation. Vaughan's bushy brows knitted in a fierce frown as he stared at them both. Then quite suddenly, he emitted a loud and raucous cackle of laughter. Both Lionel and Marcus were taken aback. This was not at all the reaction they had expected. Anger yes. Fury even. But laughter?

Vaughan barked out another laugh. "That scapegrace! You think I would have any dealings with that sorry excuse for a man that is my nephew?" He cackled again. "I have not seen nor spoken to the boy, not since he saw fit to swindle me of fifteen pounds after I had generously offered him employment in my trading house. I do not look kindly upon thieves, Mr Reeves, and I certainly never have them in my employ once their theft has come to light."

"You deny then that you are the one who has tasked Mr Boyle with the threats against my friend?" Marcus demanded.

"Most assuredly so. I have nothing to do with any of it, but I will not voice any false sympathy for you, Mr Reeves," he said, addressing Lionel. "Your family's slogans about slavery are not helpful to my business, and I would gladly see you put a stop to them. Now, if there is nothing else, I will bid you both good day."

As he made to stand, Lionel responded haughtily, "Not so fast, Mr Vaughan. If you have nothing to do with it, all well and good. But let me assure you of one thing. If our suspicions turn out to be correct and you are indeed involved not only in the threats against my business but against my person, then we Reeves will leave no stone unturned to have our revenge, and we will not be gentle about it."

Vaughan scoffed. "Again, I will bid you both good day."

Something flickered in Lionel's eyes. A moment of panic? Marcus could not quite decipher it. Curtly, he asked, "Would you be so kind, Mr Vaughan, as to tell me the time?"

Marcus gaped at Lionel in surprise, for he knew full well that he kept a timepiece in his pocket. Why was he asking this now and looking so nervous about it? There must be a reason. Marcus cursed his sluggish mind as Vaughan irritably took out his pocket watch to read the time. Then Marcus caught sight of the circular timepiece, the polished glass gleaming bright, and he was struck by a memory of something else circular-shaped and transparent. All at once, he knew—and he had to act.

"Mr Vaughan, may I take a closer look at your watch? I do believe it is of the type I am meaning to purchase for myself. Is it from Arnold & Son?"

Vaughan could barely mask his impatience, but he complied with the request, not caring to rebuff a duke of the realm. "Yes," he replied tersely, detaching the watch from its chain and handing it to Marcus.

Marcus made a show of examining it and exclaiming over it, turning his back to Vaughan. "Lionel, what do you think?" he asked, handing the piece over to him but still obscuring it from Vaughan's vision with the broadness of his shoulders. There were times when his large physique was quite the boon.

Lionel took it from him and made a noncommittal sound, something that sounded like, "Hmm," as he turned towards the window, ostensibly for more light.

Wanting to distract Vaughan, Marcus began to babble meaningless words, giving a good impression of a bumbling, clueless duke, which to be fair, was something he was an old hand at. "I am minded to favour the plain white backdrop and black lettering over the enamelled gold watch we saw the other day," he said, letting out a gay laugh. "By gad, that was an awfully pretty piece. To be sure though, this one has understated elegance. Oh the tyranny of choice! I find that I really cannot decide."

Lionel turned around and passed the watch back to Marcus, his lovely dark eyes examining him intently, for he very well knew that they had not gone to the shops together nor admired any enamelled gold watch. Marcus could see the wheels turning in his mind as he wondered... What did Marcus know? What had he given away?

An amused smile curved Marcus's lips. He took the watch from Lionel, giving it a cursory look. It appeared unchanged, yet he felt certain that Lionel had somehow tampered with it. With a flourish, he handed it back to Vaughan who took it from him, brows knitted both in annoyance and suspicion. He examined his watch briefly before re-attaching it to the chain and returning it to his pocket. Behind him, Lionel said, "Your Grace, it is getting late, and we must be on our way. Do remember we agreed to chaperone your sisters on a ride through Hyde Park."

Marcus sighed volubly. "Indeed I have not forgotten." He sketched a bow and pasted a false smile to his face. "Good day, Mr Vaughan," he said.

"Good day," the man replied in clipped tones, eager to be rid of them both.

They emerged into the hallway and waited while the butler retrieved their hats. Awkwardness returned as they stood in silence, not knowing where to look. Not too long ago, they had made their final goodbyes, and yet here they were again, brought together in some stranger's house. There was so much that needed to be said, but they were unable to utter a word. Lionel stared at the floor; Marcus stole the occasional glance at him.

Finally, the butler returned with their hats and ushered them out the door. They stepped onto the narrow pavement and stopped. Lionel's gaze flew to where his horses were tethered and to Galok standing nearby, then continued on to scan the surroundings until his eyes returned to Marcus, looking puzzled. "You did not come in your carriage?" he asked.

"I walked to your house," Marcus replied, "and when I did not find you there, I thought to look for you here at Mr Quinn's suggestion. We came by hackney."

"Mr Quinn? He told you of Henry Blunt's connection to William Vaughan?"

"Yes," Marcus said. Then he could not help but chide, "It was foolhardy of you to come here on your own, Lionel. You should have waited until your cousins could go with you."

Lionel wrinkled his nose, muttering, "The matter could not wait."

"Then it is a good thing I came to join you."

Lionel's eyes flew to his, a serious expression on his countenance. "Why did you come, Marcus? We said our goodbyes this morning."

"Pfft," Marcus huffed. "Those goodbyes were one of the stupidest things we have ever done."

Lionel was silent a moment or two, then murmured, "What did you think of William Vaughan? Do you believe him?"

"I am minded to," Marcus said. "The contempt he had for his nephew seemed genuine."

Lionel heaved out an irritated sigh. "If it is not him, then who is behind this?"

"I am not sure," Marcus replied, equally disheartened.

Under his breath, he heard Lionel say, "Precious time wasted, and a wasted device if so." He did not seem to be aware of what he had inadvertently given away, though it was as Marcus had suspected. Lionel had placed one of those transparent contraptions on Vaughan's watch, one that could miraculously convey speech to another device. Lionel stood still, head cocked slightly to the side, eyes far away as if listening to something—listening no doubt to William Vaughan! Who could the man be speaking to? A family member? A faithful servant?

Marcus watched Lionel closely, observing a look of intense concentration on his face until his shoulders deflated. "No," he said at last. "It is not him." He tapped his ring discreetly and repeated himself. "William Vaughan is not our man." *Ah yes, transmitting the information to his absent cousins.* How well Marcus was beginning to know Lionel's ways. It seemed he was listening to their reply, for his eyes again took on that far away expression—until they came back into focus once more. Looking at Marcus, he asked, "Do you by any chance know the directions for the residences of George Hibbert and Enoch Miles? They are the other two men high on our list of suspects."

"I do not, but I am sure that Mr Quinn shall have that information," Marcus responded, quickly scoping the surroundings in the hope of catching sight of the Bow Street Runner. And once more, as if the man read his mind from afar, Marcus saw him scuttling towards them.

"Your Grace," he said on his approach. "I fear from your demeanour that William Vaughan has proven to be a wild goose chase."

"You surmise correctly, Mr Quinn," Marcus replied, then made the introductions. "Lionel, this is Mr Quinn, the Bow Street Runner working to solve our case."

Mr Quinn bowed, and Lionel acknowledged him with a quick inclination of his head, followed by a sharp question, "Mr Quinn, do you have the directions for George Hibbert and Enoch Miles?"

"Of course, Mr Reeves. I believe George Hibbert resides at a house called The Hollies on the north side of Clapham Common. As for Enoch Miles, his home is not far from here, just north of the Tower on the Crescent in the Minories."

"That must be where Ralph Boyle is heading—to the house of Enoch Miles!" Lionel exclaimed, eyes lighting up. He did not realise he was once more giving himself away, for how could he know of Ralph Boyle's movements if not for the communication contraption in his ear? No doubt his cousins were somehow on that scoundrel Ralph Boyle's tail, and they had told Lionel that they were heading in the direction of the Tower. The mystery was fast unravelling. It seemed it was Enoch Miles who was behind all this, not William Vaughan as they had initially suspected.

Mr Quinn made no comment, though Marcus could see that his sharply intelligent eyes were taking everything in, despite the fact that he could not have knowledge as he did of the voice transmitting contraption in Lionel's ear.

"We must go there now," urged Lionel. He glanced at his horses then back at Marcus. "Best to walk, as it is not far. Galok will follow us with the horses."

And once more, they were on the move, three of them now rather than two, bound this time for the house of Enoch Miles—slave trader, sugar plantation owner and most likely the man that had put Lionel's life in jeopardy.

CHAPTER 28

A DRAMATIC TURN OF EVENTS

THEY WALKED AT a brisk pace in the direction of the Tower of London, then to the north of it towards the house of Enoch Miles. Precious time had already been wasted in their visit to William Vaughan, who had turned out to be something of a red herring; his connection to Henry Blunt merely coincidental. No, it was Enoch Miles that they wanted.

Through the listening device in her ears, Liora had listened to Simor as he relayed the latest developments from their end. Her brothers had waited while Boyle read Blunt's missive then stayed at the tavern to partake of a luncheon. Now, he was on the move, walking in an easterly direction, her brothers discreetly on his tail. It could mean only one thing. The man was going to see Enoch Miles—for their other suspect, George Hibbert, had his residence in quite the other direction, south of the river.

As they walked, Simor spoke into her ear. "What shall we do once Ralph Boyle reaches Enoch Miles's house? We do not have a listening device in place to record their conversation."

"What we need is evidence of their criminality which we can take to the proper authorities," added Horis.

She tapped her ring discreetly and broached the subject with her companions. "If when we get to Enoch Miles, we find Ralph Boyle in conference with him, will that be sufficient evidence of Miles's culpability in this matter?"

It was Mr Quinn that responded first. "Circumstantial evidence at best," he said. "Nothing that would hold up in a court of law."

"Then what are we to do?"

Marcus now replied, "I believe we need to confront the two men and extract a confession, which Mr Quinn can somehow be a witness to. Subsequent to that, he may put them under arrest. Is that not so, Mr Quinn?"

"Hmm," murmured the Bow Street Runner noncommittally.

"They are hardly likely to confess in the presence of a representative of the law," she protested.

"No indeed," said Marcus. "Mr Quinn will need to somehow eavesdrop on the conversation."

"That is easier said than done!"

"We are three, and with the addition of your cousins, we shall be five to convene at the house," continued Marcus, though she did not see how he knew about Simor and Horis's movements—unless, had she inadvertently blurted it out? Marcus went on, "Surely with such numbers, there is some plan we can hatch to bring our object to fruition?"

"Hmm," repeated Mr Quinn.

Time was running out to think of a plan, as they were now emerging onto The Minories, off of which was the Crescent, where Enoch Miles's house was located. It was not the most salubrious of quarters, lined with various lodging houses and small businesses such as the gunsmith they were now passing, but she supposed what recommended it was its proximity to the London Docks and to Enoch Miles's places of business.

What would they do when they got there?

"I have been to Mr Miles's house once before," remarked Mr Quinn conversationally. "It was some months ago, on rather an interesting case concerning the smuggling of brandy in false-bottomed wine barrels, but I digress, for what I mean to say is that I recall an interesting piece of furniture in the drawing room. It was a folding screen, rather gaudy in my view, with four tall panels inset with a silk motif. Unless things have changed, the screen is positioned not far from the door to the drawing room. If one or two of you could create some sort of commotion, something to distract the occupants of the room enough for me to slip inside and hide behind the screen, then it is possible our plan could work."

"How shall you enter the house without being announced?" Liora asked.

"Oh, that is the easiest part," explained Mr Quinn. "I shall simply show myself at the servants' entrance, display my credentials as an officer of the law and demand entry. Do give me a few minutes' grace to do so before you start with your distracting commotion."

Marcus appeared to be deep in thought, a frown forming on his handsome face. Did he not think well of the plan? But then, what else could they do?

"Good plan," said Simor in her ear. "We are now circling the Tower, so we should not be much longer."

"Very well," Liora said both to her brothers and to Mr Quinn. "We have a plan."

She looked to Marcus who still seemed to be lost in thought. "What is it?" she asked.

"It is just something that occurs to me," said Marcus. "I do not think Enoch Miles is likely to confess his crime in front of several witnesses. What if I were to have an audience with the man alone and see if I can get him to lower his guard?"

"You propose to go in and speak with him alone?" Liora bit her lip doubtfully. She did not question his ability to do so. Marcus's many talents had become all too apparent to her. Yet she had misgivings too. Once more she would be an observer rather than an actor in the proceedings. And what if Marcus were putting himself in danger?

"Trust me, Lionel." There was something in the earnestness of his brown eyes that melted her resistance.

"Very well," she said. "I shall go in through the servants' entrance with Mr Quinn and slip into the drawing room with him to hide behind the screen. Can you make enough of a commotion to distract Miles and Boyle while we get into place?"

His eyes twinkled in merriment. "I most assuredly can!" he promised.

It was not long before they reached their destination. This house, like that of William Vaughan, was a showy monument to Enoch Miles's ill-gotten wealth—a stucco-fronted façade with tall, rectangular windows set below an elaborate-looking frieze sculpture. They stopped a little way from the house, on the other side of the street, trying not to draw attention to their presence. A short while later, Simor's voice in her ear announced that her brothers were close to arriving, still on the tail of the unsuspecting Ralph Boyle. It was time to get into position.

Liora touched her hand to the sleeve of Marcus's coat. "You will be alright?"

His smile was cheerful, though she was not sure if he was putting on a brave front. "I will be alright," Marcus affirmed. "Now go with Mr Quinn and be ready to slip into the drawing room when the time comes."

She pressed his arm gently, then turned to join Mr Quinn, who waited at a discreet distance. Together, they wound their way around to the back entrance of the house and entered, finding the door unlocked. A startled footman stopped midway through polishing a plate of silver and blurted, "Who are you?"

Mr Quinn stepped forward officiously, and stated, holding up a document in his hand, "I am an officer of the law. The name is Quinn, and I am here on official business."

"Official business?" repeated the footman, stupefied.

"That's right, young man, that's right. Now you go on with what you were doing and don't mind me."

"Perhaps I should tell—"

"You should stay exactly where you are," Mr Quinn spoke firmly. "We are here to gather evidence on an important case and do not wish to call any attention to our presence. Is that understood?"

"Y-yes, sir," stammered the footman. Liora observed that Mr Quinn could be quite formidable when the occasion demanded it.

"Good," Quinn nodded in satisfaction.

With a pointing of his chin, he beckoned Liora to follow him. They stepped cautiously forward. The Bow Street Runner seemed to know his way about the house—perhaps because he had visited it on official business previously. They made their way down a narrow corridor, surprising a housemaid carrying a basket of laundry, which she promptly dropped to the floor. Once more, Mr Quinn explained his presence, though quietly, not wanting his voice to carry elsewhere in the house. He bid the maid to continue on her business, which she did with a nervous curtsy.

They then reached a door that led to the main vestibule. There, Quinn paused, pushing it open a mere inch to cast a glance through the gap. Liora could not see very much, standing as she did behind him, but in her ear, Simor said, "Boyle is here." And indeed, a moment later, there came a sharp rap at the front door. Footsteps were heard as the butler approached from some other direction in the house. They heard the sound of voices, then footsteps going up the stairs as the butler presumably went to fetch his master. Liora and Mr Quinn stayed where they were behind the door, quiet as church mice. Beyond that door, Boyle waited for Enoch Miles.

Finally, they heard a heavy tread and several creaks of the floorboards as the master of the house made his way down to the hall. Then all was quiet as both men went through to the drawing room. In her ear, Simor spoke again. "Your duke has apprised us of the plan. He is approaching the house now." And in the next instant, there came a second knock on the front door followed by the sounds of the butler's footsteps once more as he went to open it.

Marcus's voice carried to where Liora was standing, as he stated imperiously, "The Duke of Coleford, here to see Mr Miles."

The butler's reply was indistinct. Quinn pushed the door open another inch, and now Liora could see the butler taking Marcus's hat then knocking on the drawing room door before opening it to announce, "The Duke of Coleford is here to see you, sir."

Marcus swept into the room, and the butler withdrew to go about his usual business, closing the door behind him. The hall was now empty. Liora and Mr Quinn took a moment to ensure the coast was clear, then swung open the door to the vestibule and tiptoed across the hall towards the drawing room. They both put their ear to the door. Voices could be heard, chief of them Marcus, who was being purposefully loud. Emboldened, Mr Quinn carefully turned the handle of the drawing room door and pushed it very slightly ajar, enough so they could now hear the goings-on inside the room.

"Good God, man!" they heard Marcus cry. "A flowery motif? Has no one informed your valet that flowers are out this season and intricate leaf patterns are in?"

"What on earth—"

"What on earth indeed," continued Marcus undeterred. Straining her neck to see through the small gap in the door, Liora spied him standing to one side of the room and looking at Enoch Miles in disgust. Liora took a quick moment to study the man. Of no more than average height, he was heavy-set with thick jowls and a pink, shiny face. A generous gut spilled over the top of his too-tight pantaloons, above which he wore an expensively tailored maroon coat, unbuttoned to reveal a quite hideous floral-patterned waistcoat. So this was what Marcus was making a fuss about.

In the next instant, Marcus pulled out a lorgnette from his pocket, one that she had never seen him use before. Lifting the eyeglass to his face, he made a grand show of inspecting Enoch Miles's flowery waistcoat. "I am almost rendered speechless in my shock at such a sight as a flowered waistcoat. An abomination—there is no other word for it. See this?" Holding the lapels of his own coat, he opened both arms wide to show off his stylish waistcoat. In so doing and with his hulking frame, he obscured both Enoch Miles and Boyle from her sight, and from sight of the door. This was their moment. She did not need to spur Mr Quinn on, for very quietly, he pushed the door open. Quick as a flash, he scurried to the shelter of the folding screen, Liora on his heels. Crouching breathlessly behind the gaudy silk of the screen, she waited anxiously. Had they been seen?

Marcus could be heard speaking in a booming voice as he showed off his own waistcoat. "This gold leaf motif is all the rage in the most fashionable echelons of the *ton*." He pronounced '*ton*' with an exaggerated French inflection, but he was not yet done with the harangue. "I must implore you, sir," he drawled loudly, "to never again pollute my vision with such a sight as this. My poor spirits simply cannot take it."

It seemed they had managed it. They had not been seen. Very carefully, Liora put her eye to a small partition between two of the panels of the folding screen. At the same time, she gave her ring a quick tap so that her brothers, who must be hovering somewhere nearby, could listen along with her. Enoch Miles was staring open-mouthed at Marcus but finally recovered enough from his shock to mutter, "I thank Your Grace for the advice, but I do not think you can have come all this way merely to give me sartorial guidance."

Marcus gave a nonchalant wave of his hand. "No indeed," he said, "that was not my purpose, but I found myself curiously sidetracked." His eyes dipped down to the offending waistcoat, and he shuddered, turning around and settling himself down on a chair with great flourish, fastidiously brushing a piece of lint from his trousers. "I have come today on a matter of the utmost concern to my dear friend, Lionel Reeves," he stated. "I am hoping, sir, that you will help clear the matter up."

"Of course, Your Grace, whatever help I can be," responded Enoch Miles in oily tones. Liora perceived a touch of contempt in his gaze as he concluded that he was dealing with an imbecilic nobleman who could not possibly pose any threat to him. A grave mistake, she thought. Nobody should underestimate Marcus.

Marcus pointed an accusing finger at Raph Boyle, who stood in one corner of the room, looking on sardonically. "This loathsome person," he said in a resounding voice, "came seeking Mr Reeves with threats not just to his family's shipping concerns but also had the temerity to threaten his person. Now, sir, what do you say to that?"

Enoch Miles shrugged his shoulders and responded smoothly, "If that is truly the case, then I would suggest the man be reported to the proper authorities. I do not see how this matter could have anything to do with me."

"You do not see it?" queried Marcus. He ran his gaze back and forth in an exaggerated manner between Enoch Miles and Ralph Boyle. "Then why is this dreadful person here with you?"

"There is a simple explanation," laughed Enoch Miles, unbothered. "This man, whom I do not know, came knocking at my door demanding to see me on a matter of great importance and delicacy. I confess to having been curious and granted him an audience. I had not had a chance yet to discuss the matter when Your Grace was announced."

Boyle stood with his arms crossed over his chest, a lift of a brow his only response. Marcus put on a perplexed expression. "Well that is very odd and most puzzling," he declared. "You see, I know that a certain person by name of Mr Jocelyn came to see you some two weeks ago. It seems our friend here, Mr Boyle, had approached him with the same threats he subsequently made to Mr Reeves, and having determined through his own investigations that you, sir, were the person behind these threats, Mr Jocelyn came to have it out with you. All this is meticulously documented in his journal, which I have in my possession."

"*Good bluff, Marcus,*" thought Liora, impressed with his quick thinking.

"Not a day after coming to see you," Marcus continued, "Mr Jocelyn was dead. A man in the full bloom of health, suddenly felled. Most suspicious, would you not agree?"

Enoch Miles chuckled snidely. "Purely coincidental, Your Grace."

"I do not believe so, for the evidence, which is stacking up, speaks for itself. In his journal, Mr Jocelyn wrote in detail how Ralph Boyle came to see him with a cunning proposition regarding a shipment of sugar, unaccountably delayed at the Custom House under the instruction of the chief collector, Henry Blunt. Mr Jocelyn soon discovered the connection between this Henry Blunt, Ralph Boyle and yourself. It is all there in the journal. Compelling evidence, I would think."

"I wish you luck holding that up in a court of law," blustered Enoch Miles. "Now if that is all, Your Grace, you must excuse me, for I have a great many things to do." He made to rise, and Liora's heart sank. They were not going to extract a confession from this man today.

But Marcus was not done. Holding up his lorgnette with great affectation, he asked quite innocently, "Do you mean to say that this cunningly clever plan has nothing to do with yourself, Mr Miles?"

"That is exactly what I am saying," declared Enoch Miles.

Marcus leaned forward confidingly as he spoke his next words. "Mr Miles, I quite understand why you would not wish to admit this, but let us be blunt, for we are both men of business." At the man's doubtful expression, Marcus continued with a wide, winning smile, "Well, I shall soon be a man of business. As you may be aware, Mr Miles, I have recently come into the dukedom and a large inheritance beside, and I have bold ideas for the investing of my funds in mercantile shipping, most particularly with the East and West Indies. I have heard there is much profit to be made, but one must be canny about it." He tapped his nose knowingly.

"Yes indeed, such investments require an astute understanding of the markets," concurred Enoch Miles, a calculating look entering his eyes.

Marcus nodded sagely. "And that is why, you see, I have cultivated an acquaintance with Mr Reeves, in hopes that I may be guided in my prospective investments, but—may I be honest with you, Mr Miles?"

"Of course."

"Well, you see, it has become clear to me that Mr Reeves may not be the best guide when it comes to investing my funds, especially since this matter of the sugar shipment came to light. Five hundred pounds' worth of this commodity sequestered in the Custom House, and Mr Reeves unable to get it released into his hands!" Marcus shook his head in disgust, as if the very thought of it offended his sensibilities. Then he went on, "It made me wonder. Perhaps I should be finding some other person, more canny and wise to guide me in my investments. And so I must confess that in coming here today, I had an ulterior motive." He paused, his gaze on Enoch Miles making his meaning clear.

The man was quick to understand, his smile gloating. "Your Grace, I would be honoured to provide assistance to you with your investments."

"But you see—" Here, Marcus frowned, a look of exaggerated concentration on his face. "I do not wish to make the same mistake again. I must make certain that the person who guides me in my investments is truly capable of doing so." He stretched his long legs out and intertwined the fingers of his hands in contemplation of the matter. Then he looked up at Enoch Miles, narrowing his gaze as he went on, "I am a man of the world and do quite understand that to succeed in matters of business, one must be bold and at times, even ruthless. Customs officials must be brought under one's influence; competition must be eliminated or at the very least, much weakened. I am not here, sir, to cast moral aspersions—quite the contrary. Do forgive my earlier words, for they were meant as some sort of a test. Now do you see why I am most desirous of knowing if you are indeed the one to have hatched this cunning plan?"

"Yes, I begin to see," remarked Enoch Miles, lounging back in his seat.

Marcus fixed his gaze on the man and said, "Therefore I must have proof that I am putting my trust, and my considerable funds, in the hands of one who will ensure the most profitable return on my investment. What say you, Mr Miles to a sum of five thousand pounds as my initial stake in your shipping business?"

Enoch Miles played along, considering the matter before replying, "It is a fair amount, though I would advise doubling it to ten thousand, for as you must know, the greater the investment, the greater the return."

Marcus nodded, looking impressed. "Of course, of course. Then ten thousand it is. Now, let us talk preliminaries. I would wish you to elucidate certain matters for me, so that I may be absolutely sure that I am dealing with the right man for my business interests." Seeing Enoch Miles prevaricate, Marcus hurriedly put a hand up and said, "Mr Miles, I do understand that this matter is of a highly confidential nature. Let me presage any further discussion with a show of *my* goodwill. Here is what I propose. I hope it may not be a boastful thing to say, but I have come to wield a considerable influence over Mr Reeves. I could, for instance, persuade him to accept the terms set forth by Mr Boyle, which would put into your possession that consignment of sugar for a mere three hundred and eighty pounds. Now what would you say to that?"

"Well, Your Grace," responded Enoch Miles with a self-satisfied look, "I would say that such an action was a proper indication of your good faith and one that should be rewarded in kind."

"Precisely!" Marcus waved his lorgnette to emphasize his point. "I am glad you see it that way. So, Mr Miles, in a corresponding show of goodwill, perhaps now you may enlighten me on certain matters…"

Behind the screen, Liora had been listening to this exchange in awestruck wonder. She had not known that Marcus could be capable of such brilliant level of artifice. Why she could almost believe every word he spoke, even though she knew, of course, that he was bluffing. He had now brought the matter to a head. Was Enoch Miles about to confess?

While these thoughts flew through her mind, Marcus was continuing with his speech. "I have been curious about two things, which I hope, Mr Miles, you may explain for me. First is the matter of Henry Blunt. As chief collector at the Custom House, I am sure he must regularly be offered financial inducements to smooth matters along, but did he blink at Mr Reeves's offer of ten guineas? Not a bit. Now I ask you, how was this dubious character's complicity bought—hook, line and sinker—to the point where he did not even think to shift allegiances upon an offer as generous as ten guineas? Hmm? There must have been some sort of master plan."

At this, Enoch Miles chuckled, "Indeed there was, for it requires significantly better guarantee than a few guineas to ensure loyalties lie where they are needed."

"Then how did you manage to fix Mr Blunt's loyalty?" enquired Marcus, looking spellbound.

"A share in one of my West Indian plantations."

"Masterful!"

Enoch Miles shrugged. "It may seem overly generous, but I assure you it is a small price to pay in exchange for a willing and loyal accomplice at the Custom House, one that can smooth things along in accordance with the needs of my business."

"Indeed, indeed. I am filled with awe at the ingeniousness," observed Marcus. "And now to the second matter I have been wondering about. It is plain as pikestaff to me that this Mr Jocelyn was an impediment to your plans, and that you somehow managed to rid yourself of him. But how?"

Enoch Miles dismissed this with an airy wave of his hand. "The small matter of having someone on the inside, someone who had access to Mr Jocelyn's food and drink."

Marcus frowned in concentration then his brow cleared. "The serving maid!"

Enoch Miles merely smiled.

"How on earth did you manage to infiltrate Mr Reeves's house with this servant?"

"Some weeks ago," boasted Enoch Miles, now so disarmed as to loosen his tongue, "we had Mr Boyle's niece, Nessie, knock at the Reeves house looking for employment." His expression turned sly. "But the clincher was the artifice about poor Nessie's previous employer beating her up and dismissing her without a reference. I knew, of course, that this would move Mr Brook Reeves to compassion towards this young girl, for despite his ruthless reputation in the business world, he is known to be soft-hearted when it comes to his servants. I was proved right, and she was employed on the spot." He sat back, looking well pleased with himself, and unaware that he had by this point provided enough evidence of his criminal misdeeds.

Then, everything happened all at once. Mr Quinn emerged from his hiding place brandishing a set of handcuffs and calling out, "Mr Enoch Miles, you are under arrest for fraud and conspiracy to murder." He marched towards him and very quickly grabbed hold of one of his wrists, locking a set of the cuffs around it.

"What the devil? Unhand me at once!" cried Enoch Miles. "How dare you touch me!"

"I dare alright," huffed out Mr Quinn, taking hold of Miles's other arm and clamping the remaining cuff on that wrist.

"This is outrageous! You have no right. Unhand me now!" shouted Enoch Miles at the top of his voice.

Liora watched with morbid fascination as the portly and ill-dressed merchant continued to resist arrest, his face turning beetroot red with anger at the realisation he had fallen into a trap of the duke's making. Coarse words of fury spewed from his mouth as he swore both at Marcus and at Mr Quinn. She felt little sympathy for the man. He had met his just deserts for what he had done to Jos and her family. In the midst of the hubbub, she sensed movement to her left. It was Ralph Boyle, who had stood quietly in the corner all this time, taking advantage of the uproar to run for the door. She dived forward, barring his escape with her body.

The man, however, was determined, feinting this way and that to make his escape. Too late, she saw a glint of steel as a small but sharp knife came slashing at her. Remembering her *raiko* training, she twisted away from the blade, but she was out of shape and too slow to avoid it altogether as it ripped into her bodysuit and gashed at her shoulder. A roar sounded in her ear. "No!" In a flash, Marcus had thrown himself between her and Ralph Boyle's knife. An instant later, the knife embedded itself into the fleshy part of his arm, evincing a moan of surprised pain from Marcus. No! No! No!

All thought of Ralph Boyle forgotten, she grasped hold of Marcus, and brought him down to the floor with her, anxious to inspect his wound. Copious blood gushed from his arm, staining his jacket a dark red. Distantly, she was aware of Simor wrestling Ralph Boyle to the ground. Horis was already kneeling at her side, assessing Marcus's injury with a trained eye. "How bad is it?" she breathed.

Horis carefully eased the knife out from where it was buried in Marcus's arm then ripped open the jacket and shirt beneath to expose the wound. She hastily undid her cravat and handed it to Horis to help staunch the blood. After a moment, her brother responded, "Just a flesh wound. Your friend is a lucky man." *Yol be thanked!*

Marcus stared at her dazedly. "Lionel," he murmured. "Your shoulder—"

"—is fine. It is just a scratch. Let us worry about you."

"So much blood," he mumbled, his face going white as a shroud.

"Marcus! Stay with me!" she cried, but already, his eyelids had fluttered shut. His head slumped back in a dead faint.

"It's alright, Lior," Horis reassured her. "Sometimes the sight of blood can have that effect on people, but he is fine. His pulse is steady and already, the blood is clotting nicely."

She brushed back a lock of sandy hair that had fallen on his brow. "Marcus," she whispered. "Marcus."

"Lior," said Horis briskly, "we need to get him home, then I'll clean and dress the wound and give him a sedative." He leaned close to her and spoke softly so no one else could hear. "You have to go now with Galok. Your bodysuit is deflating, and you do not have much time. Go home, dress back as a female, and let Galok drive you to where we hid the drone. As soon as it gets dark, you must fly back to Reeves Hall."

"No," she protested.

"Yes," he whispered, his tone firm. "Your bodysuit is irreparably damaged. You cannot pass as a man anymore. You have to return home."

"But Marcus."

"He will be in good hands. I promise you. Now go. Be quick."

She cast an agonised look at Marcus. His face was still pale, although his breathing was steady. Logically, she knew he was in good hands with Horis, and that she had to go before her true identity was unmasked. But she could not seem to peel herself away from his side.

"Lior!" This time it was Simor's voice that broke sharply into her stupor. "Go. Now."

Slowly, she released Marcus and rose to her feet. Across the room, Mr Quinn was observing her speculatively. Beside him, in handcuffs, Enoch Miles hung his head, having temporarily exhausted his fury.

It was Mr Quinn that finally set her in motion. "Mr Reeves," he said. "I believe your brothers are right. Go now. We have everything in hand." *Her brothers, not her cousins.* How did he know? She was too befuddled to work it out, or even to care. Liora looked at Marcus, lying on the floor, a peaceful expression on his handsome face. So, this was it. The final goodbye. It was not how she had expected it to be.

With an effort, she tore her gaze away and walked out the door, ignoring the gawping servants, then exited the house. She crossed the street to where Galok stood with the horses. He took one look at her shoulder, and understanding dawned on his face. "Quick," he said, "let us get you home."

CHAPTER 29

TWO LETTERS AND HEARTBREAK

VERY SLOWLY, MARCUS came to his senses, his mind sluggish from the effects of a deep sleep. His head felt fuzzy; his mouth dry. Had he overindulged in wine yesterday? He searched the recesses of his memory. Nothing at first came to mind. Then gradually, snippets of memory trickled in. A man dressing a wound on his arm. That same man giving him a draught of something bitter tasting which soon had him sink into unconsciousness.

He shifted on the bed and felt a dull pain in his left arm. A knife wound. Ralph Boyle wielding a knife against Lionel. His instinctive reaction, jumping in front of Lionel to protect him. A stab to his arm and lots of blood. It was all coming back to him now. *Lionel.* He sat up quickly, wincing at the sudden stab of pain in his arm. Never mind that. *Lionel.*

Marcus reached over to pull the bell cord and summon Stubbs. When the valet knocked at the door a minute later, he found his master already on his feet, reaching for the chamber pot.

"Your Grace," cried Stubbs. "You are not supposed to be out of bed."

Marcus glared at him. "What hogwash!"

"But your injury—"

"Merely a flesh wound. Now enough arguing, Stubbs. Help me dress."

Wisely, his valet refrained from any further protest and assisted him into his clothes. As he tucked the shirt into his pantaloons, Marcus asked him, "Is there any news from Mr Reeves?"

"If Your Grace means Mr Lionel Reeves, then no, I am afraid not. However, Mr Harry Reeves it was that saw to your wound. He left another draught which he said you were to take in the morning."

Marcus wrinkled his nose in displeasure. "No, I am not taking any more draughts." Especially not if they put him into a deep, drugged sleep as before, and not when it was urgent he go to Barton Street as soon as possible.

With barely restrained impatience, he waited while Stubbs adjusted the ties of his cravat then helped him into his boots. As soon as he was dressed, he thanked him curtly then strode out of the room. His head had cleared, and apart from a dull, aching pain in his arm, he was as fit as a fiddle.

Down the stairs he went, stopping briefly in the dining room to guzzle a cup of reinvigorating herbal tea. The hour was late, just after ten o'clock, which explained why there were no other occupants in the dining room. Just as well, as he was in no mood for conversation. Side stepping the front parlour, from whence he could hear the sound of female voices, Marcus headed straight to the front door. Denby was there, opening it for him. The butler hazarded a question in his master's direction. "Your Grace, what shall I tell Mrs Cavendish?"

Marcus paused at the threshold and turned to say, "Tell her I have gone to visit Mr Reeves and shall be back in due course."

Then he was away, walking in brisk strides towards Lionel's house. Some minutes later, he knocked at the door and waited impatiently for it to be opened. The housekeeper peered at him in confusion, but stepped back and allowed him in. "I am come to see Mr Lionel Reeves," he stated crisply.

"I am very sorry, Your Grace," she replied in her accented voice. "Mr Lionel Reeves has left."

"Left? Where to?" Marcus was already retracing his steps to the door, anticipating a journey to the docks or to the business offices on Threadneedle Street.

He was shocked into a moment of stupor when the housekeeper replied, "He has left London and returned to Cornwall." He stared at her in astonishment laced with pain. Lionel had gone. Lionel had left without a farewell. Why?

"Your Grace, good morning," a voice called out from above. It was Harry Reeves, making his way down the stairs. He came towards him and bowed. "I had hoped you would spend another day in bed to recuperate," he said, ushering Marcus into the front parlour.

Marcus followed him into the room stiffly, his mind focused on one thing. "Where is Lionel?" he asked abruptly.

Harry motioned for him to sit, then responded, "It is as Esa said. Lionel has returned to Cornwall."

"But why?"

Harry sighed, casting him a look full of sympathy. "Perhaps," he said, "that question is best answered in Lionel's words." He pulled a sealed letter from his pocket and handed it to Marcus. "Lionel wrote this for you before he left."

He took the letter in hands that were not quite steady. With little finesse, Marcus broke the seal and unfolded the two sheets. On first perusal, he could see that Lionel had written in large and clear lettering. His heart squeezed in his chest at the thoughtfulness of the gesture in making the letter as easy as possible for him to read. He took several moments to decipher its contents.

Dear Marcus,

The time has come to say goodbye. It is not the way I would have chosen to part from you, but there could never be an easy way to do it. It is a painful step I must take, but do it I must, for the impediments that stand between us are far too great to overcome. I have thought it over and over, and come to the same conclusion each time. It is best, for both our sakes, that we part.

Horis tells me that your wound is already healing nicely and that you should make a full recovery in no time at all. Let me assure you too that the wound I received on my shoulder is a mere scratch, and that also is healing well.

Marcus, I must thank you for so many things. First of all, I am deeply in your debt for your help in bringing Ralph Boyle and Enoch Miles to justice. Nessie Boyle too will soon face the strong arm of the law for what she has done. I do not think we could have managed to extract a confession from Enoch Miles without you and your quick thinking yesterday. I smile each time I remember the role you played, pretending to be a foppish duke without a clue, wanting to make a profitable investment. It was done to perfection, and it serves as a reminder, if ever I needed one, that you are a man of many talents.

I also wish to thank you, Marcus, for some of the happiest times I have ever experienced in my life. I am a better person for having known you. I will never forget the magical week I spent in your company. If only we could have had more time...

I know the way your mind works, Marcus, and no doubt you are thinking that there must be a way for us to be together. It cannot be done. Please take my word for it. There is something I cannot reveal, something that makes it an impossibility for us to be lovers or even continue as friends. There is no other choice but this—to say goodbye. I wish you every happiness and will continue to keep you in my thoughts in the days, months and years ahead.

Adieu.

L. Reeves

Marcus read the letter twice over, his heart so full it could break free from his chest. When he was done, he dropped the sheets to the floor and buried his head in his hands, uncaring of his audience. Each breath he took felt raw and aching. In and out he breathed, not knowing what else to do in this moment but the most basic thing to survive—breathe in, then breathe out.

"I am sorry for your pain," said Harry Reeves gently.

Slowly, Marcus lifted his head and looked at him. "I still do not understand why he had to leave," he rasped out. "What is this great secret that I cannot be privy to? Why cannot he trust me?"

Harry sat forward with his hands clasped together. At length, he said, "Sometimes, we start a pretence or a lie—for a very good reason—and then find ourselves embroiled in situations where it seems there is no possible way out of that lie."

"I would forgive Lionel anything, if only he would come clean."

Harry examined him curiously. "Would you?"

"Yes," Marcus stated firmly.

"Hmm." Harry observed him with a penetrating stare, as if he could determine the truth of his statement. "Perhaps you would," he murmured almost to himself. Then he shook his head. "This is neither here nor there. The fact of the matter is that Lionel has chosen to leave, and he will not return. My brother is to stay on in London to take over the running of our shipping business. I myself will remain here a few more days until all matters pertaining to Ralph Boyle and Enoch Miles are resolved." He paused, then inclined his head. "Your Grace, we are immensely grateful for your help yesterday in bringing down that criminal. It is not something we shall forget. If I or my brother can assist you in any way, we should be honoured to."

"Can you tell me what it is that Lionel is running from?"

Harry sighed. "That, I am afraid I cannot do."

Marcus bent down to pick up the discarded sheets of Lionel's letter, folding them neatly and slipping them into his pocket. Then he stood, readying to take his leave. Harry rose to his feet too, and without a word, walked him out. Marcus turned to face him one last time, but there was nothing to say. He simply nodded, then turned away and started the dreary walk back to his house on St James's Square.

"THERE YOU ARE!" Julia stepped gingerly around the mound of cuttings and weeds he had gathered and approached him. "Should you be doing this with your injury?" she asked, sounding doubtful.

"I am well," he said shortly. "Besides, the cut is on my left arm, and I work with my right."

She crouched down to his level, taking care not to soil her petticoats. "Our belongings are packed and ready to go," she informed him, "but Mama says we must delay our departure a few more days for your arm to heal."

He shook his head irritably. "There is no need to coddle me. I am well enough to travel if we wish to leave tomorrow. It is not as if sitting in a carriage all day will do the injury any more harm."

She nodded in acquiescence. "I shall tell Mama." But she did not make to go quite yet. Instead, she asked, "What happened with Lionel? Have the two of you quarrelled?"

He was in no mood to discuss the matter. Curtly, he replied, "He has left London and returned to his home in Cornwall."

"Without saying goodbye?"

"He wrote his goodbyes in a letter," he said.

"Does he explain why he has left in this letter?"

Marcus huffed. It seemed he was going to have this discussion about Lionel like it or not. His sister was ever persistent and would not cease to pester him until she had the full story. So, as briefly as he could, he gave her the gist of what was said in the letter. At the end of his sorry tale, he could not help bemoan, "Why can he not trust me with this secret, Julia?"

She considered the question with care before replying, "Perhaps it is because what he is hiding is something big, massive enough to shatter the trust and love between you."

"What could it be? Do you think he has a secret wife hidden away in the country? Is that it?"

"I cannot say, Marcus," she answered gently. "What is clear is that Lionel, the one person with all the facts, has concluded it is something immovable in the way of your friendship. I do not like to say this, my dear, but mayhap it is best to respect his wishes. He has said goodbye, and now you must accept that this brief and intense affair you had with him is over."

It was not what he wished to hear.

Abruptly, he stood, brushing away the dirt from the front of his buckskins. "Tell Mama to have us ready to leave at eight o'clock tomorrow morning," he said, ending the conversation. With a brief nod, he turned away and strode back into the house.

Some time later, washed and changed, he sat at the great desk of his study, a sheet of paper before him. He dipped the pen into the ink and painstakingly began to write.

Deer Lionel,

I am mad at you for leeving as you did. Even more than I am mad, I miss you.

Why are you letting this grate seecret come between us? Dont you knoe that I wud forgive anything, if you wud only trust me? Pleese, Lionel. I urge you. Tell me what it is, and we will find a way to be together agane. Darling, pleese trust me. I am mizzrabal without you, and I just knoe you are mizzrabal too.

I leeve tomorow with Mama and my sisters to visit Sir Luke Stafford in Oxfordshire, then I will escort them home to Ashby, after wych I shall return to Coleford Hall. Write me there and tell me the trooth—I will keep your seecret safe to my grave, I promiss.

Your lovyng,

Marcus

He sealed the letter and carefully wrote the address:

Mr Lionel Reeves,
Reeves Hall,
Penhale,
Cornwall

When he was done, he summoned Denby and handed him the missive with instructions to have it sent at the first possible opportunity.

Then, Marcus sat back in his chair and tried to think. Would Lionel respond to his letter with the truth? And if not, what should he do next? He could, of course, follow Julia's advice and leave the matter there—accept that their affair was over. Some deep instinct in him rebelled against that course of action.

No, he could not do it. If need be, he would follow Lionel to Cornwall. He would find him and have it out with him once and for all.

CHAPTER 30

⋘ ⋙

AN UNEXPECTED VISITOR

Six weeks later

LIORA WAS DOWN in the basement of Reeves Hall, in the diagnostics room, checking the latest data. It was routine work, something she did on a daily basis to ensure the proper maintenance of all the engineering systems that she had designed and installed, providing them with heating, sanitation, lighting and connectivity.

The diagnostic program alerted her to two faults that required immediate attention, a malfunctioning microprocessor in the pump room and a loose coupling in the transmission panel that provided connectivity in the drawing room. She tapped her ring and called Uzenia, a Uvonian girl who was working as her apprentice. Next month, she would be sitting the *piliaps*, an arduous examination that all engineers on Uvon must pass in order to be certified—not that she required certification here on Earth. Nevertheless, both Broek and Liora had agreed that it would give her training more rigour if she were to follow the *piliaps* curriculum, the materials for which were among their vast data banks.

"Uzenia," Liora said. "Could you check panel 5 in the pump room? We have a faulty microprocessor."

"Of course. I'll head over there shortly."

"Good," Liora replied. "When that is done, you can log off for the day."

"Thank you, Miss Liora," Uzenia said, grateful for the extra time she was being given to go study for her examination. Liora would take care of the loose coupling. It was a simple job that would not take long to do.

A few minutes later, once she had finished checking each part of the system, she picked up her small toolbox and headed out of the diagnostics room. On her way to the basement door, she passed by Broek's control room, where he spent several hours a day monitoring and managing their business affairs. The door was ajar, almost as if he had been looking out for her to pass by. At any rate, she heard him call out, "Liora."

She stopped and retraced her steps, pushing open the door to his private lair. It was a small room with several screens open all at once displaying data from across their business ventures. "Yes, Broek?"

"Come in for a bit. I wish to speak with you." He pointed to the vacant chair beside his, and she settled into it with an enquiring arch of her brow. Her elder brother took in her appearance with a rapid glance. Gone were her pantaloons and tailcoat now that she was back in her true female persona, however she was dressed for comfort rather than fashion in a serviceable calico gown of a dark shade of green. Her hair had lengthened a few inches, but it was still cropped far shorter than was befitting for a lady. No matter, as she rarely left Reeves Hall these days.

Finally, his eyes came to rest on the small toolbox, still held in her hands. "You have maintenance tasks to do?" he enquired.

"Nothing of great import," she said. "A loose coupling in the transmission panel to the drawing room. I was on my way there to repair it."

"I will not keep you long, Liora. There is just a small matter I wished to discuss." He paused and looked a little uncertain. "Liora," he began again. "It has been six weeks since your return from London."

Tension gripped her at the mention of London, followed inevitably by painful thoughts of Marcus. Her brother saw the stiffening of her posture and hurried on with his speech. "I am sorry it did not go as you had hoped, and I realise that getting involved with this duke has hurt you deeply, but Liora, I do not like to see you burying yourself alive here at Reeves Hall."

"What else is there for me to do?" she asked listlessly. "Living as a man did not answer my problem."

"No, I never thought it would, but I suppose it has opened my eyes to your situation here in ways I have neglected to notice." His expression softened. "It is a man's world out there, yet that does not mean you need to confine yourself at Reeves Hall. You deserve to be fulfilled, Liora, not live the half-life you are living."

She stared at him in surprise. He was certainly singing a different tune to that which he had been spouting all these years since they had arrived on Earth. He saw her surprise and had the grace to look a little shamefaced. "When we arrived here," he explained, "all my efforts went towards establishing ourselves financially while attempting to assimilate as best we could into the backward society we found ourselves in. For too long, I have been fearful of our family appearing different, of generating gossip, and I know this has affected the way I have behaved towards you. I am sorry, Liora. I never wished to clip your wings."

"I know," she murmured tiredly. "And I understood. I have tried as best I can to adjust to this new reality." She brought her gaze down, not wishing to see any judgement in his eyes as she confessed, "But deep down, I think I hoped that our time here would be temporary, and that we would go back home someday."

"Would you really be happier returning to Uvon?" he asked softly.

She shrugged. "We shall never know."

"If you want my penny's worth, Liora, it's this," Broek said, an unfamiliar gentleness in his voice. "A return to Uvon was never on the cards for us. We could not hope to regain the life we had before it all went so badly wrong. Always, we would be branded as traitors or the children of a traitor, the sins of our parent casting a long shadow over us. I do not think we would have much joy living there now as outcasts among the people who banished us to a planet millions of light years away, who ripped us away from everything that we knew and sent us out into the unknown." He sighed before he went on, "Much as we sometimes might wish it, we cannot turn back the clock to that time when we were happy and carefree, our position established at the top of society. What happened happened, and we can only go forward now, not back."

"You may be right." Her smile was wry.

"Which brings me to your situation, Liora. I never meant to barricade you within the walls of Reeves Hall, and I think it may be possible to enlarge the scope of your activities beyond what you do here."

He had her full attention. "How so?" she asked. "You surely do not mean that I should return to London."

A fierce scowl transformed his handsome face. "No," he grunted. "Not that." He expelled a frustrated breath before expounding, "I have been speaking to Jane about your situation, and we both think that it would do you a world of good to start socialising with local folk a little more and perhaps give yourself the opportunity to make new friends. I know that we have always thought of the local populace as backward and ignorant, but being with Jane has opened my eyes to things. While they do not have the advanced knowledge that we have, there are still some good, sensible people out there, people worthy of being called friends."

She thought of Marcus and the way she too had initially dismissed him as another ignorant Earth human. She could not say that about him now. He was wise, gentle and loyal, and most definitely worthy of being called a friend.

"Yes," she concurred. "Some of these Earth humans are not so bad."

"Jane is to pay a visit to Verity Drake tomorrow," he went on. "I have come to know the Drakes these past few weeks, and they are sensible, decent folk. Why not accompany Jane on this visit and get to know this Verity more—and perhaps also her brother?"

Liora spluttered, "Are you and Jane trying to matchmake?"

Broek smiled. "Nothing of the sort. Only to open you up to new possibilities. Will you go with her tomorrow?"

Liora wanted to say no but found herself instead agreeing. She was not on the lookout for a husband, but new friends—well that was something that might make her life less dreary.

"Good," said Broek, his tone brisk.

And without further ado, she picked up her toolbox to go fix that loose coupling. The job was a simple one, and it did not take long to do. Once she had checked that all was working as it should, she replaced the lid on the transmission panel and put her tools back in the box. Yet she did not get to her feet right away. There she sat, with only a rug to shield her body from the cold and hard floor. A lassitude had taken hold of her. This torpor had been her companion for many a week now. She was sure Horis would diagnose it as a symptom of her depressed spirits. She had left for London with high hopes of a diverting escapade. Instead, she had come back changed, marked forever in the painful cadence of her heart.

She should exert some strength of purpose to jolt herself out of this torpor. Soon, she would do so, starting with her social expedition on the morrow. But for now, she would let herself sink once more into moody melancholy. Reaching back, she pulled towards her a velvet cushion from the settee and settled her head on it. She did not know how long she reclined on the floor. Head cocooned in the soft pads of the cushion, she let her eyelids droop. Whisps of memories haunted her—the look of complete harmony she and Marcus had shared on the roof of her carriage after she had showed him how the cooling system worked, their first kiss and their last, his roar of fury and pain as Ralph Boyle jabbed his knife at her. *Marcus.* Her sweet and handsome duke who was so much more than met the eye. How she wished they could have known each other in different circumstances. But then, would he have wanted her? Or was it the male version of her that he was attracted to?

She turned onto her side, curling her body into a foetal position, instinctively wanting to feel the safety and comfort of a child in its mother's womb. After a time, she slipped a hand into a fold of her gown and extracted his letter which she carried always with her. She had read it countless times, her heart tugging at each misspelled word, sensing how he must have struggled to put pen to paper. *I am miserable without you, and I just know you are miserable too.* In this he was right. She was deeply unhappy. *Don't you know that I would forgive anything, if you would only trust me?* Again, she thought this was true. His nature was such that he would not hold a grudge. But she suspected that it would hurt for him to discover her true identity, and that he might not be able to get past that hurt nor the feeling of betrayal. It would conjure up once more the spectre of feeling foolish and naive, one that she hoped he had banished for good.

In the end, she had written back a short, purposely curt note, each word a knife to her heart. *Let this be a final goodbye. Please do not write again.*

And then, silence. He had heeded her wish.

NEXT MORNING, DRESSED more elegantly in a pale blue muslin gown, she stepped out into the mid-September sunshine, in readiness for her social call to Verity Drake with Jane. Her brother's carriage drew up outside the house, and out came Broek. Through the opened carriage door, he gave his wife a parting kiss. "Enjoy your visit, my love," he said, then made way for Liora to get inside the carriage.

He took in her appearance approvingly. "You are looking well, Liora," he said.

"Thank you." What he meant was that it made a change to see her in something other than her serviceable and plain calico gowns. She settled herself into the carriage, smiling a greeting at Jane. Broek pushed the door shut. But before they could get on their way, there came an urgent call from Threvvok, who was on duty at the main gates.

"There is a visitor here, a Duke of Coleford, come to see Lionel Reeves. I have told him Mr Reeves is not home, but he insists. What do I do?"

At mention of the duke, Liora froze, then her heart began to pound frantically. Marcus was here. What were they to do? She could not allow him to see her in her female form. What if he recognised her? Surely he would. Panic surged within her, and she stared wide-eyed at Jane.

Just then, Broek wrenched the carriage door open again, looking grim. "Come down, Liora," he commanded sharply.

She obeyed without thinking, followed by Jane.

"What are we to do?" she whispered urgently.

"You, Liora, are going straight up to your chamber," Broek spoke decisively but with a gentleness in his tone. "Wait there until the coast is clear. I will deal with the duke."

"What will you say to him?"

"Whatever is needed to make him leave," he replied sombrely.

Her heart swelled tight in her chest. Marcus was here. He had come for her. No, she corrected herself. He had come for Lionel, not her.

To her brother, she breathed, "You will be kind? Please?"

"We will fob him off as kindly as possible," Jane said soothingly. "Now quick, go hide yourself."

She nodded, unable to speak, and hurried up the stairs to her quarters. Closing the door to her room, she leaned her head against it, trying to slow the mad pounding of her heart. Marcus would be here shortly. And she could not be allowed to see him.

CHAPTER 31

❧ ❧

A SHOCKING REVELATION

THAT MORNING, MARCUS had taken added care with his appearance. Call it vanity, but he had wanted to look his best upon seeing Lionel again. Stubbs had been happy to oblige. The blue superfine tailcoat he wore was exquisitely cut, fitting his large frame to perfection. His meticulously polished boots gleamed brightly, and Stubbs had excelled himself in knotting his cravat in the *trone d'amour* style that was the height of fashion, its folds well stiffened with starch.

For the last hour, Marcus had been travelling in his carriage, having stopped briefly in Bodmin for a change of horses. The landscape had changed as he had travelled further into this part of Cornwall. Instead of enclosed fields interspersed with the odd village or hamlet, now the view was of vast expanses of wild moor. As far as the eye could see were tall grasses sprinkled with a dusting of deep violet from the heather in bloom. Despite the vibrancy of the colours, it felt oddly desolate. There were no animals, buildings or persons in sight, simply heathland, wild and free. One could get lost in a place such as this.

The carriage wheels rattled on the road, at once soothing in their regular rhythm and nerve inducing the closer they brought him to Reeves Hall. What would he say to Lionel? How would Lionel greet him? Marcus was, after all, ignoring the instructions of his last letter. *Let this be a final goodbye. Please do not write again*. Marcus had not written again, but a final goodbye? No. That he could not allow.

And so here he was, turned out like a peacock, about to pay a visit to the man he loved. The gatekeeper had said that Lionel was not home, but Marcus had not come all this distance to be turned away. He had insisted, and the gatekeeper had finally relented, allowing his carriage through. Now, they drove along a winding avenue towards a substantial three-storied house. Marcus took deep, restorative breaths and prepared himself, almost as if he was about to go into battle. Something told him that the coming interview would not be easy.

As he alighted from the carriage, the front door was opened by a butler who bowed respectfully and ushered him inside. The butler led him to a spacious drawing room and bid him wait while he called on his master. Left alone, Marcus glanced around the room. It was richly decorated with understated elegance. There were armchairs, a plush settee and a strange-looking chaise longue by the window. He was not sure what made it look so strange. Perhaps it was the panel on its side with round button-like protrusions. Probably another of Lionel's inventions. He was half minded to explore it but thought twice. Now was not the time for such investigations.

Instead, he went to the settee and sat down to wait. His hand landed on a velvet cushion beside him, and idly, he ran his fingers along the soft fabric. He stopped abruptly. The tips of his fingers began to tingle just as his senses detected a familiar aroma. He snatched the cushion up and held it to his nose. Unmistakable! Lionel's head had rested on this cushion not long ago. Marcus inhaled deeply, breathing in the unique fragrance. It was Lionel. There could be no doubt. He had spent two nights wrapped around him, breathing in his essence, and he knew it well. Lionel was close by.

Hastily, he put the cushion down as he heard the door open. He got to his feet excitedly, expecting to see Lionel, but it was not him that entered the room. A tall and powerful looking man with dark hair and a stern countenance walked in, followed by an unknown lady. The gentleman came to him and bowed. "Your Grace," he said. "It is a pleasure to finally make your acquaintance. I am Brook Reeves."

Inbred courtesy had Marcus bow in return and murmur, "The pleasure is mine, Mr Reeves." He detected a resemblance to Lionel, but only slight.

Broek turned to the lady beside him and introduced her. "This is my wife, Jane Reeves, the former Duchess of Coleford."

She curtsied and smiled brightly. "Your Grace, we meet at last," she said.

He bowed again. "Indeed," he murmured. "An honour."

Jane gestured for them to sit. As she did so, she asked, "How is your arm, Your Grace? I do hope you have recovered from your injury."

"As good as new," he replied with a hint of impatience. He was not here to discuss his injury. He wanted to know where Lionel was. He decided to get straight to the matter. "I was hoping to see Lionel," he said. "Is he not at home?"

"Ah, well," replied Jane unhelpfully.

Then her husband interjected smoothly, "I am afraid you have had a wasted journey, Your Grace, for Lionel is no longer living at Reeves Hall. Had you but written, we would have informed you of this."

Marcus's jaw clenched at this blatant lie. "Then where is he?" he demanded.

"He has gone back to his main home," responded Brook Reeves. "As you may be aware, our family holds several estates in Brazil, which is where Lionel has lived most of his life. He has returned there to manage our coffee plantation."

More lies. Marcus had grown tired of this game. In the periphery of his vision, he could see the ring on Brook Reeves's finger, almost a replica of the one that Lionel had always worn. Without thinking, he reached across and tapped it. "Lionel," he said. "I know you are here. Come down at once." Then, another thought occurred to him, and he tried again. "Lior, I know you are here. I can scent you on this cushion, the one you rested your head on not too long ago, and I shall not leave without seeing you. Come down now."

Both Brook and Jane stared at him in shock. Brook was the first to recover. "What did you just do?" he thundered, every trace of civility wiped from his face.

Marcus returned his stare unperturbed. "You know exactly what I just did," he responded calmly. "And please do not pretend that Lionel has gone to Brazil, for I know that to be balderdash."

Jane had been studying him intently. Now she spoke. "Your Grace, just how much do you know about the Reeves family?"

"Not nearly enough!" Marcus gritted out in irritation. "However, I do know that you use your ring and a device in your ears to communicate with each other."

"I see," murmured Jane.

Brook was not amused. "How did you find this out?" he asked in a sharp voice.

"I was with Lionel one morning while he was still asleep. I saw a curious transparent disk on his pillow. It was making a buzzing sound, so I picked it up and heard you speaking."

The scowl grew on Brook's face. "Carelessness," he grumbled. He was about to say more, but just then, the door opened.

At last. Lionel. Marcus jumped to his feet, then stopped abruptly. The person entering the room was a lady dressed in a pale blue gown. But that was not what arrested him. It was her face. Lionel's face, but on a lady. Could it be his sister?

"Who are you?" he mumbled.

She came to stand before him, her dark eyes—Lionel's eyes—glistening with unshed tears. "It is me," she said in Lionel's voice.

"Lionel?" his voice was hoarse.

"Yes, it's me."

He shook his head, reason warring with the reality before him. "I do not understand."

She pressed her lips together and nodded her head. "I know. It must seem extraordinary and far-fetched. Marcus, there is no Lionel. It has always been me."

He stared at her, dumbfounded. The more he looked, the more he could see the resemblance to Lionel. It was his eyes, his lips, his soft skin—and his scent. But he could not reconcile this person with the Lionel he knew. He ran his eyes over her. Where before Lionel had been stockily muscular, this lady was lithe and slim, her cleavage small but gently rounded. His gaze followed the length of her bare arms, tracing over the creamy skin and coming to rest on her elegant, long-fingered hands. Lionel's hands. But these hands matched her body in a way that Lionel's hands never did. It was one of the first things Marcus had noticed about him. The strange juxtaposition of his feminine-looking hands with the rest of him, so powerfully masculine. Now it began to make sense. Except it didn't. "You cannot be Lionel," he managed to say, his throat still feeling tight. "How is that possible?"

"I wore a disguise," she explained, her voice sounding eerily like Lionel. "It was a specially formulated bodysuit that gave me a masculine appearance."

He shook his head in disbelief. It could not be true. "I saw Lionel's bare body. He had..." He paused and dropped his gaze to the area of her groin, which even under the flowing petticoats showed no sign of Lionel's large, jutting appendage.

It was Brook who now spoke. "It was an artificially constructed penile attachment. They can be very lifelike in appearance."

Marcus was still dumbstruck. "None of this makes sense," he breathed.

"No," Brook agreed. "It must seem fantastical to you, yet it is the truth."

Marcus turned back to the lady. "So," he said. "There is no Lionel?"

"No," she smiled sadly. "It was a name I made up, as close to my real name as could be. I am Liora, though most people hereabouts know me as Laura Reeves."

"Lior, short for Liora," he said under his breath.

"Yes."

There was no Lionel. He did not exist.

Marcus could not get his mind to grapple with this fact. The lady, Liora, took a step closer to him. "Marcus," she said urgently. "I never meant to lie to you or hurt you. Although I disguised myself as a man called Lionel, everything else I said to you or did was real. Do you hear me? It was real."

Her eyes, Lionel's eyes, pleaded with him for understanding. But he could not. It was too much to take in. He felt his body start to shake. There was a buzzing in his ears. His breathing was rough and uneven. Sweat pooled in the small of his back and on his brow. He needed to get out of this room and of this house, get away from this madness. Now. As soon as possible.

Without a word, he turned and strode out of the room. Footsteps followed, then he heard a voice, Jane, say, "Let him be. He needs time to come to terms with what he has learned." Marcus did not hear the rest of her words as already, he was out the front door, running down the steps, then walking quickly towards the back gate of the estate. It opened on its own as he reached it, almost by magic. He did not stop to wonder at it but simply carried on, walking to the wildness of the moor. Earlier, he had thought it a place one could get lost in. So, he went there, walking aimlessly, wanting to be forever lost and never found.

Emotion churned in his chest and clouded his mind. There was no Lionel. He loved a man who did not exist. He had been a fool. A fool. Always a fool. Oh Great God, it hurt!

On and on he walked, uncaring of where he went. He did not know how long he had been walking when his feet stumbled over a patch of stubby grass, and he fell to his knees in a sea of purple heather. The floral scent filled his nostrils, enveloping him in its mystical spell. He cried out his pain—a harsh, ragged sound—and it was as if the moor heard him. The wind whistled in his ear, a softly soothing tune. "There, there," it seemed to say. "It will be alright in the end."

Marcus sank to the ground, his head nesting in the magically scented heather. And then he gazed at the sky, blue with small patches of fluffy white clouds. He gazed and gazed, breathing in and out, in and out, and listening to the moor speak to him in its eternal language of wisdom. "Heal my broken soul," he whispered to it.

And it whispered back, "It will be alright."

CHAPTER 32

A BOUT OF PASSION ON THE MOOR

LIORA HAD FOLLOWED Marcus, a hundred paces or so behind. She did not wish to intrude on his pain, but neither could she leave him to be totally alone. Instead, she walked with him step by step as he wandered aimlessly into the heart of the moor, watching him from a distance.

The look on his face when he had found out the truth—that was the reason why she could never reveal her secret. There had been incomprehension, followed by hurt and betrayal. She was filled with revulsion at herself for having caused it. She should never have let their intimacy develop under the guise of a lie. It had been weak of her, and now they were both paying the price.

Ahead, she saw Marcus stumble to his knees, then sink his whole body to the ground. For a long time, he stayed supine on the grassy ground, unmoving. She watched him, her mind filled with pain and worry. Would he rise again to his feet or simply stay there? She waited and waited, then made her decision.

Gingerly, Liora approached. Once she had reached him, she lowered herself quietly to sit on the grass beside him. She knew he sensed her presence, though he said nothing. After a while, she sank to her back and lay on the ground with him, her head mere inches from his. The sky above her was bright blue, speckled with a few hazy dots of white. The grass rustled in her ear, and the gentle breeze tickled her cheeks. Cocooned in their nest of grass and heather, with a wide expanse of sky above them, it felt like they were in their own world, a peaceful place where no harm could reach them. Gradually, the sharp, gnawing pain in her chest began to recede, replaced by something else. She was not sure what it was. A sense of fatalism? What was done was done. At least the truth was out now in the open—or most of it, as Marcus still did not know her true origins.

It was then that he spoke.

"Why?" That one word was filled with a multitude of hurt.

She took her time to reply. "The place I come from. It is a very different place from here. I grew up in a world where women had an important role to play." She told him then of her life on Uvon, though not mentioning it by name. She spoke of her mother, her great crime of treason and of their banishment to England. Somewhere along her tale, Marcus's hand reached over to hers. He drew circles with his thumb on her palm while he listened and studied her face, his expression grave, his brows creased in concentration. In the midst of his pain, he was trying to understand.

She endeavoured to explain the best she could. "Last month, we received word from London that Jos, the person we had put in charge of our shipping enterprises, had died suddenly. It was imperative that one of us should go there and take over the running of the business. Broek was newly married and reluctant to leave his wife. I knew he would ask either one of my younger brothers to go in his stead. You see, Broek, Horis and Simor are my brothers, not my cousins."

"Yes," he murmured. "I had figured that one out." When she said nothing more, he prompted, "So, you put yourself forward for this task."

"I did. Something in me rebelled. Back home, it was me that had been groomed for leadership, not them. And here in England, the roles had become reversed. I told my brothers that I would go. Of course, they did not take me seriously. They explained that it was a man's world out there. Oh, that made me mad! And so, without thinking the matter through, I said I would turn myself into a man."

Marcus's frown deepened. His hand left hers as he turned once more onto his back to stare up at the sky. "But how was that possible?" he gritted.

She chose her words carefully. "The world I come from has far greater scientific knowledge than even the most learned of people have here. We have the means to create things that you would marvel at—the cooling system in my carriage, for instance. In my world, there are women that live as men, and it is accepted as normal. They can choose how they wish to change their appearance, decide on the level of musculature, on the body hair, and on the preferred size and shape of the male appendage they desire. A male bodysuit is then crafted to their specifications, and the artificial appendage attached to their body in a surgical procedure. That is what I decided to do and how I became Lionel. What you saw of my body was not actually me, except for my face, hands and feet."

"It looked so real," he whispered.

"Yes, it was very lifelike. Even my brothers were struck when they first saw me as Lionel."

His hands formed into fists at his side. "I should have known," he said angrily. "There were clues aplenty. Your hands. The soft hairless skin of your face. Even your scent. I should have realised you were female, but I was blind. A blind fool."

"No!" she cried. "Do not say that."

"It is the truth, Lionel—Liora, whatever you are. Only someone as blindly foolish as me could have been hoodwinked for so long."

"Marcus, no." She reached out a hand to him, but he moved away to sit up.

"Did you laugh at my expense? Was it a thrill for you to see how far you could take your masquerade without being unmasked?" His voice was brimming with bitterness as he recalled past events. "We spent two nights together, skin to skin. We kissed and made love. And still I did not fathom the truth about you."

He got to his feet and began to pace, a furious fire raging within him—fury at her but mostly at himself. There was no greater trigger for anger than the feeling of being duped.

"I thought myself in love," he raged. "I wondered at it. How could I love a man when never before had I felt attraction for any male? Day and night I thought of nothing else. What was the matter with me? Who had I become?" He came to a stop before her, a fiery blaze in his usually gentle brown eyes. "And finally, I accepted what I thought to be the truth about myself." He beat at his chest. "I, Marcus Cavendish, was a sodomite, one of those men who desired other men, an outcast from society should I ever be found out."

He shook his head. "And even then, I was prepared to sacrifice it all, do anything to be with you." He threw his hands up in the air and shouted, "I did not even like the hair on your chest, but I made myself appreciate it because it was part of you. Could I have been any more deluded?"

"But don't you see," she cried, no longer able to keep silent. "It means that deep down, you knew who I was, and it was me, Liora, you fell in love with, not Lionel."

He huffed in disbelief. "I fell in love with a man who does not exist. Perhaps that love too was a delusion."

"No, it was not!" She clutched at the lapels of his coat as she pleaded with him. "What we had was real. You may have been mistaken about my identity, but your feelings were true and so were mine." He pulled at her hands, trying to shake her off, but she did not let go. "Look at me, Marcus," she demanded. "Look into my eyes. It is still me. I am the same person as before. Put your hands to my face and feel my skin. Put your lips to mine and taste me. It is still me." He turned his head away in protest but she brought his face back to her. "Go on," she goaded him. "Kiss me."

"This is not the time for games—"

"Kiss me!"

Then his lips touched hers, and he did as she asked, but it was not gentle. This kiss was rough and bruising, equal parts anger, pain and lust. His large hands roamed over her face as his tongue plundered her mouth with a hunger that was unrestrained. No, it was not gentle, this kiss. Their tongues swept and stroked and savoured the familiar essence of each other.

Soon though, kisses were not enough. She needed more, and so did he. His hands slipped down to cup the swell of her breasts, kneading the aching flesh. "I like the feel of you here," he growled.

"Good," she breathed, "because it is me, all me."

"Let me see you."

She did not hesitate. They were out in the open on the moor, and there was nobody here but them. She pushed down on her gown, releasing her breasts to his avid gaze. They were not very large, but they were softly rounded and pert.

"Oh, dear Lord!" he groaned. His large hands covered her, holding each breast in its entirety. The possessive feel of his hands enveloping her had her core going slick.

"Marcus," she pleaded.

Their eyes met.

"Please," she begged.

In an instant, his mouth was on one peak, licking back and forth, and when that still was not enough, he took the whole thing into his mouth and sucked.

"Ah," she moaned. He sucked harder, rubbing the nipple of her other breast with skilful fingers. Her hands threaded through his hair, holding him to her. "Oh, Marcus," she cried again. "Don't stop." He heeded her words, worshipping the breasts she had kept hidden from him, swapping from one to the other with great strokes of his tongue, then sucking strongly almost to the point of pain. She gloried in the feel of his mouth on her. A tide of slickness dripped from her core. Still, she needed more.

"Inside me," she moaned breathlessly. "I need you inside me."

He raised his eyes to her. In one quick move, he had her hand pressed to his swollen cock. "Is this what you want?" he rasped.

"Yes," she gasped.

"Then take it out."

Needing no further invitation, she fumbled with the fastenings of his pantaloons, and soon, she had them undone. She pushed them down eagerly until his cock sprung free, thick and strong. Then she looked back up at him expectantly.

"Where do you want it?" he demanded, his eyes glittering with anger and lust.

Wordlessly, she put a hand over her aching cunt.

"Show it to me. Last I saw, there was a cock there." His words were biting. Yes, there was still plenty of anger in him despite his evident desire.

Very well. He wanted to see her female form naked. It was understandable, after the way she had disguised her body as a man. Without a second thought, she pulled her dress over her head and threw it down. Quickly, she unlaced her stays and took off her petticoats until she stood naked in front of him, with the exception of her stockings. He stared, examining her closely as each garment was removed. At the same time, he undid his tailcoat and threw it off, though he left on the rest of his clothes, his rigid cock jutting out impudently from the gap in his open pantaloons.

"Show it to me," he rasped again.

She sank to the ground once more, her body bare this time, and lay down on a bed of grass and heather. It tickled her back a little, but she did not care. Keeping her eyes fixed to his, she slowly eased her legs wide, showing him what he wanted to see. He stared greedily at her feminine cunt, palming his cock with a rough, jerky hand. A moment later, he dropped to his knees, his eyes not straying from the folds of pink glistening flesh before him.

"Liora," he groaned, calling her by her true name for the first time. "I am almost beyond rational thought. This is your last chance to tell me to stop, for I mean to fuck you."

"Then fuck me."

Barely were the words out, than he was on her. With practised fingers, he guided the tip of his cock to her opening. Keeping his eyes on her, he pressed in. Great Yol, he was large. He filled her, inch by thick inch, until his entire shaft was seated inside her, stretching her. Leaning down, he pressed his lips to her, demanding entry. She welcomed him greedily. And with the thrust of his tongue into her mouth, he began to plunge deep into her core in a fast-paced rhythm. *"He is good at this,"* she thought wonderingly. Then jealousy hit her at the thought of him fucking anyone but herself. She drowned the feeling in kisses, lifting her body to meet his every thrust.

"Oh yes," he growled into her mouth, then kissed her harder. His mouth swallowed her cries as his large cock drilled in and out of her. They were not gentle with each other. Their need was too strong. Her hands clasped his buttocks and pulled him to her with desperate need, wanting more. He gave it to her, hard and fast. She forgot where she was. On the moor? If so, this moor was a haven of sensation. With each hard thrust, she felt herself get closer to the precipice. Already, she was nearly there. The feeling grew and grew like an unstoppable wave as Marcus pinned her under him, driving his thick shaft in and out with a force that had her core throb and ache. And then the wave engulfed her. She pulsated around him, pleasure flowing through her veins. Her grip on his cock was so tight that he roared in pain or delight, or perhaps both. His shaft swelled as he thrust wildly a few times more before he too reached his peak, pouring his seed into her.

Time stood still. Above her, he caught his breath, keeping their bodies joined as they both came drifting down to earth.

Then slowly, he pulled out and sat back on his heels. Liora was too drained to do anything but lie on the grass, her legs splayed decadently, looking the epitome of a fallen woman. In the eyes of this world, she probably was for having lain with a man unwed. She felt his spend seep slowly out of her and drip to christen the ground. He saw it too and was momentarily mesmerised. Then he became brisk, reaching over to his tailcoat and extracting a handkerchief which he used to gently clean her up. Once that task was done, he refastened his pantaloons and shook out his coat before putting it back on.

Liora sat up and began to dress without a word. He watched her quietly, brushing away bits of heather from her gown. When they were both presentable again, by mutual consent they began to walk back in the direction of Reeves Hall. With each minute, their silence became heavier. Evidently, their frantic lovemaking in the heather had not reconciled them. They still had a barrier of hurt and distrust to overcome.

"As soon as it can be arranged, we will marry," Marcus said stiffly, interrupting her thoughts.

"Marry? Why?"

He looked at her as if she had gone mad. "Liora, if there is even the slightest possibility that we have made a child, then we must marry."

"Hmm," she huffed. Of course, the offer of marriage was not romantically inspired. He was doing the honourable thing, proposing to give his unborn child a name. He did not know yet that there would be no child.

She replied coolly, "There is no need for marriage, though I thank you for the kind offer. I am protected and cannot conceive at this time, so there will be no child, I assure you."

"Protected? How?"

"Every six months," she explained, "I receive an injection of a special substance into my body that prevents any unwanted pregnancy. It is something else that my scientifically advanced world can do."

He scowled darkly, digesting this information. "I cannot begin to get my head around how that can be done," he said irritably, "but are you taking steps to prevent pregnancy because you engage in licentious activity with other men? Galok perhaps?"

Ah, so now he thought she was a whore. Excellent. Angrily, she lashed out, "If I did, it would be none of your business."

"So much for being in love," he sneered. "The ugly truth is coming out now."

"You know nothing of the truth," she hissed.

"And whose fault is that? I see that keeping secrets is your great talent."

She whirled around to face him, reminding herself that it was his hurt that was doing the talking. "Stop this, Marcus," she said with as much dignity as she could. "It ill becomes you to speak so to me. And I was at fault too for what I just said. In truth, I have not engaged in licentious activity with anyone but you. It has been many years since I have lain with a man, and yes that man was Galok. I have already explained to you before that my relationship with him ended long ago."

Like a dog with a bone, he did not let go. "This other world you come from, is it acceptable there for women to engage in licentious behaviour?" he asked pointedly.

"I do not like the term *licentious*," she snapped in reply. "However, it is true that in my world, women and men can engage in sexual relationships without the necessity of marriage."

"And did you?"

"Before coming to England, I had several lovers, yes," she said evenly.

He did not reply, choosing instead to resume walking. Greatly annoyed, she caught up with him and posed the question, "Are you going to pretend that you had no lovers before we met?"

"No," he muttered.

"So, it is alright for you to have had lovers but not for me?"

He expelled a frustrated breath. In a low, gritty voice he said, "I do not like to think of you with others, Liora, because I am a very jealous man."

"Jealous? Does that mean you still have feelings for me?"

He did not deign to respond. Why should he, when the truth was there for both of them to see? Hesitantly, she told him, "I too do not like the thought of you with anyone else, Marcus, because I am a very jealous woman."

He huffed again, but as they walked on, his hand reached for hers. They continued their journey in silence, though this one was less fraught than before. A small part of her heart was singing with joy. "*He is mine,*" she thought. Then she corrected herself. Someday, he would be hers. She could be content with that.

A long time later, he asked, "You keep speaking of this strange world you come from, Liora. Where is this place you speak of?"

"It is a world very far from here," she began.

"Further than Brazil?" he asked.

"Much, much further. It is called Uvon."

"Not Luxzuc?"

"Luxzuc is my home city on Uvon," she explained.

"Ah," he murmured. "I have never heard of such a place."

"Nor would anyone else." She drew a breath, then took the plunge. "It is in a different universe, on a planet millions of light years away."

He stopped and frowned. "I do not understand."

"Do you sometimes look up at the sky at night and see distant stars?" she asked.

"Yes, of course."

"Imagine a world that revolves around one of the stars you see in the sky. It is so far away as to be a tiny point in the sky."

He looked at her strangely. "And that is your world? The place you call Uvon?"

"Yes," she said.

He considered this extraordinary revelation. She would give him credit for the calm way he was digesting the information. Then, he came to the next logical question. "If your world is as far away as the stars in the sky, then how did you get here, Liora?"

"Remember I said that my world has vastly greater scientific knowledge?" He nodded. "Well," she said. "We have the knowledge to construct machines that can fly in space and travel from one planet to another."

"You came here on one of these machines?"

"Yes," she replied. "We travelled on a space ship. It took us several years of travel in space to get here."

He began to walk again, deep in thought, though he glanced at her a few times in wonder. "You travelled from a world as distant as the stars," he repeated.

"Yes."

He frowned again, thinking of something else. "The people on your world. Do they look like us?"

"Yes, they do. We are all of the same human race even though our planets are light years apart."

"How is that possible?"

She laughed. "One day, Marcus, I will explain it all." Then doubt set in. "That is, if you will still be my friend in the days and years to come."

"We are more than friends, Liora," he said sharply.

"Then… what are we?"

"At present, I cannot say." More humorously, he added, "You have rejected my offer of marriage, so I suppose we shall have to be something other than husband and wife. I cannot tell how it will be with us, only that I do not ever want to sever my ties with you."

"Neither I with you," she said shakily.

His hand squeezed hers. They walked on, their hearts several degrees lighter. Soon, they were at the gate to Reeves

Hall. Liora pressed her ring to the hidden panel, and the gate swung open. Marcus observed this with interest. "Hmm," he said, as they passed through into the grounds of Reeves Hall. "Another use for your ring, I see."

She smiled. "You have seen nothing yet, Marcus. But I will show you, never fear."

"Good," he said with satisfaction. "I want you to teach me about your world."

"I will." That was a promise.

CHAPTER 33

CONNECTED

AS THEY ENTERED the grounds of Reeves Hall, he found himself feeling a good deal calmer than when he had left, though still dazed and bewildered. What Liora had told him was so fantastical as to be beyond belief. Part of him doubted— but then, he could not discount the evidence of his own eyes. He had already seen what scientific marvels this family had in its possession.

Nevertheless, every certainty he held about the universe had been shaken to the core. There were people living on a world as distant as the stars in the sky. They were able to travel unimaginable distances in ships that flew in the endless space above him. It was an extraordinary notion.

These revelations had served to distract him from the maelstrom of painful emotion he had undergone in the last few hours, or at least in part. The hurt, the disappointment, the betrayal of Lionel not being Lionel was still there.

He supposed he should have been feeling relieved. He was not, after all, a sodomite. Instead of Lionel being a man, he was a beautiful woman named Liora. One who he had ravished in the wildness of the moor. One who he could not wait to ravish again. But hurt he still was. Could it be possible to hold pain and disappointment alongside joy and elation? For while he undoubtedly found this new incarnation of Lionel attractive, he still recalled the appeal of Lionel when he had been male. There had been something special about their friendship. As well as lovers, they had been comrades going on mad dash adventures together. Through their friendship, Marcus had transformed into someone else—a more wordly and assertive version of himself. He did not know if he could still experience such camaraderie with Liora as she was now.

He also missed the way Lionel had looked with his hair cropped short, emphasizing the perfection of his face. There had been something strangely seductive in the contrast between his ethereal beauty and his powerfully male physique. It was shameful to admit it, but Marcus had felt a thrill in dominating such a powerful man and exerting a male aggression that he would never have dreamt of doing with a lady. Except he had just done so, in that frenzied bout of passion on the moor. Guilt nagged at him. Had he been too rough with her? He certainly had not been gentlemanly in his behaviour. He had been coarse and demanding; not at all gentle. And he had enjoyed every moment of it. What kind of a man did that make him?

A thousand questions and thoughts flew around his head, enough to frazzle even the sanest of minds. Chief of which… what happened next? That, he could not tell. All he could say was that the despair he had felt on learning Lionel's true identity had been replaced by a tenuous hope of something else.

They reached the house and entered, finding both Brook and Jane Reeves long gone. The butler informed them that Marcus's valise and valet had been conveyed to Penhale Manor, where Brook Reeves and his lady would be honoured to have him as their guest. Marcus had not gone as far as to think where he would stay the night, but it seemed it was not to be at Reeves Hall. Liora caught his look of confusion and explained, "Broek and Jane have resided at Penhale Manor since their marriage. It is a comfortable house, but we have not installed there all the Uvonian devices that we have here, so it is possible for us to entertain guests there who do not know the truth about us."

"But I do know it."

"Yes, but not your valet. I am afraid we cannot risk having Stubbs here to witness the way we live at Reeves Hall."

"I see." He did see it, and he was beginning to understand the reasons why the Reeves family guarded their privacy so fiercely, but he was also disappointed. Had he hoped to share a bed with Liora tonight? Of course, that was out of the question, despite their earlier intimacies.

"We have missed our luncheon, but I can have our cook send up something for us to eat," continued Liora.

His stomach rumbled in reminder that he had eaten very little since his breakfast repast at the coaching inn that morning. "That would be agreeable, thank you," he replied, a stiffness returning to his demeanour. What happened next? How was he to comport himself with this lady, Liora not Lionel, after he had so brazenly taken her in the open space of the moor?

She smiled and led him to a private parlour, saying along the way, "There is a water closet down the hall, if you would like to refresh yourself."

"Thank you." He was certain his appearance was not quite as polished as it had been when he first arrived here. Excusing himself, he went to make use of the facilities. He glanced about him curiously as he entered the water closet. It was a brightly lit room though he knew not how, for he could see no candles or lamps. Over to one side, he spied a commode and wash basin similar to those he had seen in the house on Barton Street. There was also a large looking-glass above the basin. Quickly, he did his business and tidied his appearance as best he could. The grass stains on the back of his tailcoat, he could do little about.

When he returned to the parlour, he found Liora waiting for him—how odd it still was to call her this when he had held the name Lionel so close to his heart this many weeks. She beckoned him, and he took a seat beside her on the settee. At once, her distinctive scent enveloped him, bringing with it a sense of familiarity as well as a sharp stab of desire. His recalcitrant cock reacted, stiffening in the confines of his pantaloons. He tried to will it down, and his eyes landed on the curious contraption she held in her lap. It was rectangular-shaped and flat, with a glassy surface.

"What is that?" he asked, curiosity beginning to take precedence over his desire.

"That is my console," she said, her dark eyes sparkling.

"And what does this console do?"

"A great many things," she smiled. He saw her swipe her finger across its surface, and at once, it lit up. Marcus reared back instinctively, causing her to laugh. "There is nothing to fear, Marcus, truly," she assured him.

Abashed at his show of weakness, he came close once more and cautiously examined the contraption. On the lighted surface, there appeared to be strange symbols and boxes in different colours.

"This is my starting page, where I can decide what I wish to do by selecting one of the boxes," she said. She pointed to some of the symbols. "And this here is Uvonian script. It was designed by a group of scientists, artists and intellectuals some two centuries ago when it was decided that we should replace the many different written languages we had on our planet with one universal script that would be accessible to all. We have five main spoken dialects on Uvon, but everyone can read this script and interpret it in their own language."

"Would this apply to any language, even English?" he wondered.

She grinned. "Yes indeed, that is the beauty of it! You would need to receive instruction in how the symbols work, but it is not a burdensome task. The people who designed this script were intent on making it truly accessible to all, including persons who had experienced difficulty deciphering letters in our previous written languages. It took decades to research, test and design this script so that it could be learned easily and understood by all."

He felt a flurry of excitement. Could he, thick-skulled as he was when it came to letters, learn to read this Uvonian script? He pointed to a symbol under an orange-coloured box. "What does this say?" he asked.

"It says 'connect'. See how this symbol here is in the shape of a two-sided arrow? That is meant to signify the connection of two entities."

He looked at the symbol, and he saw what she meant. It seemed simple and obvious, but there was still more he needed to know. "Connect to what?"

"Ah, look what happens when I tap on the box." She demonstrated, and immediately, the box moved, leaving the surface of the screen to rise and float in the air before them. He stared at it in fascination, no longer feeling any fear but intense curiosity. The orange box floating in front of them divided into three little capsules in a deeper shade of the same colour, each with a symbol attached to it. "This one," explained Liora, "is for sending messages. See this symbol here? Again, there is the double-sided arrow to signify a connection, but it also includes the symbol for our universal script, so this can be read to mean 'connect to someone using script'. This will allow me to send a written message to someone else's console."

It made so much sense to him that he felt the urge to whoop in delight. Without hesitation, he reached a finger across and tapped the capsule for sending a message. At the contact, he felt a pleasant little tingle to his fingertips, and a moment later, the console screen transformed into a list of symbols which he studied eagerly. At once, he knew what they were. Each symbol denoted a person. One was in the shape of a four-legged creature, perhaps a dog? Then he understood. He pointed to it and said, "Is that the symbol for sending a message to Galok?"

Her smile was full of pride at his acuity. "Yes, quite right. Galok chose this symbol for himself as it shows a four-legged creature that could be a horse." She turned to him. "Can you identify any of the other symbols?"

He studied them once more. The one at the top looked like a figure of a man standing in a powerful stance. He pointed to it. "Your older brother, Brook?"

"That's right."

The next symbol depicted the form of a woman wearing a headdress and looking quite regal. It took him a moment to work it out. "The duchess, your brother's wife?" he hazarded a guess.

"Indeed, it's the symbol Broek chose for Jane, who by the by, started learning this script only a few months ago and is already quite proficient at it."

Intrigued, he decided to tap on the symbol for Jane. A new box emerged, a blank white page, waiting for him to write his message. He turned to Liora and asked, "What now?"

"What message do you wish to convey to Jane?" she enquired.

"I would like to say good day from Marcus, Duke of Coleford, and to thank her for her kind hospitality."

Immediately, symbols appeared on the screen. At his look of confusion, Liora elucidated, "The console is programmed to act intelligently. It heard what you said and transposed your message into Uvonian script."

He gazed at the symbols with interest. The first one had the shape of a smile. The next symbol beside it looked like the sun. "Good day," he deciphered, pointing to the symbols.

Liora beamed at him proudly. "Absolutely right, Marcus. You are quick to learn."

They spent the next few minutes going through the remainder of the symbols, which all made perfect sense to him once Liora explained their meaning. "Would you like to send it now?" she asked.

At his nod, she spoke to the console. "Send message." The symbols flew off the screen, as if they were indeed flying off to their recipient. He stared in wonder as not a minute later, the screen lit up again with a new set of symbols. "Jane has replied," said Liora.

He read the first line, "Good day, Marcus." Liora nodded encouragingly and helped him decipher the rest of the message. *I am honoured by your visit and look forward to welcoming you at Penhale Manor. Dinner is at eight o'clock. Jane.*

What an impressive contraption! And so easy to use even a simpleton like him could make sense of it. "This is amazing!" he could not help but cry out.

"Yes, I suppose so," Liora replied. "It is something I have had all my life, so for me, it is commonplace. Seeing it through your eyes though, makes me realise just what a marvellous invention it is."

There came a knock at the door, heralding the entrance of a servant bearing a tray of food, which he placed on a side table. Once he had left and shut the door, Liora went to the tray and prepared a plate with small, triangular sandwiches and something else which he could not quite identify. It was a flat, pancake-like food and purple in colour. She brought the plate over to him and saw his look of misgiving.

"I thought you might like to try a food from my home world," she said with a chuckle at his wary expression. "These are Uvonian pancakes, and very popular in this household. Do give them a try."

He took the plate from her and eyed this strange pancake curiously.

"Go on, try it."

Cautiously, he cut a piece and lifted the fork to his mouth, not sure quite what to expect. What he got was a light and moist bite of something delicately flavoured with just the right level of sweetness.

"What do you think?" Liora was keen to know.

"I like it." So saying, he took another mouthful and chewed the food consideringly. "What is it made of?"

"It is made with a Uvonian grain which we grow in our glasshouses. It is similar to wheat but has a deeper flavour and colour."

"I should very much like to visit your glasshouses, if you will allow me," he blurted, thinking just how many things at Reeves Hall he was eager to explore.

"Of course." Liora served up a plate for herself and joined him on the settee. She glanced in his direction then asked, a trifle warily, "How long can you stay?"

And just like that, their convivial mood was punctured by the realisation that their time together was finite. On setting out for Reeves Hall, he'd had no ambition except to see Lionel and make it clear that he would not accept an end to their friendship. He had hoped for more than friendship too, though in what way that could be managed, he did not know. And then, of course, he had found out there was no Lionel, but a beautiful lady that had been masquerading as him.

Again, he asked himself the question. What happened next?

Matters ought to be simpler now. He could get down on one knee and propose marriage. Whatever impediment had been in the way of their love was no longer there. He found, however, that he could not do so. It was difficult to explain why, even to himself, only that there was still doubt in his mind.

Liora watched him intently as he considered his response to her simple and yet complex query. In the end, he replied, "A week, maybe two at most. I must be gone by the end of the month to attend Portia's nuptials."

"To Sir Luke Stafford?"

"Yes," he smiled. "Thank the Lord, she ended the season with a match."

"I am sure your mother must be very pleased about it," Liora remarked.

"Indeed she is." He paused. "Liora, I did not come all this way so that I could talk about my sister or my mama with you."

"Oh?" she arched a brow. "Then why did you come?"

The air thickened around them. "You know very well why." His voice, regrettably, sounded like a growl.

"No, actually I do not," argued Liora. "I know you expected to find Lionel, not me, but as to your purpose in coming, I am not clear."

"Neither am I, except that I wanted our relationship to go on."

Liora set down her fork and returned the half-eaten plate to the tray. Standing with her back to him, she enquired in an expressionless voice, "And now that you know who I really am, do you still want our relationship to go on? Or would you much rather I had truly been a man?" On this last word, she turned to face him.

He stared into her eyes, so much like Lionel's. Why was he still thinking of Lionel when she and he were one and the same person? Was it because, as she suspected, he would much rather she were still a man? His gaze travelled down her body, lingering on the subtle curve of her breasts then down to the slim waist hidden under the fabric of her gown. His cock answered the question, rising stiffly to attention. "I want you," he admitted, both to her and to himself.

Liora said nothing for an endless time. Then very softly, she breathed, "Come with me." She walked over to the parlour door and opened it, looking over her shoulder to make sure he followed. He swallowed the hard lump in his throat. Good God, why was he so tense? It was not as if they had not done this before.

His feet took him towards her. Once she saw he was following, she continued on her way, exiting the parlour and walking to the main hallway. They passed by a footman, the same servant that had brought in their tray of food. Liora nodded to him in passing. He inclined his head respectfully but betrayed no surprise or any emotion on seeing his mistress lead a man up to her bedchamber—for that must be their destination. He recalled what she had told him of her world.

Women and men can engage in sexual relationships without the necessity of marriage. Here at Reeves Hall, the outside world's rules of conduct did not apply. There would be no moral judgement nor stain on Liora's reputation for what they were about to do—and what they had already done. For a moment, he was stunned at the wondrous freedom of it all. How liberating it was to simply follow their own desires with no fear of retribution.

Up the stairs they went, then along a corridor until they reached a sturdy oak door. Liora glanced over her shoulder at him, as if to ascertain his willingness to embark on this sensuous affair. What she saw in his face must have reassured, for her lips curved in a slight smile as she opened the door and ushered him inside. He followed her into the room, giving it a cursory look. It was spacious and uncluttered, permeated with her heavenly fragrance. Liora came to a stop and turned to face him. Wordlessly, she began to undress, first removing her shoes and stockings, then lifting the gown above her head and tossing it over the back of a chair. He watched, drunken with desire, until it occurred to him that he too should be discarding his clothes. He did so clumsily, kicking off his shoes and throwing off his coat. Heat coursed through his veins as each garment was removed. With it too, he shed every last remnant of indecision. He wanted this woman—Lionel or Liora, it mattered not.

Totally bare, they stared at each other once more, then he took a step forward, and so did she. They met in the middle of the room. Slowly, Liora lifted a hand and rested it to his chest, her palm stretched wide. He imitated her gesture, his right hand enveloping her left breast. Her breath quickened at his touch, but they stayed like this, not initiating anything further.

On the moor, they had been wild and uninhibited. Here, they were intentional and deliberate, each touch speaking in a language without words. He glanced down at their intertwined hands, the shape of their stance reminding him of the Uvonian symbol he had learned earlier. "Connect," he whispered.

She grasped his meaning instantly. "Yes," she said softly, "we are like that symbol."

"We are connected," he said again. "What we did on the moor was… it was not like this."

Again, she understood. "No, on the moor, we were not thinking, just reacting to the pull of our emotions. Here, we are making a conscious choice to connect to one another."

There was no room now for anything but absolute clarity about what they were doing. Filled with a sense of urgency, he bit out, "We are bound together now, Liora. Never shut me out of your life again. No more secrets, no more lies, no more doubts. Accept me."

"I do." Her whisper was soft but sure.

"Then let us go to bed." He dropped his hand from her breast and led her to the wide divan-like structure that was unlike any bed he had seen before, except at Barton Street that night they had spent together. He knew what to expect. A mattress sprung so well as to make one feel weightless. Sheets as soft as silk.

They lay facing each other, heads resting on the featherlight pillows. Rays of sunlight filtered into the room through the half-opened blinds, reminding him that it was daytime, and that most people at this moment were going about their everyday business while they lounged naked on this bed. He searched her face, so familiar and dear to him, and traced it with his fingers, caressing the fullness of her lips. She parted them, allowing him to plunge his thumb into the moist heat of her mouth. She sucked on it gently, and the sight of it had him conjuring a vision of her sucking on something else. Never had he plunged his cock into any lady's mouth, but now the idea of it was planted firmly in his mind.

It seemed he could not hide his thoughts from Liora. Pulling his finger away to free her mouth, she murmured breathily, "One day soon, we shall do it."

"You would like that?"

She touched the roughness of his cheek with her hand. "Yes, Marcus, I would. It is a wonderful act of intimacy, and I will take great pleasure in seeing you go wild with ecstasy as I feast on your beautiful cock."

"Oh!" he stuttered, lost for words. His cock was rock hard merely at the mention of it.

She smiled. "But for now, I would like us to fuck."

"I would like that very much too." Needing no further urging, he kissed her, sealing their bargain. This kiss was different too. He took his time, angling his mouth to hers and seeking out her tongue. They explored each other languidly, exchanging open-mouthed kisses and the occasional nibble, pausing once in a while to look into each other's eyes before coming back for more. His hands stroked the softness of her skin, roaming along the curve of her hips, down her back and over the rounded fullness of her bottom. He drew her to him, letting her feel the hardness of his erection. She moaned in pleasure, the sound muffled by his mouth on hers.

Needing to take matters forward, he rolled them over, covering her body with his. The tip of his cock nudged her opening, but he did not enter her yet. Instead, he reached his fingers down to her cunt, stroking the slick folds until he found the spot that brought her the greatest sensation. He rubbed her there, gently back and forth, and brought his mouth to the tantalising tip of one breast. He licked it, then could not resist taking a bite of the taut flesh. "Ah!" Liora moaned. He sucked her sweet breast, knowing by now how much his girl enjoyed it. He did not stint on lavishing the other breast too with the lap of his tongue. His mouth travelled up to taste the sensitive dip of her throat, raining soft kisses along the way. All the while, his hand was busy at her cunt, and the sounds she made spoke to him of her pleasure. He could not wait any longer. He needed to be inside his Liora.

Taking hold of his shaft, he guided it to her opening and pressed himself home. He did not stop until he was fully sheathed inside her. Glancing down to where their bodies were joined, he was reminded once more of that powerfully evocative Uvonian symbol. *Connected*. Their eyes met, and he could swear she read his mind again.

"Yes," she whispered.

He pulled out slowly and thrust again, his eyes fixed on hers. *Connected*. That was what they were, and not just with their bodies. He had asked Liora to accept him and she had said, "I do." It was as good a vow as any they could take in a church. And this joining of their bodies was a sealing of that vow.

Deliberately, he drove his cock as deep as he could and held it there, savouring the sweet heat of her cunt clamping around him. He dipped his head down, giving first a kiss to each breast before bringing his lips to hers. On their next kiss, he plunged deep into her core once more, commencing a slow and steady rhythm, hypnotic in its power. All he could think was this one word. *Connected*. A thread that ran from him to Liora and back again to him. *Connected*. Their lovemaking on the moor had been passionate and satisfying, but this... this was on another level.

"Connected," she breathed on his next thrust into her tight heat.

"Always," he breathed back, driving in deep, over and over until he felt her pulse around him. Then, his control at an end, he pounded his release with a loud groan of intense satisfaction.

CHAPTER 34

THE MATTER IS SETTLED

THEY LAY TOGETHER in the aftermath of their passion, her head tucked comfortably on the broadness of his chest. She ran her fingers idly over his body, enjoying the feel of the hair that graced his forearms and chest. Occasionally, she stopped to drop a kiss over his smoothly tanned skin. *Connected.* That was how they had felt just now when they had made love, and how she still felt, even after their desires had been sated.

All was not yet settled though. She lifted herself onto her elbow to gaze down at his sleepy face. "Marcus," she murmured.

His eyelids lifted. "Mmm?"

"Have you forgiven me?"

He sighed and stretched his arms over his head. Finally, he said, "It is easy to forgive, Liora, now I understand how it all came about."

She exhaled the breath she had been holding, but he was not done. "It is harder though to eradicate the hurt I felt on learning the truth, and the sense of having been a fool not to have seen it."

"You are not a fool!"

He smiled sadly. "I still feel like one sometimes, but yes, when thinking rationally, I know I am not."

"Then you must always be rational, except when I have you in my bed," she returned saucily.

"Is that so?" He flipped her over to her back, imprisoning her wrists above her head. "Are you saying, Liora, that you like it when I act like a wild beast and defile you?"

"Maybe."

His eyes gleamed with mischief then darkened as an idea occurred to him. "In that case," he growled, "I think we should try something out." He lifted himself up to his knees, straddling her, and inched his way up her body, stopping just above her shoulders. His thick shaft jutted out, already coming back to life. He wrapped a hand around it, keeping the other over her restrained wrists. She did not tell him, of course, that her *raiko* training meant she was quite capable of liberating herself should she wish to. He guided the engorged shaft towards her. "I believe you wanted to feast on it," he said by way of explanation.

Oh yes, but she would not go easy on him.

He tapped the tip of his cock to her lips. "Open up," he instructed in his most imperious, ducal manner.

She did not comply.

He regarded her closed lips then dropped his eyes to his appendage, still held in his hand. "Aye, I get it. You are having second thoughts now that you are getting a closer look at the great beast in my pants."

"Ha!" she scoffed, still keeping her lips closed.

"I do not blame you. It is, admittedly, on the large side, though nothing quite like the fake cock you gave yourself as Lionel," he remarked.

She gave a little shrug of insouciance.

"No, I see now that this great thing would not fit in the daintiness of your mouth. Now if this were Lionel—"

He did not get to finish his sentence. Her mouth was already clamped around the tip and sucking gently.

"Ah yes," he grunted. "That is good."

Oh, Marcus, you have seen nothing yet. She smiled to herself as she licked the salty sweet tip, letting the taste of his musk invade her senses. Then, she opened her mouth wide and drew in another inch of his length. His reaction was priceless. He groaned, staring in fascination at the juncture of his cock with her lips, as if he could not believe what he was witnessing. She signalled to him with her eyes that she could take more. He understood perfectly the silent language of their bodies—it was only the English letters of the alphabet that defeated him. Carefully, he eased in further, watching her reaction like a hawk. Despite his talk of acting like a beast and defiling her, he was being the perfect gentleman, at least to her mind.

She spoke to him with her eyes. *More!* After a moment's hesitation, he gave her more, surging further into her mouth until his tip hit the back of her throat. Deliberately, she took a breath through her nose and relaxed her throat. Another advantage to her *raiko* training was that she had learned to use the power of her mind to direct the muscles of her body. She focused her gaze on him, on seeing his pleasure. An invisible thread ran from her eyes to his. *Connected.* Even as he fell under the spell of intensely pleasurable sensation, he kept his eyes on her. She knew instinctively that one look of pain from her would ensure his immediate withdrawal.

Eventually, he began to move, shallow thrusts at first then gradually deepening the movement. He made guttural groans of satisfaction, surging in and out of her throat. She felt herself slipping into a semi-hypnotic state, only distantly aware of the discomfort as she kept her focus on him. His eyes flared, the pupils dilating. So connected were they that she felt the sensation of his pleasure in the throbbing at her core. She knew the instant when he was about to reach his climax. His thrusts quickened, and his shaft swelled in her mouth. He began to pull out, but she sucked him in more strongly. It was too much for him. With an unfettered cry of joy, he spurted into her mouth, and she swallowed him down, licking him clean of every drop. She filed away in her mind the unique taste of his spend. It was one she would never forget.

Slowly, he pulled out of her mouth and sat back on his heels, still unable to look away from her. Silent tears flowed their way down his face. She gazed at them in confusion then hurriedly sat up to catch a rivulet on the tip of her finger. Her eyes questioned him. Why the tears?

He took in a harsh breath, tamping down on the swell of emotion. "That was beautiful," he murmured hoarsely. Then he swallowed and tried again. "I cannot put it into words. It was… something transcendental. All at once, I felt a deep knowing— of you, of us. I could see into our past, our present, our future, and we were indelibly intertwined."

"I felt it too," she said on a breath.

He drew her to him and kissed her reverently. After a time, he pulled back to look at her. "Liora," he said.

"Yes?"

"Is the matter settled between us?"

"Yes," she said, wiping away the last remnants of his tears.

"The important thing is settled, though we still have much to discuss," he mused. "For instance, where shall we live? Here or at Coleford Hall, or somewhere else?"

She smiled. "As you say, the important matter is settled. The other things, we can debate in the fullness of time."

He frowned. "There is also the matter of marriage. I feel as if we have already sealed our vows, but in the eyes of the world…" He shook his head. "I am doing this badly. I should be on my knees and proposing with eloquent, romantic words."

"You are already on your knees," she reminded him with a laugh.

His eyes twinkled in amusement. "So I am."

He cleared his throat, but she hastened to tell him, "I am not bothered about marriage, Marcus, as we have already sealed our mating bond through the vows we made to each other. My family will not care one way or the other about it unless it has a bearing on my reputation in the outside world."

He eyed her quizzically. "Would you have any objection to us getting married?"

"None," she replied.

"Well in that case, Liora and Lionel, my dear loves. Will you consent to being my wife?"

"Liora and Lionel," she repeated, a question in her voice.

"Is it wrong of me that I still think of you as both?" he rumbled. "In time, I am sure that will change, and you, Liora, will dispel all notions of Lionel."

She cocked her head to one side. "What if I do not want to dispel all notions of Lionel?"

His eyes narrowed. "Your meaning?"

"My meaning is this. In the time that stretches before us, there may be occasions where I wish to be Lionel. We can have the freedom to do things together that are otherwise difficult for a female in this world to do. Travelling far and wide, attending boxing matches and gambling dens—even riding astride a horse rather than side-saddle."

His eyes lit up. "I think I should like to have adventures with Lionel again," he declared. He kissed her nose. "Liora/Lionel, you have not answered my question. Will you marry me?"

"Yes," she responded without hesitation. "I will."

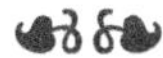

MARCUS

Of course, I did not waste any time making Liora my bride. The very next morning, we went to the small church in Penhale and posted the banns, and in another two weeks, she became my duchess. There was no time for Mama or my sisters to be present at our wedding, as they were already in Oxfordshire, preparing for Portia's nuptials to Sir Luke. This happy event I attended with my new duchess at my side.

Portia was not much impressed that I had pipped her to the post.

LIORA

It was nerve-inducing to meet my new family in my real guise as Liora, or Laura as I became known to them. On our meeting, his family immediately noted the striking resemblance between myself and Lionel, but our story—that Lionel was my twin brother and that Marcus had met me on his visit to Cornwall— seemed to satisfy them.

The only person we were unable to hoodwink was Julia, and eventually, Marcus felt compelled to take her into our confidence. His youngest sister was much surprised and not a little shocked at the revelation that all this time, I had been masquerading as a man, though I fancied the surprise was soon replaced by a trace of admiration and envy at my exploits. In any case, Julia was sworn to silence on the matter, and she has kept her promise ever since.

EPILOGUE

A TRANSFORMATION AND A HONEYMOON

Six months later

SHE ROUSED SLOWLY, stretching her arms and legs under the covers. As she did so, the ball of her foot encountered a warm, solid object. "Mmm," she groaned sleepily, rubbing her foot along Marcus's leg. His large hand dropped to her chest, unerringly finding her breast and drawing lazy circles with his fingers. He did not otherwise respond to her waking.

With an effort, she lifted an eyelid to have a quick look. It was as she thought. Marcus was sitting in bed beside her, his console held in his lap, engrossed in reading the second book in the Veloris saga, an immensely popular Uvonian series of historical books. They were packed with adventure, suspense and some very spicy romantic scenes that had at first shocked her prudish husband, then delighted him. He had even put some of the things he had read into practice, which she could not complain about at all.

It had been a revelation, seeing Marcus learn to read Uvonian script and immerse himself in books—a pastime he had previously felt excluded from. It was as if he were making up for lost time now. Nearly every spare moment, she found him with the console in his hands, reading from his book.

With a yawn, she finally sat up and tucked her head into the crook of his shoulder. "Morning," she murmured, dropping a kiss to the line of his throat.

He set down the console and gathered her to him, kissing the top of her head. "Morning, my duchess," he replied. "Are you ready for the start of our adventures?"

"I shall be once I have had coffee and something to eat," she sighed lazily.

"I am sure that can be arranged, but in the meantime, there is something else we can do to sate your hunger."

She hid a smile. "Such as?"

"Such as this," he stated, easily lifting her to straddle his lap. "This position is very useful," he casually observed. "Not only is it perfect for you to sit comfortably on my cock, but my hands are also free to roam over your delightful curves while I kiss your sweet lips. I do believe it to be a wonderful way to start the day."

"Hmm," she pretended to consider his words. "I suppose we could put it to the test."

"I think we most definitely should," he concurred, dipping his head to capture her breast into his mouth.

It was at least another half-hour, probably more, before they made it to breakfast in the dining room of Marcus's townhouse on St James's Square. Mrs Cavendish—her mother-in-law—and Julia were still lingering over their coffees when they finally made their appearance.

"Ah, here you are," said Marcus's mama. "I was about to send someone up to fetch you. There is no time to dally if you wish to depart for Dover and catch a crossing to the Continent."

"We shall make it in time, Mama," Marcus assured her, "and if not, we shall simply sail the following day."

Liora exchanged a knowing glance with Marcus. What his mama did not know was that when they made their farewells later this morning, it would not be to travel to Dover, at least not directly. For several weeks now since the start of the season, they had been in London. As his new duchess, Marcus had escorted her to several balls, soirées and card parties, including a rather tedious evening at Almack's, a stuffy bastion of the *ton*.

Their social duties fulfilled, today they would leave to go on a belated honeymoon trip. There had been little time for it since their marriage, busy as they had been with improvements to Coleford Hall, installing the plumbing and connectivity Marcus had deemed necessary for their living comforts in his ancestral home. It had taken ingenuity to upgrade their living quarters in ways that did not draw attention to her superior Uvonian technology, but it had been done, with the changes being attributed to the new duke's known penchant for eccentric behaviour. Then they had come to London.

Later this morning when they left, they would be making a small detour on their way to Dover and the Continent; namely they would be going to the Reeves townhouse on Barton Street, where Laura Cavendish, Duchess of Coleford, would be mysteriously transformed into Mr Lionel Reeves. A fresh wardrobe of masculine clothes had been sent for and delivered for this purpose, and a new bodysuit had been created to the same specifications as before, though with a slight difference. This one had an external penile attachment, lifelike in appearance but not fully functional as the one Liora had had before, which had been surgically attached to her body. She and Marcus were both in agreement that in the privacy of their bedchamber at night, she should be able to remove the bodysuit and return entirely to her female form. Nevertheless, taking on the persona of Lionel during the day would provide them with more freedom to explore the sites as they completed their own version of the Grand Tour. It would be another adventure for the two of them.

They finished their breakfast, then it was time to load their baggage in the carriage, bid their farewells and depart, but only for Barton Street. One person who would not be joining them on this trip was Stubbs, Marcus's stalwart valet. The man may have had his suspicions about her, but they had never revealed to him Lionel's true identity, and to keep that secret intact, it was best that someone in the know took on the job of manservant on this trip. To this end, they had enlisted the services of Tivok, a young lad that worked for her family at Reeves Hall, and given Stubbs a well-deserved paid vacation.

The journey to Barton Street did not take very long. Once they arrived, the trunks containing her female clothes were unloaded—for the duration of their absence, they would be stored in her London townhouse. In their stead, a fresh set of baggage containing her male wardrobe was loaded onto the carriage. While that substitution took place, another, more important one needed to occur in the privacy of her bedchamber. She greeted Esa, who had continued to work as housekeeper here despite numerous offers for her to retire at Reeves Hall. Then, Marcus led her upstairs, for there was no time to lose if they were to make a crossing to Calais later today.

Her new bodysuit was already laid out on the bed in anticipation of her arrival, as well as the full complement of clothes she would be wearing today as Lionel Reeves.

"Ready?" asked Marcus.

"Absolutely," she assured him.

He came to her and began to help her undress, layer by layer, until she stood totally bare before him. He took his time to admire her naked form, tracing the fingers of his hands over her breasts and down to the juncture of her thighs, covering her mound with one large palm.

"I shall miss this," he mused.

"You will still see me like this at night, when we are alone."

"True." He smiled, a hint of playful humour in his eyes. "And I'll get the prurient delight of seeing you in your male form, knowing what hides beneath."

"Then let us do it."

He retrieved the bodysuit from the bed and helped her into it, watching with fascination as she sealed it into place. When she was done, she turned in a circle for him to admire her new manly form. He stared, a little stupefied.

"Good Lord, Liora, it looks so unbelievably real!" he blurted.

"It is Lionel from now on," she said pertly. Then she added, "But yes, it is very real looking. You do see now, don't you, how nigh on impossible it would have been for you to fathom my true sex."

"Yes," he said.

"No more berating yourself for not guessing my true identity?"

He shook his head. "No more. And now, I am reassured too that your disguise will hold over the course of our trip, with no one else being the wiser."

"Will you help me dress?"

"Of course." He picked up the shirt laid on the bed and handed it to her, then held out a pair of cream-coloured pantaloons, assisting her with each layer of clothing until she stood before him, fully dressed as Lionel Reeves.

"There is one more thing we need to do," she reminded him.

He pulled on a loose curl of her hair, his expression regretful. "It seems a pity to rid yourself of these."

"You once told me that you miss the way I had looked with my hair cropped short," she pointed out.

His smile was wry. "There is no logic to it, my darling. I am both eager to see you with cropped hair and sad to see your lovely locks go."

"They will grow back," she said soothingly, picking up the scissors on the dressing table. He took them from her and watched thoughtfully as she sat down on the stool. "I am ready," she prompted him.

He stayed unmoving some moments more, then finally came to stand behind her. With a frown of concentration, he began his task, shearing off each of her locks and arranging her hair into the fashionable Brutus style. He was meticulous in his work, achieving a creditable haircut—another of his many talents she needed to file away in her mind.

When it was done, he busied himself with tidying things up and brushing away any stray pieces of hair from her tailcoat.

She stood then and faced him, studying his face. "Well," she queried. "What do you think?"

His molten eyes shimmered with untold emotion. "This is how you looked when I first fell in love with you," he declared hoarsely. "You are beautiful, Lionel." He pressed his brow to hers, and they stayed together like this for several moments as he worked to regain his composure. Finally, he stepped back with a fond smile. "Ready to go?" he asked.

"I am ready," she said.

IT WAS LATE, and they had both retired to their separate rooms at the Calais coaching inn where they were staying the night before they began their journey to Paris the following day. In her nightshirt and robe, she stepped quietly out of the room. She walked a few paces to her right and knocked gently on the next door. It opened at once, and she entered quickly on soft feet. The Duke of Coleford locked the door and turned to her.

"Mr Reeves, what is the meaning of this late night visit?" he enquired with a lift of a brow.

She stepped towards him, placing a delicate hand over the solid broadness of his chest. "Your Grace," she purred. "Please do not think me forward, but I believe we should enjoy each other's company this night."

"Enjoy? What did you have in mind, Mr Reeves?" his voice was low and breathless.

In response, she dropped to her knees and looked up at him enticingly. "I have a great wish, sir, to enjoy your cock," she said brazenly.

He let out a long breath. "Then by all means, Mr Reeves, enjoy my cock."

Much later, they came together in the bed, though not before she had removed the bodysuit and become Liora again.

"Liora my love, thank you. That was incredible," he whispered. "But you have not yet had your pleasure." So saying, he slid his hand down to her mound, finding the bud of her clitoris. He stroked her there, patiently, lovingly, painstakingly until she too convulsed and reached her peak. Then he settled her to his body, draping them snuggly in the blankets before blowing out the candle for the night.

"Well," murmured Marcus. "That was quite a start to our adventure. I think we are going to have a grand time, you and I on this trip."

"I think so too."

She was drifting off to sleep when he spoke again. "Do you recall what you once said to me on that fateful journey to London?" He repeated her words. *"If I could have one wish, it would be to find a mate, someone who loves me unreservedly and with whom I can build a life with, a family."* Then he kissed the top of her head and whispered, "You have your wish now, my love."

"Mmm," she murmured drowsily, but she heard him and in the realm of her nascent dream, she smiled.

AFTERWORD

Dear reader,

Thank you for reading *My Masquerade With the Duke*. I hope you enjoyed Marcus and Liora's adventures in Regency London.

Although this is a work of fiction, some of the characters, such as William Vaughan, were based on persons that actually existed. Vaughan was one of the twelve investors in the London Docks and was given compensation when the slaves who worked on his plantation were freed in the 1830s. Although Enoch Miles was a fictional character, there was a Richard Miles who was one of the leading slave traders in the late eighteenth century—I simply made up a fictional son for him and named him Enoch.

Another thing that was based on historical fact was the slogan "East India Sugar, Not Made By Slaves". This was widely used on sugar bowls in the 1820s as part of a boycott of West Indian sugar grown on slave plantations, examples of which can be seen in this excellent post by the V&A museum: **https://www.vam.ac.uk/blog/museum-life/an-anti-slavery-sugar-bowl**.

And finally, in the early part of the story, Julia referenced some scandal about a bishop that had been stripped of his see after being found in a compromising position with a soldier. That too was based on fact. The bishop in question was a man by name of Percy Jocelyn, and you can have a look at the cartoon caricature Julia spoke of on this Wiki link: **https://en.wikipedia.org/wiki/Percy_Jocelyn**.

Continue this series

Next in this series is *A Not So Convenient Marriage*, Horis's story, and how he finds himself married—most inconveniently—to a very inquisitive lady named Verity Drake. You can read an excerpt from it in the following pages.

Stay in touch

Want to hear about new releases, exclusive extras and special offers? Join my reader list on my website:

→ **mw-author.com**

Loved this book? Please leave a review!

Reviews help readers discover indie authors like me. A quick rating on **Amazon** or **Goodreads** makes a huge difference—thank you!

Happy reading, and I hope you'll return to Reeves Hall with me soon.

M.M. Wakeford

ABOUT THE AUTHOR

M.M. Wakeford lives with her husband and son in a London terraced house that gathers dust while she loses herself in her writing. A lifelong reader of romantic novels, she writes in many genres including contemporary, sci-fi and historical romance.

Her stories capture that heady feeling of falling in love, with emotionally rich characters whose journey to a happily ever after is lined with dilemmas, desire and difficult choices. If you're looking for a page turning romance with high emotion and a good dose of spice, you're in the right place.

To be the first to hear about new releases, sneak previews and exclusive extras, sign up for M.M. Wakeford's mailing list at mw-author.com.

A Not So Convenient Marriage

A Sensual Regency Romance With a Sci-fi Twist
(AN EXCERPT)

THE REEVES OF REEVES HALL
– BOOK 3 –

M.M. Wakeford

PART I:
IN WHICH WE MEET VERITY DRAKE

CHAPTER 1

A MOST MYSTERIOUS FAMILY

April 1821

THERE WAS VERY little that occurred in the small Cornish village of Penhale that escaped the attention of Miss Verity Drake. She had long ago made it her mission to know everyone's business and had consequently developed a friendly acquaintance with a great many people, in all walks of life, as a means to acquire this knowledge.

It would be an unkindness, however, to call her a busybody, for she certainly did not engage in any idle gossip. No, indeed not. The information she gleaned through artful questioning and very attentive listening, she kept firmly to herself. A busybody she was not, yet it would be true to say that she had a great curiosity about the lives of the people that lived in her vicinity, and that she took great care to indulge that curiosity.

And thus, when the Reeves family had moved into the locality some seven years ago, purchasing a large and crumbling estate on the outskirts of the village, she had naturally been most keen to find out all she could about them. In this, she was not alone, for the arrival of the Reeves clan into their midst had excited much interest among the residents of Penhale. But to their collective disappointment, very little knowledge was to be discovered about this mysterious family. The Reeves kept themselves apart from local society and hid behind the sturdy walls of their estate, which was guarded by a surly gatekeeper who made sure to keep all curious visitors out. Other than a brief appearance at church every Sunday and the occasional sighting in the nearby town of Newquay, few opportunities were to be had for discourse with any member of the Reeves family.

As is often the case when the true facts are obscured, stories soon began to emerge about this family, the rumours spreading like acorns flying in the wind, becoming more outlandish with each day, month and year that passed. The very latest tale making the rounds was that the Reeves were members of a pagan cult that practised the dark arts. Verity had listened to these reports with the scepticism of a gentlewoman grounded in good sense. To her mind, there was no credible reason to suppose that the Reeves were involved in witchcraft.

This did not mean, however, that everything about the family was above board. She had conducted her own lengthy investigations into the matter and come to the conclusion that the Reeves were not who they claimed to be. Soon after their arrival, they had let it be known that they were descendants of a Cornish gentleman named Phineas Reeves who had travelled to Brazil several decades ago and there made his fortune. Verity doubted the truth of this very much. Over the course of these past seven years, she had painstakingly studied the records of births and marriages in Penhale's church register and in every neighbouring parish that she visited, finding no mention at all of any Phineas Reeves. She had spoken to elders in the village and beyond, probing their long memories for any knowledge of a Phineas Reeves. None was forthcoming. The man was an obvious figment of the imagination, or if he had indeed existed, he had not been a gentleman from these parts of the country.

What this could mean for the true identity of the Reeves family was anyone's conjecture. Perhaps they were French spies, settled near the coast so they could convey smuggled messages to and from their home country. The Napoleonic Wars were over, that was true, and peace had been restored, yet there was still immense distrust between the two nations. The Reeves being French spies might also have explained the strange hint of a foreign intonation which Verity had detected in their speech. English, she was sure, was not their mother tongue.

That was one possibility. Another was that the Reeves were not descended from gentry but from more humble stock, that they had somehow amassed a substantial fortune in the shipping trade and were now anxious to join the ranks of the landed class. They would not be the first rich merchants to want to wash off the stink of trade through the purchase of land. If that were the case, however, then would it not make sense for them to be more sociable with the other landowners of the county rather than live reclusively as they did? The Reeves had made no effort, seemingly, to bolster their social standing. They had declined the handful of invitations to dine with the Drakes, the nearest landed family, and the Drakes had not received any invitation in return, much to Verity's frustration, for she would dearly have liked to see the inside of Reeves Hall and have an opportunity to probe further into the mysteries of this family.

At length, Verity had mulled over these two possibilities and found them both wanting, for they did not explain the other strange things about the Reeves family. For instance, the fact that they were very tall, much more so than was common, and that they all possessed a gleaming set of perfectly white, straight teeth, which was so far out of the common as to be quite remarkable. This last circumstance had helped to fuel those rumours of witchery, for how else could a family achieve such dental perfection other than through magical means? Even so, Verity, being a lady of good sense, could not bring herself to believe the rumours, and so she strived to use logical reasoning to solve this mystery—a resolution of which still evaded her.

Such was her preoccupation with the matter that she immediately set her teacup down and paused in the partake of her breakfast when, one April morning, her brother, Timothy Drake, casually dropped these words. "I came across Brook Reeves yesterday, when I was in town. Had a drink with him at the Red Lion."

"Oh?" inquired Verity, pretending a passing interest, though she was unlikely to fool her brother. He knew only too well of her continuing interest in the Reeves family.

"Damned uncomfortable business it was too," replied Timothy.

Verity arched a delicate brow in enquiry, silently urging her brother for more. He readily obliged. "The tavern keeper was unbearably rude to the man. I had half a mind to give him a set down, but then, to make things worse, Brook Reeves noticed my discomfiture and quizzed me on the matter."

"Did you tell him about the rumours?"

"Well," said Timothy, scratching his side whiskers uncomfortably, "I had to, didn't I?"

"Naturally," replied his sister good humouredly. "And how did he take the news?"

Timothy huffed. "I could tell he was surprised by it, and not a little displeased." Quickly, he added, "I told him, of course, that I did not set much store by these rumours and that they were most likely prompted by the differences in their ways, no doubt due to their having lived abroad for so many years."

"A sensible conclusion," approved Verity.

"Though I almost did end up believing something of those rumours," continued Timothy with a snort, "when I saw the scowl on Brook Reeves's face. The man looked positively menacing!"

"Yes, he can be quite terrifying," sighed Verity dreamily.

Her brother sent her an arched look. "Don't tell me, Verity, that you have developed tender feelings for the man."

"I am far too sensible for such things," she replied briskly, "but I would have to be in my dotage not to find that man other than appealing."

Timothy laughed. "I know only too well just how sensible a person you are, so it is heartening to see that even you can occasionally succumb to a gentleman's charms." After a pause, he added, "I'll allow that the man does have a formidable presence, and he is mightily handsome too." He shook his head, as if to dispel the matter from his mind, and dropped his eyes to the knife and fork in his hands as he neatly cut through a slice of roast beef.

Verity too dropped her eyes, wanting to spare her brother's blushes. With her proclivity for finding out everybody's business, she could not but be aware of Timothy's preference for persons of his own sex, though they never alluded to the matter openly. It was not something one talked about, but of course, she knew something of it, and knew too that her brother would most probably always remain a bachelor. This suited her well, for it looked as if she too was likely to end her days a spinster—not out of preference, but out of circumstance. And thus to be assured of a comfortable home with her brother in the event she never did marry, was a reassuring prospect.

"What do you suppose he will do, knowing that the good folk here believe his family to be involved in witchcraft?" asked Timothy, after a moment of silence. "Surely he cannot ignore the rumours, for they will not go away otherwise."

After a moment's consideration, Verity replied, "If it were me, I would host a dinner party or a ball, and invite people into my home to show them I have nothing at all to do with any sort of wizardry. It is the fact that they hide themselves from view that makes the people here so curious and predisposes them to believe the rumours."

"Hmm," her brother grunted, not entirely convinced.

In this, however, she was to be proved right, for not two days later, an invitation arrived in the post for them both to attend a dinner party at Reeves Hall.

A NOT SO CONVENIENT MARRIAGE

A gentleman sworn to protect his family's secrets.
A young lady determined to uncover them.
And a marriage neither of them planned.

"Beware of poking your nose into our affairs," he growled menacingly. "Do not doubt there will be hell to pay if you breathe one word of what you saw last night to anyone."

Verity Drake knows the Reeves family are not who they claim to be. Ever since they arrived at Reeves Hall—an isolated estate in the Cornish countryside—she has sensed something strange beneath their polished manners and guarded ways; and she is determined to uncover the truth.

Harry Reeves is equally determined to stop her, turning her curiosity into a battle of wills neither of them intends to lose.

But when scandal threatens to destroy Verity's reputation, there is only one solution: an inconvenient marriage to the very man who has been her adversary.

Bound together by duty neither anticipated, their simmering tension gives way to desire—and then to something far more dangerous: love. Yet the secrets Harry guards are not merely his own, and when the truth emerges, it will force them both to confront an impossible question.

What truly makes a family—blood, law, or love?

Because some truths cannot be hidden forever… and some bonds are stronger than fate itself.

What you'll find inside:

- A Regency romance with a sci-fi twist
- Enemies to lovers
- Marriage of convenience
- Open-door romance with emotional depth
- Found family and chosen bonds

A Not So Convenient Marriage is Book 3 in **The Reeves of Reeves Hall**, but can be enjoyed as a standalone.

ALSO BY THIS AUTHOR

THE VISCOUNT'S SCANDALOUS AFFAIR
BOOK 1 – THE STANTON LEGACY
— SERIES COMPLETE —

A high-heat, open-door Regency romance about a scandalous affair and unexpected love.

"Why not have a short dalliance with me? In the cold desert of my spinsterhood, I assure you I will not treasure my virtue half as much as the memories of sensual pleasures with you."

Charlotte Harding has little to expect from life. Orphaned, penniless, and painfully aware that society finds her forgettable, she survives on the charity of kindly relatives.

Then she meets the Viscount Stanton—handsome, wealthy, and entirely out of her reach. He barely notices her… until one reckless night changes everything.

Charlotte accidentally witnesses the viscount in a secret liaison, and her silence is bought with a single, unforgettable kiss—one that awakens a longing she never dared hope could be fulfilled.

And when later, an opportunity presents itself, **Charlotte does something truly scandalous: she makes him an offer.**

> → A discreet, temporary affair
> → No promises. No future
> → Stolen weeks of pleasure—memories to sustain her through a lifetime of spinsterhood

But the viscount soon discovers the quiet, overlooked woman he never noticed is the one he cannot forget. Desire deepens, and both must decide whether society's rules are worth denying their hearts.

The Viscount's Scandalous Affair is the first book in *The Stanton Legacy*, a completed Regency romance series. Each book features a full romantic arc, explicit open-door love scenes, and a guaranteed happily ever after.

Praise for The Viscount's Scandalous Affair:

"A beautiful story… and the ending was perfection." ★★★★★ Goodreads review

"A stunning read and a great story… compelling and very steamy." ★★★★★ Goodreads review

"Excellent book to curl up with and enjoy. What a way to start a new series. Would strongly recommend." ★★★★★ Goodreads review

"Charlotte enchanted me completely… a superb romance with twists and turns and a stunning HEA." ★★★★★ Goodreads review

"It's hard not to fall in love with Charlotte… This was a charming book and I loved every second of it." ★★★★★ Goodreads review

"I loved reading this book! Right from the beginning I was invested in the story. The writing style is not rushed, so detailed and so well executed. I loved being immersed in the story of how the main characters fell in love." ★★★★★ Goodreads review

"It's hard not to fall in love with Charlotte… This was a charming book and I loved every second of it." ★★★★★ Goodreads review

www.ingramcontent.com/pod-product-compliance
Lightning Source LLC
Chambersburg PA
CBHW071135180726
48291CB00007B/2185